BETWEEN HERE

AND THE

YELLOW SEA

BETWEEN HERE
AND THE
YELLOW SEA

STORIES BY

NIC PIZZOLATTO

DZANC BOOKS

5220 Dexter Ann Arbor Rd.
Ann Arbor, MI 48103
www.dzancbooks.org

Library of Congress Cataloging-in-Publication Data

Pizzolatto, Nic, 1975-
  [Short stories. Selections]
  Between here and the yellow sea : stories / by nic Pizzolatto.
    pages cm
  ISBN 978-1-59692-168-9
  I. Pizzolatto, Nic, 1975- Ghost birds. II. Title.
  PS3616.I99A6 2015
  813'.6--dc23
                                    2014041155

First published in 2006 by MacAdam/Cage Publishing, San Francisco.
First Dzanc Books edition: May 2015

Several of these stories have appeared elsewhere, in some cases in a different form: "Ghost Birds" in *The Atlantic Monthly*, "Amy's Watch" in *Shenandoah*, "1987, The Races" in *The Missouri Review*, "Between Here and the Yellow Sea" in *The Atlantic Monthly*, "The Guild of Thieves, Lost Women, and Sunrise Palms" in *Quarterly West*, "A Cryptograph" in *Stories from the Blue Moon Café, Volume IV*, "Haunted Earth" in *The Iowa Review*, "Graves of Light" in *Ploughshares*, and "The Wanted Man" in *Oxford American*.

Printed in the United States of America

10 9 8 7 6 5 4 3 2 1

For Nath, my brother

CONTENTS

GHOST BIRDS

THEN THE CITY ENTERS ANOTHER TORPID AND simmering May. Parents grimace while pulling their kids through the Museum of Westward Expansion, and barges moan down the Mississippi. Something erupted at the Dowling Industrial factory and the gases are making our sunsets plum and plutonium orange.

I work from eleven at night until six in the morning. The park is deserted, and I keep watch from a small window in a wall of steel 630 feet above the ground. Ninety acres of grass and trees on the east, bridges over the river and the lights of St. Louis to the west. I patrol under purple sky (you can't see stars this month), and after surveying the grounds with my official U.S. Park Service binoculars, I squeeze out my window and drop off the top of the St. Louis arch.

I use a Perigee II, a Velcro-closed, single parachute container made by Consolidated Rigging. It holds an ACE 240-square-foot canopy and my gear is black: helmet, knee and elbow pads, a black scarf over my nose and mouth, but my goggles are the blue glass of fourth-generation NVT night-vision. The arch is Pittsburgh steel, called "The Gateway to the West," and when my leg hangs out the window and high winds break on my face I can stare down at the dark forest or turn to the far window where St. Louis smolders, and in that moment I feel I might be straddling the sleeping intersection of a country's dreams. Gichin Funakoshi tells us that truth is contained in dreams.

Wind explodes so hard and loud you might be disintegrating. Three seconds of free fall, about four more guiding the canopy down. Sometimes I revolve in descent, like water going down a drain.

At the base of the arch, the Museum of Westward Expansion has the dimensions of a football field. In its lobby I keep a bag and ranger uniform, hustle in after a jump and emerge seconds later as Ethan Landry, park ranger. Those times, it always takes the quiet darkness to remind me that the park is closed, and I am alone.

The old workers' elevator jostles and squeals softly bearing me up.

A radio plays music and I listen to breaks in static on the black call box. Hours crawl toward morning. Since I don't drink anymore, I break the tedium by reading. Stuff like *The Book of Five Rings. Hagakure: Way of the Samurai*. The *Tao Te Ching*. I enjoyed the writings of Black Elk and some of Emerson's essays, but the Eastern mind seems a lot clearer to me. Clarity, I think, is the chief thing. Find a road and walk it.

Which as much as anything explains my jumps. The literal definition of BASE jumping is to parachute off a stationary object (building, antennae, span or earth), but for me it means narrowing your senses and joining the void. The great samurai Miyamoto Musashi says it is necessary to lose the self and become one with Mu, the emptiness at the heart of existence to which everything returns. Thus the warrior finds life in death. That's tougher than it sounds, and I've really come close only once. Three years ago, kayaking on the Buffalo River in northern Arkansas, I overturned and kicked loose. I smacked into a rock and the kayak shot at me, broke my ankle, whipped around and knocked a molar out and vanished downstream. Pounded by waves, swallowing water, and nearly blind from pain, I clung to the rock, knowing if I got washed away, I was over. On the bank of the river I noticed a squirrel staring at me. It cocked its head, as if asking what I thought I was doing, then spiraled up a tree where I lost it in the branches. I remember a sense of calm then, stillness, and thinking, This is my death. Interesting.

The moment was a glimpse of the true universe, a galactic procession that marched on without me. What Dogen calls "The Ten Thousand Things." My ankle healed, but rafting lacked something after that, and I discovered skydiving, which led to

BASE jumping. I started kayaking in the first place because one of the basics they tell you in rehab is that if you're going to stay sober, you have to get physically active.

But if none of that makes much sense, let's just say that with the hours I keep, my chief relationship is with gravity, and we're intimate every moonless night around three a.m.

And we're in May. The skies are hued amethyst and green and, like I said, I can see no stars. At night the woods lose their depth, take on a flatness and seem to stretch out in a single plain like the overgrown grazing fields on the farm where I grew up. The two spotlights at the bottom of the arch aren't a problem—I fall between them. Though there's no moon tonight, I'm a little wary of the illumination the strange sky creates, as BASE jumping is effectively illegal in the U.S. Many jumpers take falls in national parks, and park rangers are their traditional nemeses. The irony of my life is so obvious, I don't even think it's irony.

Before I jump I check the park with my binoculars: clipped grass, patches of pine and broadleaf poplars, concrete walkways converging at the Old Courthouse to the east. A gleam—behind a tree, I spot a shining flash. I zoom in and see at least two people huddled in the shadows. I'm about to call it in on the radio, but then I see what was gleaming: glass lenses. One of them is looking up at the arch with binoculars. Three o'clock has brought something new tonight; I shed my rigging and become a park ranger.

The elevator chugs me down and I creep between trees and crouch behind tall shrubs. I find three people—a girl and two boys, pretty young, and I remind myself to take it easy on them. At twenty-eight I can still remember the thrill of sneaking around at night. I had a girlfriend who loved exploring forbidden places. Our nerves humming along on whatever we copped, Mabel would lead me through dark spaces crammed with steam pipes and No Trespassing signs, staircases to rooftops that ended in a kiss. I hold off on my flashlight and move closer, because I can hear voices and want to know what they're saying.

A burly kid with fat cheeks and glasses is speaking to a thinner boy in a ball cap and trench coat.

The girl has been looking at the arch with binoculars. She lowers them and interrupts the boys, "I think I saw a ranger up there."

Then a human moan breaches the air. I look around and see outcroppings of shadow everywhere. Ahead of this grove, people fill the park, at least a dozen of them. A girl and boy are lying on their backs, the girl pointing to the sky. Another couple making out against a pine tree explain the moan I heard. I've stumbled upon some dream of youth and lust. For vague reasons this angers me—these young people intruding on my sacred and necessary moment.

The flashlight ignites and my deepest voice comes with it. "What's going on here? The park is closed." Everybody bolts and I trap the three in my beam. Leaves rustle and the dull reverberations of footsteps run through the ground.

The boy in the trench coat raises his hands, slowly lowers them, and steps forward. "Um, hi. We know the park is closed. We're sorry. We're on assignment for a class. We all go to Washington University." Over his shoulder, the girl watches me.

I'm still angry, and as the boy steps into my circle of power I ponder various angles of *kokyu nage* I could use to throw his body over the shrubbery. "You're all trespassing."

"We're in this class, Modern American Myth and Legend, um, we're working on our final project...see..."

Now the girl speaks up. "There's this urban legend that on nights without a moon something flies down from the arch." I can't make out the shade of her eyes, but they're pale. "Frank thinks it's a guy with a parachute, but the descriptions sound like a ghost bird."

"What?"

"Ghost birds. Native American thunder spirits. Gigantic, black with glowing eyes. People have seen them for centuries."

"Nothing flies off the arch."

Frank (I guess) interjects, "I personally know three people, who never met each other, and told me stories of seeing this thing fly off the arch. All three described something in all-black, with glowing red eyes. Another connection? There was no moon either night. I researched this. Six hundred feet is a totally plausible BASE jump. You can't be watching all the time."

"Listen, kids. You are trespassing. This is illegal. You're on government property."

"We're sorry. Really. It was just—you know."

"We wanted to see if it was true."

"It's not," I say. "You need to leave the park."

They shuffle off, mumbling apologies. The girl turns her head and glances at me. Soft features gleam on her face—eyes, lips. Then the students vanish.

I trudge back to my office with memories of my own college experience in mind. I was the first person in my family to attend a university, and I remember the students there, so like these kids— tan, smiling, walking through stone quadrangles holding hands, and they all had different haircuts than me, different clothes. I learned that I did not know how to talk, or dress, or even smile.

I remember feeling like a fraud that first year, picturing conspiracies around me, but I had a roommate who bought pot in bulk and he showed me ways to relax and let the world go. My spine shivers a little when I remember those days, before I learned the necessity of control and found my path.

As the elevator takes me up, my mind's eye keeps replaying the girl's parting glance. Miyamoto says the true bushi divorces himself from desire, but in tonight's shadows her eyes tugged at something in my lungs that ran down to the place behind my abdomen where chi is stored, and I'm compelled to think of Mabel, so I spend the rest of my shift practicing guided meditation. In the lotus position, I close my eyes and focus on the Blue Triangle where I store the egoless self, trying not to remember Mabel's laugh and the cleft at the base of her spine, the taste of her sweat or the purple bathwater that covered her on our last night together. Dead air from the call box hisses, and I block it out.

Morning is a loud wash of white sun and I hear St. Louis waking up as I ride the tram down. Birds wake, barges wake, everything calling to everything else. A girl stands at the bottom of the arch in a sleeveless white blouse, wind wrapping brown hair around her face, and even before she brushes it away I know who she is.

"The park doesn't open until nine," I say. She looks at me with faded green eyes and her brown hair is streaked by shades of orange. "Can I help you, ma'am?"

"It's you, isn't it?" she says.

"I'm sorry?"

The wind keeps playing with her hair. "You're the ghost bird, aren't you? You know there's a Web site about you?"

The morning grows noisy, feels too bright. "What?" If I keep lying, what are my odds? She's much smaller than me, and I consider a *yonkyo* nerve pinch to make her unconscious. But I'd still have a problem when she woke up. "What do you want?"

"I'll tell you in a second." She looks around at the park and up at the arch. "Can we go talk somewhere?"

A coffee shop that smells like butter and icing. She wears a lot of silver, and rope bracelets on one arm; dusky-hued freckles spot her nose and cheekbones. Her name is Erica Gleason, and she's telling me the history of ghost birds, working toward an explanation for something she hasn't said yet. "In our class one of the myths we studied was how throughout history, in every culture, an unexplained thing people see are black, ornithologic figures, enormous bird-things with glowing eyes. They're called different things, but a lot of theory insists names are meaningless."

"Erica—"

"I mean, angels, demons, monsters, whatever."

"Erica." I lean over the table. "What do you want?"

She deflates a little, and I'm instantly sorry I interrupted. She sips coffee and looks out the window. People bustle under traffic lights. Horns bleat, brakes squeal. I'm usually in bed right now, preparing to sleep through the day.

She turns back to me. "I'm just saying, I was disappointed when I figured out it was only you."

"How did you know, by the way?"

She bows her head and stirs her coffee. "I could tell by the way you acted…and I saw a guy dressed all in black looking at me with binoculars from a window in the arch." Her eyes meet me with consolation. "I didn't tell anybody."

"Right. So. What do you want?"

"Okay. Here's the thing." She puts her spoon down. "I want you to teach me."

"Teach what?"

"BASE jumping."

I try to tell her it doesn't work like that. "You don't just go out and BASE jump. It takes years to accumulate the knowledge needed to do your first jump. It's a continual learning process. I still walk away sometimes."

"I've skydived before."

"How many times?"

"Twice."

"Jeez." I'm wrong to describe her hair as brown. It's more like burnt wheat with copper and russet highlights. "This sport isn't about proving anything. It's very personal. People get killed. Very experienced people get seriously injured and killed. Why do you even want to do this?"

"Why do you do it?" she asks, and the image of Mabel floating lifeless beneath lavender soap bubbles flashes across my mind.

"You have to master skydiving first. Even after, there are other people who can teach you."

"Look, I didn't say anything to anybody, okay? I didn't turn you in or anything. I mean, then why are you talking to me about it? What are you waiting for?"

She knows that by deliberating, I've already agreed. Silver jangles on her wrist; her lips are thin and faded; her collarbone spreads like a shadowy albatross above her chest and I'm thinking, Blue Triangle, Blue Triangle.

At my apartment the answering machine blinks, showing several messages, which makes me uneasy because I don't know who could be calling. After ten months in St. Louis, my acquaintances encompass a landlord, a mailman, and two park rangers who think I'm crazy for pulling the hours I do. In *Hagakure*, Tsunetomo writes that there is deep power in the solitary man.

It's my father's voice on the machine: "Ethan, it's your dad. I can't find your mother, son, and I been trying to get hold of you. You need to bring the horses in."

The next message is from an hour later, his voice guttural and slow, twanging words out. "Ethan, it's your dad. I can't find your mother, son, and I been trying to get hold of you. You need to bring the horses in. It looks like rain." Three other messages say roughly the same things, along with suggesting I gather up some potatoes and carrots so my mother can make vegetable soup. Our farm was sold some time ago, after my mother died.

I call Green Grove and speak to the head nurse about these messages. She puts me on hold, comes back and explains that a temporary nurse was working my father's floor yesterday, and that's why he was able to make so many phone calls. She apologizes for the inconvenience. In my room, I lie upon a bamboo mat in the center of the floor and place a sleep mask over my eyes to block out sun filtered through the blinds. When I attempt to envision a beach where I can align my heartbeat with the breaking of waves, I instead see my father one particular morning, during my first summer home from college: at dawn my mother and I found him standing in a field of scrubgrass with only a blanket wrapping him, staring at the sun. Brightness engulfed him that morning. We thought he was kidding around at first, but in the intervening years I've wondered what, exactly, he was seeing.

So the ocean in my mind becomes the sounds of warblers and wrens at dawn on my father's farm, and then Erica starts lecturing me about eternal spirits disguised as birds while unbuttoning her white blouse. Unable to sleep, what I really want to do is jump off something.

We enter an AFF course—accelerated free fall. It's a seven-step program designed to teach skydiving basics; after that she has twenty jumps till she's a novice jumpmaster. She has money for all this. Her father's a litigator for Dowling Industrial. We start on a small single-engine Cessna whose air tastes like aluminum and petrol. Our bench rattles and dips; the engine sputters. Beyond the door is a roaring radiance. While we're waiting to be flagged out, Erica eyes her static line and says, "Here we go. Geronimo."

"Don't say that. Everybody says that."

"What do you say?"

I admit, reluctantly, "Banzai."

She nods and keeps her gaze steady, being tough, betraying no awe or excitement or fear.

At 12,500 feet a jump doesn't even feel like falling—more like being at the center of a cold explosion. You can see the curvature of the planet, the spherical surface that tugs you down. I watch her body tumble, bright red jumpsuit, limbs arched back in perfect form. She shrinks, breaks into white clouds, and I lose her. My arms go straight at my sides and I dive. At about 140 miles an hour, I see her canopy, a ruffled red square below me. My cheeks billow with wind.

On the ground, she can't stop smiling, looking up at what we traversed. She cheers and laughs and suggests we go do some shots. I explain that it's just the adrenaline rush and that I don't drink.

May's air is thick and heavy, trapped under this purple vapor we're enduring. At night I worry. Surveying the park grounds, I wonder who's out there, watching for me. Erica's told me about a Web site: "Bird Man of St. Louis." There's a picture on it of a fanged black bird with burning, phosphorous eyes, along with message boards and testimonials from people who have seen me. You can order a T-shirt.

Skydiving doesn't compare to BASE. Out of a plane you're too high and have no real sense of the bottom. Mu, the void, is not so immediate; you can't even glimpse it, and gravity's embrace is more like a languorous tug than a violent slam. I press my hands against the glass and ponder the fall, and the dream life of a sleeping city seems awfully far away as my reflection looks back in the window and parallel light beams shine up from the arch's base like a Zen ladder.

Five jumps later Erica tells me her mother is an artist who gives lessons at their home, and who lost her left breast to cancer three years ago. We're eating ice cream, walking in the mall because she wants to get new shoes. She says, "You know, I was really hoping you were some undiscovered animal, like a ghost bird."

"I know. You believe in that stuff?"

She shrugs and licks her cone, swinging her bag from Foot Locker. "I guess. Probably. There's always stuff we don't know about. Once, in the 1920s, in Texas, there was a series of sightings of a black bird as big as a city, perched on the moon. I love that."

She wipes caramel off her lip with a finger that she licks while grinning at me and my chi thrums against my diaphragm like I've swallowed a tiny bomb.

Her school lets out for the summer, so we start diving more. Three times a week. Evening sets in as we walk off the airfield. She says her father is working long hours now. The EPA is giving Dowling Industrial hell.

"What is that stuff, anyway?" I ask, tracing an arc across the lavender sky.

She takes my hand, and we stop walking. "I don't know what it is."

At first I'm embarrassed, because I don't have any furniture in my apartment, and my bed is a bamboo mat with a single thin blanket. In fading light from a window the fuzz on her chest and stomach is lucent and blond. Sweat gathers in a salty pool at her navel. Her skin is darker than Mabel's, and she weighs less.

A certain anxiety dissipates as we progress. Touching is fine. Like I remembered, but different.

"Tell me about your first time," she says, face flushed and glistening, tips of her hair sticking to my chest.

I tell her about jumping off Bethel Bridge in Cypress Park. I don't mention my perverse curiosity that cold morning, the clear idea I had as I dangled my foot off the bridge, to hold onto the bundled chute the whole way down and never release it from my hand.

"Really," she says. "Why did you start doing this?"

I shrug and feign sleepiness. I don't mention the time four years ago when I bought half a gram of heroin, or the night Mabel used it, passed out, and slipped under the bathwater we were going to share when I got home.

I want to explain that I'm not just some thrill-seeker, that the arch is the nexus of civilization and wilderness, and there I inhabit a space between spaces, where city and forest are separated by a perfect geometry of solid steel. But we don't talk, and when I close my eyes, burning scarlet fissures erupt and crack the perfect symmetry of my Blue Triangle.

The next morning I call my father at Green Grove. He asks the same two questions four times.

Erica wants me to come meet her mother and "see something." I can guess what.

Her mother, Carol, has hair the same color as Erica's, but much shorter. She asks me what working for Park Services is like, and looks at me softly when I explain myself as a nature lover. Erica is quiet. When she faces her mother, they don't make eye contact long, and I find some similarities in their faces. Carol asks me about my hobbies and has a distant look in her eyes. Her voice seems to tremble when she speaks; she absently fingers an earring, as if she's worried about something but doesn't want to trouble anyone. I remember that she lost a breast when she was ill.

A garden in their backyard is elaborate and well pruned. A tiny creek burbles through it. I take a deep breath and confess: "I don't want you to do this."

Erica's mouth opens, but before she can answer I say, "It's too dangerous," and I reach for her hand.

She crosses her arms and steps back. "I'm good. What are you talking about?" In the kitchen window the back of her mother's head is visible. "Where's this coming from?"

"It's too soon. It's too soon and it's too dangerous. I don't want anything to happen to you." What I don't mention is that I can't possibly handle killing another girl.

The little creek sloshes between us. "No," she says. "I'm still doing it. Forget it. I'm going." Then she breaks our date at 10,000 feet, and I know we won't be up in any more airplanes. She leads me to her bedroom, where her equipment is sprawled on the floor.

"This is what you wanted me to see?"

It's an ACE 240 canopy and a Perigee II container. Black. "Just like yours," she says, moving toward me. "I know how to do it," she says. "And I will. But I'm asking you to."

"Please, Erica, c'mon." I'm allowed to hold her hand.

"I'm doing it regardless, okay? Whether you do this for me or not. But I trust you." She puts her head on my chest. "I'm still doing it, but I trust you, okay?"

I nod.

I rotate the Perigee II on the floor, harness down, and stow the break lines solemnly. It is grim business. I divide the line groups and run the slider up toward the canopy, observing that the leading edge of the canopy is hanging at my knees while the trailing edge faces away from me. She sits on the bed, watching over my shoulder. The room smells like her, like a young, living girl: some combination of flora and powder, lotion and fruit.

I work the fabric between the line groups to the outside of the lines, and continue flaking it that way for all sections of the canopy. It's like folding an accordion. The idea is to keep all of the line-attachment points toward the center of the packjob, with the fabric folded to the outside. The bed squeaks behind me, and her fingernails rub the back of my head. I carefully redefine my previous folds, bring the center of the trailing edge up and hold it under my thumb. Next I dress the tail and fold it around itself. I stow the lines in the tail pocket and place the canopy in the container. Then I breathe.

She kisses the top of my head. "Thank you."

We sleep apart tonight, and I spend two hours in a straight-backed lotus, mentally defining my circle of power, trying to reconstruct my Blue Triangle.

The very beginning of sunrise. False dawn after the moon vanishes. By now the gases in the air have finally begun to settle, so while the sky is a fairly normal indigo, a thick fog under the Bethel Bridge is opalescent, glittered with pinks and purples. She wears loose black pants and a tank top, with the Perigee hunched on her back, pads on her knees, her hair tucked under a helmet. I've got my gear on too.

We both look down at the fog, which twinkles and undulates beneath the bridge. Pine trees and shrubbery are hushed.

"You can't even see the bottom," I tell her.

She's looking down. "So? I count off three seconds, right? I'll see it when I get down there."

"I wouldn't do this." My hands start twitching as she climbs onto the railing. "Erica—"

"You don't have to do it. I am. I'll see you down there."

She's taking quick, shallow breaths and can't stop looking down. Her eyes are panicked, and remind me of her mother's. Then, when I see that similarity, I understand what it is between us, what must have drawn her to me and why we're out here.

"Erica, wait. If you think this will keep you from being afraid—it won't. The fear doesn't stop. It never does."

She looks confused and shakes her head. "What? I don't—I never said that." Her eyes remain fixed on the fog. "I never said that."

Background noises rise: twittering birds, things scraping in trees and rustling the grass. The trestle begins to rumble from far-off automobiles.

Atop the railing she grips her pilot chute with white knuckles. She glances at me and fakes a smile. "Okay. I'll see you at the bottom." She takes one giant breath and steps off, leaving a splash of fog lingering where she pierced it.

I rush to the rail and look down. No, listen, I want to say, what we think is a gesture of freedom, see, is a symptom of our cage. But she's gone. I can't see beyond the mist, already closing the hole she made, and I climb on top of the railing.

What can I do but follow her down?

Before human beings, a deep river lived here, carrying tons of life between oceans. Now fog below the bridge conceals only a pebbled canyon of cool, dry stone. A garden under purple gas. Rocks thump against my feet as I stick the landing.

At the bottom she's on her knees, the canopy flapping around her. My chute trails like a black flag. We're small among giant ferns and ivy growing inside the jagged walls of this chasm. I lift her and start undoing her harness. She's shaking. She reaches around my back to undo mine. A tear streaks behind her goggles. She says she thought she was going to die. The straps slide down, and I feel the dead drag of my own chute drop away.

We promise never to do it again.

I purchase a gel-filled mattress that promises to conform to the contours of my spine. I buy cotton sheets. Erica brings me more pillows than anyone could ever need. I change my schedule so that I'm only working three graveyard shifts.

Erica wants me to teach her martial arts, so I use my empty living room to show her what aikido I know. All the *kokyu nage* body throws end up with us wrestling and then getting pretty dirty on the carpet.

At work, I still appreciate the view, but when I contemplate Mu and the bushi's goal of joining the void, my feet feel heavy. There's slight vertigo as I gaze down from my office window. Concerning my relationship with gravity: I start to wonder if it even exists, since "gravity," after all, is just one name ascribed to a particular phenomena. Instead, I ponder isolation as the governing physics of this universe: mass attracts mass because singularity isn't natural, sentience or no, and the basic unit of life isn't one, but two. Planets and moons form, and people stick to them because something in the cosmos is trying to keep itself company. Below the arch a slight lilac tinting of air is all that remains of the once heavy cloud that distorted our skies these last two months. Dowling Industrial ended up settling with the EPA for five million dollars and a new system of air vents that could suck the eyes out of your head.

Near the end of July, Erica's father leaves her mother.

The lobby at Green Grove is antiseptic in a deceitful way. The rosy wallpaper and carpet are okay, but the plants are plastic, and Muzak plays at a hushed volume. Ms. Teschmaucher, the head nurse, approaches me sympathetically. The nurses at Green Grove wear light-blue uniforms with navy aprons, and they smell like nurses, like Ivory soap and rubbing alcohol.

She takes my arm as she escorts me past the smiling elderly who gaze up like I might be someone they once loved. "I just want you to be prepared," she says, patting my elbow.

My father's room is an eight-by-fifteen space with beige walls and salmon-colored carpet. Two tall chairs form a V to the left of the television, which sits on a standard wooden dresser. A bookshelf stands against one wall with pictures of my mother and me, his own parents, a Bible, and some flowers. His bed is made in military style, sheets so tight you could bounce change off them. He made his bed like that my entire life, and I wonder then if certain things never go away, movements so right that they can never be unlearned.

He sits in a rocking chair, wearing his robe and pajamas, staring out the window at the far side of the room.

"Jacob?" Ms. Teschmaucher says, guiding me toward him. "Ethan's here. Your son, Ethan."

He turns from the window and looks up at me. My father's face is a lost expanse of wrinkled flesh and liver spots; he has a still-noble jaw and a white crew cut thinning at the crown. His blue eyes search the space where we stand. He smiles slowly and nods. His hand, dry, stretched taut, reaches out and takes mine.

"It's good to see you. Really good," he says, with the kind of emotional tone you wouldn't use unless you were faking it.

"Hey, Dad."

He turns back to the window and watches the bucolic, parklike area that exists at the heart of Green Grove's compound. Ms. Teschmaucher and I exchange glances, and then my father looks back at me.

"I'm worried about the grass out there. It looks dry this season."

I crouch beside him and stare out the window. "It's not so bad." He smells the same: musky traces of the Brut cologne he splashed on every day I ever knew him. I put my arm around him.

He asks, "Do you know Susie Frenesi?"

"No," I say.

He turns back to the window, then looks down at me again. His eyes blaze with sudden joy. "Bill? Where have you been?"

I used to have an uncle named Bill, my father's younger brother.

"Around. You know."

"I'm worried about the grass out there."

On the way to the lobby, Ms. Teschmaucher says this deterioration will continue and I shouldn't let myself feel hurt by his inability to remember me. I don't feel hurt. He's the one who's having everything gradually peeled from him, his identity falling away, years dropping like skin being shed in preparation for a new spring. As I pull away from the building, I glimpse my father standing at his window, inspecting the grass, and I have a sudden vision of Mu claiming him, its bright void drawing him closer with the most deft and sinister grasp, taking everything he ever was into its light.

It's a time when things are taken away.

A time when I find a brochure for Bridge Day among Erica's textbooks. Bridge Day is an annual gathering of BASE jumpers in Fayetteville, West Virginia. For one day in October, BASE jumping is made legal off the New River Gorge Bridge.

She walks into her room wearing a black tank top and jeans, her hair tied back and cheeks slightly sunken. She's thinner.

I brandish the advertisement. "You're not really going to do this, are you?"

She shrugs and starts picking things up, moving loose clothes around and stuffing them into drawers.

"Hey. You're not doing this, are you?"

She looks at me and plops on her bed, throws an arm over her eyes. "I don't know. I was thinking about it."

"I thought we stopped all this. I thought we talked about it."

She keeps her arm over her eyes. "You don't have to do anything you don't want to," she says. Not changing position, with one hand she uses a remote control to turn on her stereo. The Pixies start playing too loud for conversation.

That night I toss and turn on my new, obscenely comfortable mattress. My thoughts center on a girl's body falling through space, on a chute that opens a split second too late to slow her fall. Her body breaks on rocks and stone, the canopy drifting delicately down upon her. People crowd around, and when that shroud is pulled away, the face I see is Mabel's. My stomach hurts, a cramping I haven't felt since I first went cold turkey, four years ago.

I sleep on the floor.

It's a time of transition, when the eyes of summer close and open on autumn. The *I Ching* says my dominant yin is Earth over Fire, which means "Injury to the Enlightened." Confucius advises, "It will be beneficial to be steadfast and break through distress."

Because she asked me to, I pack Erica's chute in preparation for Bridge Day. Then I explain that we can't see each other anymore.

She gets angry. "What? Are you serious? Just because I won't do what you tell me?"

That's meant to goad me, but in my mind I am a perfect Blue Triangle, and my heart is the steady, slow lapping of waves on an inner shore. "Because I don't want to be there when you die."

"What? When I—" She raises her arms. "Nobody's ever died at a Bridge Day."

"That's not true: 1983 and 1987."

Erica puts her hands on her hips and stares with mock disgust. "Whatever. I'm not going to be, like, some mad BASE jumper. I mean, look who's talking. What's your problem?"

My Triangle holds. I am three lines of perfect order, pulsing with a cool sapphire glow. "I can't handle losing anyone else," I say, and what I'm thinking is, *I am so tired of everyone disappearing.*

"So, okay, wait." She sits on the bed and makes a tiny box with her hands. "To keep from losing me, you're breaking up with me?"

I don't expect her to understand the logic. She calls me a coward. She says that I'm the one who's afraid. I turn to leave, and she says I'm like an addict: I can't deal with life so I insulate myself with habit and ideas. I don't turn around, because there's nothing else to say.

What can you say to someone you love who won't abide her own fear?

I take to driving past Green Grove during the day, spotting my father sitting at his window where he watches tree limbs rustle with squirrels. It isn't often that I think of her.

One day my father isn't at his window. I look, make a U-turn, and pass again, but in his place I see only a pane of glass that shines back the sun. I know he must be in a different part of the home at that moment, yet I stop to stare, and in that window's flat, radiant square I ponder my father, perhaps for the first time, with true clarity.

I get my old schedule back at work.

I stand at the window when three a.m. comes, tightening my harness. Through the glass, the woods are still and mysterious, stretching boundlessly into darkness, while on the other side of the arch a city beats brightly, steaming and vibrating with implied movement. I raise the scarf over my nose and lower the blue glass of my NVTs and the world becomes a hazed impression of emerald spectres. Now I tell myself that I don't straddle the dreams of my culture, but that I stand within them.

I'm like the giant black bird perched on the moon, an idea existing between rumor and imagination, the shape you hope to see when you chance to look up after a late night.

Now I'm like myth, a UFO, a thunderbird, and this role carries its own concessions, its promise of ritual and discipline, while below, somewhere in the wilderness or in apartments across the river, with telescopes pointed out windows, people wait to see, ready to mold me into whatever they decide to believe I am. I raise the window and let my leg slip out. Wind caresses me. I clutch the pilot chute.

Now I am a ghost.

Banzai.

AMY'S WATCH

TWO HOURS BEFORE SHE LEARNED THAT HER BROTHER was dead, Amy tried to aggravate North Godcheaux by bringing up the subject of her sister. Amy worked at a drugstore in the afternoons, and North picked her up when her shift ended. To avoid being noticed, North parked his truck a few blocks away when waiting for her. She told her mother a friend from school gave her rides. In the truck North had been silent, had hardly looked at her, and this irritated Amy.

She said, "I found you and Kara's prom picture last night."

He stopped rolling the toothpick in his mouth. "What are you telling me?"

"Nothing. I was unboxing pictures from our attic. I just found it."

"What are you telling me this for?"

"Nothing." The truck braked at a red light, and he held his palms up in a way that reminded her of Father DeBlanc at Nana's funeral mass.

"Why are you talking to me about her?"

She shrugged and, having irritated him, turned to stare out the window. North looked much different in the prom picture. His face had been rounder, jaw smooth, hair in a crew cut. Now his cheekbones were hard edges, black hair curled down from under his fishing cap, and by this time of day his stubble was much thicker than any of the boys' at Laughton High. In the picture, his hands rested gently on her sister's hips. Kara, she thought, probably looked the same. Amy had not seen her sister in seven years. Kara had eventually gone to college and married a man in computers, and now they had three houses in two countries. Amy sometimes imagined the houses, and they would be extravagant, vain, so nice they bullied visitors with slippery marble and dramatic lighting.

North's truck eased up a shallow hill. They passed a field where for years an abandoned station wagon had sat on cinder blocks instead of tires. Perched on the old automobile, two cattle egrets glowed white through the khaki haze of dried cutgrass.

"I just want us to have fun," North said. "I don't want to talk about her." He put his hand on her arm.

Amy knew her demeanor today—sharp, distant—was confusing North, but felt no pity for him. The day before, she'd learned she was pregnant, and that knowledge, unshared, permitted her strength, a new reserve of depth and weight. She stared out the window.

Plants broke through every surface. Weeds divided concrete parking lots into segments. Grass veined the road's black tar. Oak, pine, and sumac grew in the spaces between buildings. Every building they passed was a single story and had rust-colored water damage staining its edges. Over two centuries old, the town of Laughton remained a harsh, humid wilderness. Amy fit its spaces. Sixteen, she had muscular thighs beneath her denim skirt, a solid, compact girl with a strong back and a wide, open face. She had soft black hair, combed straight, a good shade, what she thought of as her best feature.

They descended into wooded terrain bordered by cane fields. Beyond the cane rose the courthouse's thin clock tower, and beyond that meadows and the small oil derricks that bowed up and down all day like feeding birds. She saw North's trailer park through the forest vines.

Her older brother, Christian, had gone hunting with North in this truck, back when it was a shiny sky blue. The paint was a more powdery color now, almost gray against the reddening sunset. Rust flayed the truck's edges, and the door squealed when she opened and closed it. Amy saw that North had left a black thumbprint on her arm. She stared at the greasy oval before wiping it away with spit.

Smells crammed the air inside the trailer. Cigarettes, gasoline, sharp odors from the chemical cleansers North used at his job. He folded his bed down from the wall and took off his shirt. In the dim lighting Amy thought he looked once more like the athlete her sister brought home when Amy was six. He'd become leaner in the ten years since, more shrunken. When she took off his cap hair fell around his face and she liked that. She took off her T-shirt, and he moved her skirt up around her waist. She draped her bra over one of the chains that held the bed.

She touched his arms, the humidity of his skin, ashy taste from his tongue. The bed jostled on its chains. His face was turned up and his eyes closed tightly. Amy watched him from below. At these times she believed that he was thinking about Kara, but she could never bring herself to mind that. She was thinking about Kara too, remembering the night she first saw her sister's breasts. She often thought of that night.

Kara had stood in front the bathroom mirror wearing only a pair of purple panties, preparing for a date. In the mirror, she'd smoothed lotion over her gold skin, and her chest shined. Her breasts sloped firmly, curved up to their tips. Her blond hair had been pulled back. Kara patted her stomach and cupped her breasts when she leaned forward to inspect her teeth. Amy had stood beside her with a toothbrush hanging from her mouth.

Kara had asked if Amy wanted some lotion, too, and she'd squeezed Nivea into her sister's hands while Amy stared at her nipples. They were dark brown, the size of silver dollars. Amy mimicked her sister when Kara propped one foot on the toilet and began rubbing the lotion into her legs, giving them a white glow. On the bathroom mirror, their mother had inserted prayer cards where the fixtures held the glass. The three children were met by the painted faces of St. Michael and the Blessed Virgin, each morning and night.

Amy had asked her sister, "Who are you going out with tonight?"

"North Godcheaux. You remember him?" Kara had looked in the mirror while she talked. She undid her hair and let it fall. She patted Amy's head and went to her room. Kara had bumped into Christian in the hall, wearing only her drawers, and moved around him and shut the door to her room. Later that night a sheriff's deputy would bring her home. She'd been sixteen then. Christian was fourteen, Amy six.

Immediately after he'd finished, North sat on the edge of the bed and pulled up his jeans. He rose and walked to the toilet. Amy zipped her skirt and lay on the sheets. A green-gold ray filtered through the narrow window above the bed, coloring the hand she rubbed lightly over her stomach.

Amy hadn't decided whether to keep the baby. The newness of the pregnancy created a calm that still felt surprising. Beaumont had clinics that could end the life for little or no money, but for now it was her secret, a thing that made her more powerful.

North stepped out of the bathroom and said, "I'll drive you home."

Amy barely heard him. She was trying to imagine what it would be like, the moment the baby left her body, what she would feel.

When they were back in his truck, North asked, "Nobody's heard from Christian?" He lit a cigarette.

"Not since Easter," Amy said. The last they'd heard, her brother was mountain climbing in Washington. Christian had not been home in three years, and then his visit was compelled by a fractured leg and arm he got breaking horses in Brenham, Texas.

"Every October I take the bows down, I think about that stag. First time out." North had said that to Amy at least three times since they'd been going out, but she didn't think he realized. North was four years older than Amy's brother. After Kara had broken up with him in high school, North had maintained a relationship with her little brother, a blatant attempt to remain connected to her life. But real friendship developed between the two boys, or as much friendship as Christian allowed anyone. North took him fishing and taught him to bow hunt. Amy remembered, as a little girl, seeing them leave one morning before sunrise, wearing camouflage jumpsuits and holding brawny bows in their hands. She'd thought of them the rest of the day, the way they'd looked in the blue morning, their weapons, the clothes that looked like tree bark. She'd wanted to go with them.

The truck motored past barren lots of scrubgrass and fireweed, moss held like handkerchiefs by branches, farther into the country, past marshes thick with cattails and cypress, stagnant scents drifting through the curtains of ivy. The truck stopped at the top of the street. He let her out and she walked downhill toward her house.

The neighborhood was a tidy arrangement of single-story homes bordering a large basin of muddy grass. Their parents had bought one of the first five houses here, but a planned lakefront community was aborted when the Corps of Engineers diverted the Vermillion River, eventually making the neighborhood's small lake into the weedy basin at the end of the street. Her mother's old Cougar was parked beneath the live oak in their yard, where it had not moved in over a week, as far as Amy could tell. The lawn tangled past the boundaries of porch and driveway. Weeds had cracked through the driveway, splitting its slabs. A four-bedroom with flaking auburn paint around its sides, the house had a front door of thick, burnished wood, and five diamonds of glass built a larger diamond at its center. She called, "Mom?" when she opened the door. She lived in the house with only her mother. Her parents had divorced less than a year after Christian left.

She crossed the foyer, where pictures lined the walls. More pictures, like the ones she'd found in the attic the night before. Her family's pictures were disconnected from her own life. From the time they were children, her brother and sister had been recognized as two of the best-looking people in Laughton. They were both tall, had blond hair and bronze skin, lean faces above wide shoulders and thin hips. Amy's own black hair framed a heart-shaped face, the kind people described as "pleasant." She had broad hips and eyes that slanted faintly, as if an Asiatic presence shimmered in her genes. Her eyes were blue and her pale skin blushed easily. Her parents said she resembled one of her father's aunts, a woman she'd never seen. The pictures in the hallway—her brother and sister and parents, most taken before she was born—always carried accusations, made her feel like a trespasser.

Her mother was sitting in the kitchen, in a floral nightgown. Through bay windows the evening cast a dowdy blue light on her slouched figure. A retired schoolteacher, her mother often sat there, her Bible replaced by books of crossword puzzles she solved while smoking cigarettes.

"Hey, Mom?"

Her mother's head twitched, hands dangling at her sides, a yellow pencil on the linoleum floor. Amy heard a soft bleating from the cordless phone that sat on the table. Beside the ashtray on the table lay a cigarette with a long tube of ash above its filter. The cigarette had burned a shiny black oval into the table's wood finish.

When her mother finally spoke, she began crying. "Christian died."

Amy fell into a chair. She said "why," though she'd meant to say "how." Her mother kept weeping and put her head into her arms, folded on the table. Amy reached out and turned off the phone, an almost unconscious gesture. She watched the burnt black spot on the table as though expecting it to shift in size.

II.

THE SUN SHINED RELENTLESSLY ON THE DAY OF THE funeral. A stiff gulf breeze caressed the few mourners with briny, soothing air. Her mother sat in a formless black dress, frowning with some terminal surrender. Amy's father, Arthur Placide, stood several yards away, his spine rigid in a dark gray suit, his head lolling now and then. Twice she saw his legs buckle and straighten. His wife, Suzanne, helped him both times. She was a small, extremely thin woman with deeply tanned skin and frazzled orange hair. Her father had married her with no warning, three years after his divorce. He was now a personal injury lawyer in Baton Rouge. He had received the body and made the funeral arrangements.

A plain brown coffin enclosed Christian. It took three days to get the body from Washington. "I don't understand," Amy had asked her father. "They just found him on a street?" The undertaker had cut his hair and shaved his beard. She tried to remember him as he'd been when they were children, but she kept seeing the brooding teenager, the young man with the scar over his lip. "What do you mean he was lying in the street?" she'd asked, voice warbling.

Altogether, she counted sixteen people at the funeral, most of them old friends of her mother. North stood farther back than anyone else. He wore dark brown corduroy pants and a blue blazer over a white shirt. She watched the wind toss his hair. His face was still handsome, gaining some dignity from its gauntness and the angle of the sun. Amy had cried hardest when she'd told him about Christian.

She told him they didn't know who had done it, but her brother had been stabbed. The words had brought out convulsive tears. She remembered her brother showing her how to set crab traps back when Vermillion River still flowed into the lake at the end of their street.

"Hey," North had said. "Is Kara coming to the funeral?"

Amy shrugged. "I guess."

After high school, Kara had taken a scholarship to SMU, and three years later she moved to San Francisco and got engaged to Jim, an older man with a company. It had taken her mother an entire day to track down a number where Kara could be reached, her husband's representatives at first unable or unwilling to provide the information.

And Kara was not at the funeral today. Sun flared in the priest's glasses. He made the sign of the cross as the coffin lowered. Alone, Amy's mother dropped a handful of dirt onto the casket. One of her friends, a very old elementary school teacher, held her by the arm and shoulder as she let the dirt fall.

On that night when Amy first saw her sister's breasts, a sheriff's deputy had woken the family at a very late hour. He'd brought Kara home. Amy and Christian had crept out of their rooms, peering around the corner to the front door. They saw the deputy talking to their parents, Kara silent and furious-looking. Their voices were murmurs to Amy and Christian, but they both understood that the deputy had caught their sister parked in a car with a boy. There was some offense beyond that, though, because the boy didn't sound like North Godcheaux. When the deputy left, their father locked the door and slapped Kara's face. He said he didn't raise her to be a nigger-lover. He'd called her names while their mother remained silent nearby. She stood in her long white nightgown, hands on her big hips and her head bowed, the rosary she took to bed still gripped in a fist.

Kara pushed past her parents and down the hallway, past Amy and Christian, and she slammed the door to her room. Their mother followed, going to her own room and leaving their father alone in the foyer. A tall claims lawyer in a small town full of lawyers, Mr. Placide's neck bowed from looking downward his whole life. Most nights he watched TV alone in the living room, where he would sleep on his recliner. He came into the hall and saw Amy and Christian. Their father would be at a loss to explain his next action. He had meant to say something to the two children, something about how late it was, but instead he struck Christian across the mouth with the heel of his hand. He seemed confused a moment, then told them both to go to bed. He walked back to the living room. They heard the television turn on. Somebody said something and a laugh track played.

Lying in the dark of her own room, Amy had felt dread, fear for a vague thing that would be worse than what just took place. Her room seemed different around her. She didn't recognize the shapes on her walls.

North's face glistened, freshly shaved. When he'd arrived at the church, Amy had seen him searching the small crowd for her sister, the girl from whom he'd never recovered. She felt his disappointment. She remembered when he came in the drugstore a month ago, bought a box of Band-Aids and at the register said, "Hey, you're Kara's sister, aren't you?"

Her father appeared at her side. Amy was standing outside the circle of people that had gathered around her mother, and he stumbled forward a little, pressing her close to his chest. He smelled like gin. "It'll be all right, sweetheart." His hand thumped her back too hard. Suzanne conveyed sympathy. "He was a tough kid," her father said, turning his head to his wife, keeping his hand on Amy's shoulder. "He really was."

Amy nodded. He had been. In his later adolescence, after Kara left, Christian brawled continuously. Twice, families of other young men had threatened legal action. When he was seventeen, he'd had to have two teeth replaced and acquired a scar between his nose and lip.

Her father said, "I'm going to get to the bottom of this. I'm going to figure it out." He was silent a moment and he turned abruptly to Suzanne, attempting to smile. "I used to beat the hell out of him." His lower lip trembled. His face collapsed, slowly, like a child who realizes his knee is skinned. "I did."

Amy stepped gently out of his arm. He told his wife, "I did," as though she didn't believe him. She held onto him as he walked away unsteadily.

Amy was left alone, watching the drab, fat women offering her mother consolation. The cemetery was small and bordered by thick woods. Over the tree line the white spire stood against the sky like a pointing finger. North stepped behind her.

"Are you all right?"

"No," she said. "I'm really not." She spoke briefly, because she'd found that if she spoke she started crying.

"Where's Kara?"

She rubbed the bridge of her nose, taking a long, frustrated breath. "She's in France. They said something about not being able to get a flight out so soon. Or something like that. I don't know."

He shook his head. "That's her all over, isn't it? Who can't come to her brother's funeral? I'm sorry, but that's—it ain't right."

Amy felt a blush of hatred swarm her face. "You're so stupid."

"What?"

"I mean, do you even know how many times she cheated on you? The police brought her home one night 'cause she'd been doing some black guy in a car."

He stuttered, shrank back. "What are you talking about?"

"Nothing." She wiped her eyes. "Just—I don't want to talk to you now, okay? Go away."

He tried to approach her, but she held up her hand as if halting a bus. "Please go away right now."

Hot tears were rising and she turned away. Her mother was still surrounded, and in the parking lot she could see Suzanne helping her father into the passenger side of their old Lincoln. Christian's face in the coffin had looked too calm to be him. She remembered that when she was eight, she saw him washing blood off his hands in the hall bathroom. His eye was cut, and he'd stopped shaving. Amy had asked him, "Are you trying to make yourself ugly?"

He hadn't said anything, but slammed the door. Eventually, his eyes would become so stormy and intense that their father would shy away from physically confronting him. The mourners were dispersing. The fields of stones and flowers emptying people. Amy was supposed to drive her mother's car to the wake, being held by a Mrs. Abrams, the old teacher who'd stood beside her mother all day. It was still too bright outside, the white, glaring sort of sun that makes a person squint no matter where they're looking.

Amy drove through Laughton's small main strip, the grocery store, Dollar General, and three-screen cinema. She turned toward the high school. This group of six brick-and-stone buildings was the same school where Kara and North had met, where Christian won the writing award each year, and where Amy was beginning her final year with the same diligent anonymity she had long ago assumed as her chief characteristic. She felt as if the town and her family were a story that had already been told, and, their parts played, everyone had exited the stage, leaving her alone with the backdrops.

She stood outside the car in the school's parking lot. The large flat field where teams practiced was empty, goalposts lying like solitary H's on the ground. A flock of blackbirds erupted from the field, swirled upward in unison and held above the field like a swaying thumbprint. The gray dress she wore had a slimming effect. She ran her hands over her hips. She imagined her hips expanding if she chose to keep the child. Any thoughts about her body implied her sister's body, but today when she thought of her sister, she imagined for the first time what it might have been like to be stared at your whole life. Amy knew how intrusive other people's eyes could be. She understood it was those eyes, always staring, that had molded her sister. It suddenly made proper sense, the way her sister's beauty had seemed vindictive, the way she spent half the year in France with her rich husband, even the way she could in good conscience miss their brother's funeral. It wasn't that she resented their family. Kara resented something about the world, something about the way it was always looking at her. The blackbirds hung above the field, swaying back and forth, and Amy wondered why they wouldn't move on. The sun was setting behind clouds.

She traced a circle on her stomach. She planned to gradually convince herself to abort the baby. Then she wondered if it might be possible for part of Christian to reappear in her own child. Was there a chance she could have a blond and dark son, a child whose dormant traits must exist somewhere in her own blood? She imagined her brother flickering like an electric current along the ladder of her own chromosomes. The parts of him that were her, the blood they shared. She imagined an explosion of stars, his life inside her like a small galaxy spinning itself into existence, and the thought made her belly warm. The flock of birds flew up and dove down, scattering, fading into the brush.

III.

THE LAST TIME AMY HAD SEEN KARA, HER SISTER HAD come home to claim a set of luggage in preparation for moving to San Francisco. Their father had just moved out of the house, and Kara's only comment on the divorce was, "It should have happened a long time ago." "You'll leave too," Kara had told her. She'd squeezed Amy's small hand as if the statement were meant to be encouraging. "You'll see."

But Amy didn't want to leave. She didn't understand why everybody else did. Here was home. What else was there to find?

Amy parked her mother's car under the live oak in their yard. All the lights in the house were off. Inside kept the familiar stale smell of potpourri. The pictures in the hallway. The living room's carpet was gray-green, two gray couches forming an L against one corner. Heavy shadows, blue light. A darkened lamp, a ceiling fan, two crucifixes, porcelain statues of the Blessed Mother gazing down in repose beside the exposed heart of Jesus. The answering machine's light blinked rapidly, showing several messages. Amy breathed in the silence. She felt pierced by the house's history, this weight that would not admit her. She didn't turn on a single light.

The kitchen. She remembered Christian scrambling eggs. He was maybe ten. He'd put jelly in the skillet and after he made her taste them, he threw the eggs away and they'd both laughed. It was hard to remember his smile, and she was grateful for the memory.

Or Kara strolled through the kitchen in a long white T-shirt that hung below her underpants. She'd sat at the breakfast table and propped her golden legs on Christian's lap while he ate cereal, his speech and gestures becoming awkward and nervous. That amused Kara. She maintained a feline regality in the house, frequently stretching, lounging with the bored look of a house cat. Sometimes she'd twist a finger in Christian's hair.

The counter was lined by tall glass containers of peppers soaking in olive oil, a porcelain goose that held sugar, red and white salt shakers.

The phone rang out of the silence. She moved to the counter and lifted the receiver.

"Amy?" North's voice, deep, sorry sounding.

"Hey."

"Are you okay?"

"I don't know."

"Do you want to come over? Do you want me to come get you?"

Amy pressed a palm to her stomach. She could imagine the vanished sounds of the family. Things remaining over time, voices accruing in the corners.

She told him not to come get her. He apologized for what happened at the funeral, and she told him it was okay. She thought maybe it would be, that they would hang up and see each other later, but he broke the silence by revealing himself. "When you said, what did—you said she cheated on me. Do you know, I mean—"

"She cheated on every boy she ever went out with, North."

"But you don't know, I mean, as far as who with and all that? I always thought she'd done something with Matt Clark, but I couldn't prove it."

Amy sat down on the floor, shadows blanketing her and a heavy glow deepening in the empty, muted kitchen. "I don't think we should see each other anymore, North."

He stuttered, argued. He said it was just that today was a bad day.

Amy thought of what she should say. She should tell him about the baby. She should explain to him that he doesn't even really like her, that he's blinded by something that's gone. She should tell him because he isn't smart enough to realize it on his own. He's not even the saddest man she knows. But he has given her a baby. He has given her a baby, and she will not see him again.

She didn't want to deal with that, then. She told him she'd call him tomorrow. He protested but she provided reassurance. "We'll talk later." She hung up the phone and sat back on the kitchen floor.

She knew she would keep it, she admitted to herself, had always known. Because she deserves something that is hers, a purpose and family. She told herself that the birth might finally initiate her own history, that it might signal the arrival of her true life. She felt the lost ground of her family could be recovered. She felt she no longer needed to merely wait, like one of those war brides keeping watch at a window. This wait would pass, the way everything here passed.

Amy stood and walked to the answering machine. She pressed the button just below the blinking red light, and messages played in the dark. Family friends, the parish monsignor offering his services to the woman who'd attended his masses for over forty years. Then a strange voice, female, that said one word in greeting: "Mom."

It was Kara's voice, cracked and frayed by the old machine's recording tape. She apologized several times. In the message she said "hi" to Amy and apologized to her too. She said they have to call her, to please call her, and she recited directions for how to make international calls. Her voice was brief, direct, then there was the low beep that announced the end of new recordings.

She played her sister's message twice more, trying to recognize the voice. She would've liked to phone her sister and hear her explanation for missing the funeral. She would've liked to tell her about the inheritance of haunted men she left in her wake. What happened, she'd like to ask. Tell me everything that happened. She sat on the couch in the dark, hands on her stomach.

Once she graduated in May, she thought, she'd be able to get more hours at the drugstore. Her mother could watch the baby while she's at work. Amy began to make plans, telling herself again, more sure this time, that yes she'd known that she would keep it, known from the moment the first test showed its blue dot.

Amy stood up and walked to the living room. She turned on the light. She walked from room to room, turning on all the lights in the house.

The child would depend on her, clutch her fingers with its tiny hand. The baby could sleep on her chest, coo softly at the sound of Amy's voice as she talks about her day. Once a mother, she thought, certain vanities would disappear. She imagined her hips expanding, her breasts swelling and falling.

She imagined her hair cut short, like most mothers she knew. An impulse toward prettiness was already leaving her. She will never allow herself to cultivate her own beauty. Amy knew she couldn't let herself care about something like that, not if things were to be reclaimed.

1987, THE RACES

OAKLAWN DWARFED THEM, WHITE AND HAUGHTY AS a plantation, four tall stories with flags waving out front. Police directed traffic around the building, blowing their whistles in its shadow. His father drove an entirely red car that was eleven years old. The boy, Andru, knew this because his father bought the Continental the year he'd been born. A few black flies hovered around the floorboards of the big Lincoln, where French fries and pieces of trash trembled in the gutters. He usually saw his father two weekends a month, and from February till mid-April they usually went to Oaklawn. The building had a time-capsule quality to the boy, because he mainly associated Oaklawn with the mobsters who ruled it in the '40s and '50s. He liked the stories his father told about those gangsters: Lucky, Meyer, Bugsy, how they met in Hot Springs for conferences, dividing up fortunes during mineral baths and over rare roast beef in one of Oaklawn's dining rooms. He pictured men in fedoras and long coats moving through the crowd, bearing violin cases furtively under their arms. It was almost one o'clock and they parked a few blocks away from the track. He wasn't paying attention to what his father was saying, but later he would realize he'd heard every word.

"Handicapping is predicated on the principle that the future will repeat the past. Okay? So all the numbers—you have to be mathematic. Okay?" The father, David, turned off the car and held a cigarette near the top of his window, where a thin breeze entered. Black, round burns spotted the red upholstery bordering the glass. Sometimes if the boy concentrated, one of the cigarette burns would become a black fly and circle their heads before landing in the same spot. "Do you understand?" The father's voice was slightly hoarse. He squeezed his cigarette through the crack in the window and a small flurry of orange sparks burst into the car.

"Okay." The boy squinted as sparks died toward his face.

David dusted ashes off his gray suit, picking shreds of tobacco from the white shirt whose seams were yellowing. The elbows of the suit were thin, but it was all neatly pressed and smelled strongly of Polo for Men, a bottle of which sat on the backseat next to some clothes. He smoothed back his hair. On his thick, hairy hand was a large gold ring that had his initials, DS, spelled in diamonds over one knuckle.

"Hey, Dru?" he said. "Do you not want to be here?"

The boy sat up and glanced at him, then toward the brick wall beyond the windshield. A long crack sprawled across the glass. "Sure. I mean, I don't care. It's fine."

"A lot of people would like to visit Hot Springs twice a month."

"I know." His father's voice made his face hot.

"We're having fun. We're the guys, right?" He ruffled his son's spiky brown hair.

His son grinned.

The smile was so forced it infuriated the father. The boy could tell because his father clenched his jaw, climbed out of the car and slammed his door. It was a panicked sort of anger, visible at moments like this, when faced with evidence that these visits were something the boy endured. The son sensed fear as well as anger, and he wanted to alleviate the pressure, but could not move himself to utter any words to placate his father. He wouldn't realize until over a decade later that the fear was part of his father, a thing that lived in its own time, growing within him and needing nothing to engender it.

People swarmed the racetrack, like Indians around a fort in one of the John Wayne videos his father rented for them to watch with a bucket of fried chicken or a pizza. Old people, families, single men, and the young girls, the debutantes from Little Rock in expensive dresses, hair shining in the sun, the sun in their teeth. The boy watched them like he always did.

Now his father no longer seemed angry. He smoothed down his suit and ran a hand over his dark black hair, thick and swept back. "All right, my man. Day at the races." He punched his son's shoulder softly.

"Yeah." The boy watched his father, the energy that always gathered in him as they approached the entrance. Today it seemed stronger. He kept shooting his cuffs as they walked, fingering buttons at the ends of his sleeves, closing and stretching his fingers as if he were about to play the piano. He winked to a policeman.

Inside people bustled, white slips of paper in hand, eyes absorbed in racing sheets, an electric voice speaking over the garbled din. Many people faced up, watching statistics play on dozens of monitors overhead. His father bought a form and began looking through it while they leaned against a wall. The light in Oaklawn was faded and artificial, inhabited by smoke and voices.

"Isn't this something? All these people." Before his son could answer, David picked up his head and began looking around, scanning the crowd, it seemed. "Hey, let's walk around some."

They walked to the other end of the first level, through the commotion of bodies, but when they reached the end, near a souvenir emporium, his father turned and directed Andru back the way they'd come.

"Come on." He strode fast, with a hand on his son's back, racing form curled in his fist.

They walked to the upper paddock, where more people were mingling and coming to see the horses. His father craned his neck slowly across the crowd, sucking his bottom lip.

"Are you looking for someone?" the boy asked.

"No, not really." Then David studied his son, hand on the boy's jacket, the boy calm, still preadolescent and smooth-skinned under his shocked hair. "Hey, pal. Let me ask you something. What would you think if I started seeing a lady?"

"That's okay. That's great."

"You wouldn't mind?"

"No. Not any. Really, Dad."

His father's tone stiffened. "Well, yeah—I mean, why would you?"

"Yeah."

"Your mother's got Frank, right? I should have somebody. Don't you think?"

"Yeah. Of course." Looking up at him, again his father seemed to skirt the edge of that difficult energy he ran on, but then it was gone, and the man was smiling.

He gave his son a complicated handshake and spoke in a deep, urban slang. "You bad, brother. You a bad man."

They left the paddock and went up to the mezzanine. Mezzanine was one of the words Andru had learned at the track. He liked it. It sounded like it had secret implications.

His father led him through the crowds and across the mezzanine. Then they went to the lower and upper terraces, and after half an hour, when the first live race neared, David told his son they should grab some lunch, and they went down to ground level, where an oyster bar sat between a restaurant and the betting windows. When they got there, his father smiled with relief. Therese was standing in front of the oyster bar, sucking a shell between her lips.

She was still some distance away when they stopped. David turned to Andru, emanating a feverish joy. "You remember Miss Therese, don't you? She was with us one time."

The boy remembered the woman who'd sat drinking at the Upper Terrace restaurant with his father two months ago, though she'd only been with them for a couple hours before walking unsteadily out the doors. Now she was talking over a plate of oysters to a thick man who wore a beige suit and had reddish skin. They seemed to be part of a small, smartly dressed group.

The father straightened his suit and smoothed back his hair. "She used to be a model. Did I tell you that? In New York. And she was on stage. Isn't that something?"

"Yeah."

They stood still a second, watching between people as Therese laughed at something the man in the beige suit said.

"That's Bill Hays. I think they used to go out."

"But not anymore?"

"No. They're just with a group." As if the boy offered a rebuttal, David looked down and said, "People stay friends, Dru. Like me and your mother. We're still friends, right?"

"Yeah."

They waited some more, neither saying a word, and the boy became tense, wondering what would be required of him. Bill Hays belched into his fist, wiped his mouth with a napkin he let fall to the ground, and touched Therese's shoulder before he walked to a betting window. David nudged his son's arm and said, "Come on."

She was a tall, slender woman in a green dress that fell below her knees, with thin, pursed lips and hair neatly cut into a bob. Some kind of propriety was broken by a quality in her smile, in her theatrical eyebrows, the way her mouth seemed constantly on the verge of making a joke. But on the whole she appeared sapped of all moisture, her blond hair a bright color, but without shine, like chalk dust. She lit a cigarette and exhaled into the bleached light, looking distant even after she spotted David leading his son toward her.

"Hey, Therese." His father smiled.

"Hi," she said, raising an eyebrow.

"You remember Andru, my boy? He spotted you across the floor."

Her eyes drooped toward the boy and her mouth curled. "Hey Dru. Were you this tall last time?" She turned her head to the side and inhaled. Her eyes looked back to David, but her face remained in profile while she exhaled, her lashes clumps of black.

"So we were going to grab some lunch," his father said.

"I was just thinking I'd like some fruit. I was thinking I'd like some persimmons."

"You want some persimmons?"

She seemed amused. Her perfume was so strong it stung the boy's eyes. He was watching her and his father, watching the empty space between them and the small party around them, knowing he and his father were not part of it—and sensing that part of what his father was doing involved shutting out the knowledge that his son understood they didn't belong here.

"They're my favorite. You can't find good ones around here. All the time I was a little girl, I loved persimmons." She smiled at the boy. Smoke slipped out between her teeth. "How about that? You believe I was ever a little girl?"

He blushed.

She winked at him and he looked up at his father, who was staring with a kind of blank patience at Therese.

Just then Bill Hays reappeared, solid and glowing in the beige suit. He was taller than any of them, his sunburned skin and cowboy boots of a glossy, thin hide.

"Well, hey Dave. What do you know?"

The father seemed to simultaneously shrink and inflate, his head bowing and tilting, but his shoulders back, chest out. "Got my boy in. Thought we'd grab some lunch, catch some races."

Bill Hays looked down at Andru with green, sympathetic eyes. The boy wore a black Iron Maiden T-shirt under a leather jacket and blue jeans, his hair a stiff helmet of spikes. "You like the races?"

The boy shrugged. "Sure. I guess."

Bill Hays smiled, put a hand at the small of Therese's back. "Big horse fan you got there." David was expressionless, tapping his racing form against one leg.

The party began to move. Bill said to Therese, "We should get up there."

She nodded and put out her cigarette, took up her purse and winked again at Andru. "You don't let him get you into trouble, all right?"

"Hey, hey, watch it," David said, laughing. A thing in his father's laugh unnerved the boy, a forced, excessive quality he worried over.

As Therese and Bill turned, David began walking with them. "So where you guys going to be?"

Bill smiled. "Triple Crown Room, all day."

"Oh."

Bill raised a hand like a crossing guard would. "Dave. Take care."

The boy and his father stood while the crowd moved around them and they watched the man in the beige suit and the slender woman as they walked to the elevator with their friends.

He didn't want to look at his father, whose disappointment felt smothering, and instead watched outside the entrance doors, at the sunlit street and the cars, the people walking together beyond the lucent glass.

"Hah!" His father snapped his fingers, now livid, grinning like he had a sure thing. "Hold on. Stay right here." David walked to a betting window and began flipping pages in the racing form, making a number of bets. It took some time, and the boy watched the quickness of his father's hands across the pages, the tapping of his shoe, the way he leaned close to the teller and smiled at her. When he returned, stuffing tickets in a pocket, his father said, "Okay. Let's go."

"Where are we going?"

"Shopping."

"What about lunch?"

His father directed him through the exit. "We'll pick something up." They walked outside as horns were sounding a race.

*

They started driving toward town and his father lit a cigarette. The afternoon felt crisp and chilly, radiant under a cloudless sky the color of a perfect heaven. They drove down Grand Avenue, and his father stopped at the first grocery store. He said, "C'mon, c'mon," while he jogged toward its doors, his jacket flapping like dark wings under his arms as he hurried ahead.

Inside, fluorescent bulbs enameled every surface in a sickly, diffused white. His father walked toward the produce aisles, gave his son a ten-dollar bill and told him to get a sandwich in the deli. His hand held the money behind him, while his body turned to examine the fruit laid out under thin piping that just then issued a fine mist.

Andru got a corned beef sandwich and was sitting down at a small table when his father found him, his steps fast and stiff. Hands bunched into fists, a few errant strands of hair looped down to his nose. "Hey. C'mon. We have to go. Eat in the car."

Then more driving. His father running into three more grocery stores while he sat in the idling Lincoln. He chewed his sandwich slowly as the scene became familiar, watching the automatic doors part for his father, seeing him appear a minute later, pausing to sweep his hair back. It was one of the gestures most native to his father, the hand almost involuntarily rising up and smoothing down the mound of pomaded black hair. The boy knew that he, also, had that habit of putting a hand to his hair. His father's ring gleamed when he fixed his hair in front of the grocery store.

"Okay. There's one more thing," he said, shifting the car into drive. "The guy in there told me about a farmers' market on Saturdays. He said they usually close around three, but we might make it. I can't believe nobody has persimmons in this goddamn town."

The boy nodded. He let the plastic wrap fall between his legs, to the floor where black flies shot to inspect it.

"How was your sandwich?"

"Good."

His father raised up the radio and they descended a hill, turning back toward Central Avenue.

It was close to four when they found the farmers' market, completely abandoned, a few kiosks still standing but shuttered and padlocked. Other than one man loading boxes into a pickup truck, the immense parking lot was empty, its terrain of flat, cracked concrete stretching around them. The boy had his hands buried in his jacket. His father walked over to the man with the pickup truck and spoke to him a moment, then watched the truck drive away. A wind had picked up and it caused his father's suit to ripple, pulled his hair up and tossed it around while he turned, slowly, in a circle, looking out over the lot. There was something clear and final about the moment, both of them standing on a barren surface in the sunlight, but the boy didn't know what it made him feel. His father was squinting, an almost confused expression on his face, as though stranded in the glare, uncertain.

"Shit." David trudged back to the car, head hung as his hand went to work automatically straightening his hair.

Before returning to Oaklawn, his father stopped in one of the grocery stores they'd already tried. After about ten minutes, he emerged with a full paper bag. He handed the bag to his son while he got in the car. It was filled with oranges, peaches, apples, plums, and some green grapes.

"They're no good till after the first frost, this guy tells me. At that parking lot? But I'm like, hell, somewhere in the world right now they're growing persimmons and shipping them out, right? So what the fuck?" His father lit a cigarette and didn't say anything else on the way to the track.

The Triple Crown Room was on the Upper Terrace, the highest level of the racetrack. It was next to an expensive lounge called the Arkansas Room, and was accessible only by special reservation or by dint of clout. In front of the doors stood two tall men in khaki pants and blue blazers with the Oaklawn crest on their left breasts. The doors were dark, polished wood, so shiny the boy could see his father's reflection in them as he spoke to the two men in jackets, the paper bag held in the crook of his left arm.

His father was saying he only needed to get in there for five minutes. I just have to drop something off. "Come on, Jerry," he said to one of them. His father put down the paper bag and handed a twenty-dollar bill to the man. They opened the doors and said, "Be cool, Dave," as if it were an order.

"Yeah," his father answered, lifting the bag. "C'mon, Dru." He cocked his head for his son to follow.

The Triple Crown Room smelled like rich meat and the light was warmer, more yellow in there. White-clothed tables spread between burnished wood walls with brass trimmings, and a mahogany bar with a marble top stood near the entrance. People in suits and dresses talked and laughed at the tables, cigar and cigarette smoke revolving upward. A big-screen TV showed the races and results while servers in vests and white shirts weaved around tables. His father spotted Therese sitting with Bill Hays and about nine other people at a table near the other side of the bar. He pointed to a barstool and told his son to sit down, and he walked toward the table.

Andru asked for a glass of water and idly slid a few napkins over. He started folding a napkin and watching his father.

He saw his father crouch down next to Therese, and the table looked at him, smirking as he drew her attention to the bag he held.

Therese chuckled, "Oh, jeez." She looked at his father as if he were playing a joke on her, but after staring, became somehow pitying. "Oh, come on, Dave."

His father stood. "I thought you'd like it. That's all. There isn't a persimmon in this goddamn town."

Therese looked at Bill Hays, and he stood gracefully and laid his cigar in an ashtray. He walked around her and put his hand on David's shoulder. People at the table were watching sternly. "Okay, Dave. Come here. Come with me."

"Hey, what—here," he said, extending the bag to Therese as Bill Hays gently turned him around. Therese stood and took the bag, still grinning.

"Dave, we're going to have a talk, all right?" With one arm over his shoulder, Bill Hays guided his father past the bar, and his father said, "I'll be right back, Dru." The two men in blue blazers were watching, shaking their heads as if such incidents were all too typical. They stepped aside as Bill Hays and his father walked out the doors.

The boy sipped his water. Therese laid the brown paper bag on the bar, and some of its contents rolled out, oranges in green mesh, the other fruit divided into tiny plastic sacks. She sat on the stool to Andru's right and lit a cigarette, put her hand under her chin and stared at him.

"Where'd you learn to do that?" she asked.

In his hands, the napkin had almost completely transformed into a swan. "Books."

"You like to read?"

"I guess."

"Mm-hm." She blew smoke across the bar, then reached over and patted the top of his hair. Searing heat washed over his back and neck. "That's some sharp hair you got there. That's a lethal weapon."

He made an uneasy, stunted laugh and continued folding the napkin. The oranges and cherries were lying just outside the paper bag.

"Does your dad give you trouble about your hair?"

"No. He says I can look however I want." That was true, and he felt a burst of loyalty and love for his father.

"Good for him. Do you like the races?"

"Yeah."

"Really?" Her perfume seeped into his sinuses. She scooted her stool a little closer, leaned her chin out to him on her hand. "What do you know about horse racing?"

He kept his head down, folding the napkin, and said, "Handicapping is predicated on the principle that the future will repeat the past."

"You know what that means, though?"

He stopped folding and turned to her. She had that amused grin on her face, the not-quite-benign spark in her eyes. He could see flakes of powder in the cracks above her lips. "It means you can tell how a race is going to be run by how the horses ran other races."

"Mm-hm." She inhaled, pausing a moment. "But also you can tell a horse not just by races he's run, but by how his parents ran, and on and on." She was tracing a kind of figure eight on the bar as if to illustrate the point.

"Yeah."

She put a red fingernail on the paper swan and slid it toward her. "You know, I don't think your dad's having such a good day. You should do something nice for him."

When she said this a sudden anger flooded the boy. He wanted to scream at her, to tell her she didn't know the man, not at all. Who was she? He felt a surge of pride and hope for his father so powerful that he almost spit in the woman's face. He wanted to grab the sack of oranges and beat her with them, like he'd read about a man doing to a woman in a crime novel his father had.

Instead, he began folding a new napkin, and as his anger festered he returned to his father's face as he was walking out with Bill Hays. The frantic eyes, the unsure smile. The boy sighed sadly, knowing that it would now take only the slightest disappointment to push his father into one of the silent depressions he weathered. And he knew what his father needed now was an ally, a friend, a reminder that he was important, and loved.

But just then something else happened. The boy looked at the discarded fruit and touched his hair, patting it in the mirror behind the bar. When he saw this a new fear gripped him.

He folded the napkin halfway into a flower, then stopped and asked Therese if he could borrow two dollars. "I need change for the phone. My dad'll pay you back."

"It's no problem, sweetie." She got her purse and took eight quarters out of a long wallet. She pointed to a pay phone at the other end of the bar.

When he returned from his call, he asked her to tell his father he was going to wait outside on the bleachers, where he could watch the horses run.

It wasn't crowded on the bleachers. The frosty air kept most people inside, but a few stood along the railings, smoking and checking their forms. Three girls in fur coats leaned side by side on one rail, talking back and forth while watching the horses in their gates. Andru sat near the top, away from anyone, looking down on the track and listening between indistinguishable voices. He was picking out the silences within their dialogues, as if trying to narrow his range of hearing into just those silences, where he could sit within them.

He'd only been there for ten minutes when his father appeared. He stood for a while in his suit, looking over the bleachers, the familiar, searching expression his son had seen all day. He let his father continue searching until he spotted him.

His father walked up the metal stairs, footsteps resonating through the seats. "Hey. Um, we have to go." He began taking betting slips out of his pocket and letting them fall. Other slips were stamped into the bleachers, dirty and unreadable. Andru stared down at the track. "Hey. C'mon, Dru. We have to leave."

"I can't."

"Why?"

"I called Mom. She's coming to get me."

His father's face broke, startled, eyes wide. "What? Why? Go call her back—Dru, go call her back. If you want to go home I'll—I'll take you, okay? Call her back." His high, sharp voice of panic.

His son stared at the track. "I can't. She already left. She said she was out the door."

"What? Why—is Frank coming?" His father clutched his own head and began rotating in half circles back and forth. A deep, cheery voice came over the speakers and spoke in numbers, called out the names of horses, *Merlin's Anchor*, *Desiree Blue Carafe*, *Shift Holmes Prince*. His father stuttered, let a betting slip flutter to his feet. "I don't, I don't—" his breath small tufts of white against the flawless blue sky.

"I don't understand why you'd do that, Dru!" He crouched next to his son, his face confused and distressed. "I don't understand why you did that. Why did you do that?!"

The boy didn't answer or look at him. He watched the horses. David rose and walked down to the rails. A gunshot opened the gates and the horses galloped forward.

After the horses had run one lap, his father walked wearily back up the aluminum steps. He stood next to his boy a moment, then sat down. He said, "Shit," softly, ran both hands over his head and left it bowed under them.

The boy didn't turn. He was still thinking about the instant at the bar—when in the moment he'd felt most trapped, how quickly and easily he'd deserted his father. He nursed that understanding, and watched the races with his father hunched over next to him. He liked the way the horses suddenly exploded into thunder when they passed, rumbling the bleachers, then fading quickly back to the serene, secure state of silence.

Two Shores

HOT WIND GUSHED INTO JOANNE'S CAR. CATTAILS AND wild marsh flowers passed, orchids drooping like spilt milk in the grass along the muddy banks. Beyond the banks, cypress knees spread into flat, wet land. Sam watched a blue heron keep pace with the car for a time, its tall shadow stretched across the road and flapping beside them. He studied Joanne driving. Her face was round and smooth, tiny, without Lana's angular cheeks or long jaw.

Her eyes were orbicular, dark, perceptive-looking. Beneath each a small crescent of flesh puffed slightly, which was oddly appealing. She was once a gymnast at LSU and now taught phys ed at the elementary school in Port Salvador. In conversation she often composed subtle lists. Things to do, things not to do, things to remember, things to buy. She liked to let her brown hair fall over half her face when she felt playful, and lying across her bed she'd reprimanded Sam for living here two years and never seeing the Creole Nature Trail. That was on the list of things to do.

The trail was a highway that traced the very edges of the sinking coast. Driving it, they observed nutria and alligators slinking into the water, wildflowers and large white birds beneath an incendiary sky. They rode in Joanne's Acura, with the sunroof open.

A polka-dot scarf tied her hair back, her sculpted arms shining in a blue tank top, small hands on the steering wheel. She turned down the stereo and said to him, "Did Lana ever tell you about her dad?"

She had this way of suddenly breaking long silences with nonsequiturs, as if she couldn't really abide silence for long, something in it making her uneasy. He said, no, Lana never told him about her father.

"Her parents died," she said. "Her mom first, when she was real young. Then she lived with her dad. He never worked, but he used to take her around town."

"To do what?" About fifty yards ahead of them, a brown deer bounded across the road. He waited for her to answer his question, but she watched the road awhile.

"He wasn't related to us. Lana's mom was my mom's sister. But she said that her dad used to take her to all these places. Like business offices and sometimes bars, one time a car dealership, she said. And her father would have someone's name on an index card. Someone he once knew. He'd give her the card and tell her what this person looked like. She was like seven, eight, nine years old. He'd tell her what this person looked like, and what their name was, and he'd send her into places to find these people. Then she would give them a note saying she was Burt Slaton's daughter, Lana, and the note asked these people for some money."

"Really?" Sam asked. The sun streaked in bursts over the car. Wind caused them to shout a little. "How often did that happen?"

"All the time," she said. "That's what he did. That was their lives. He collected some kind of government assistance, and brought his daughter around to all these people he once knew to get her to ask them for money."

"But he must have done something, at some time?"

"I think he was an engineer for a while, before Aunt Alice died. He drank a lot and maybe took pills too. I don't know. I remember him saying he had back trouble."

Sam saw something—a thing of savage violence that he couldn't verify. Out his window he observed a great rustling in the middle of a field of high grass. Amid that calm green, a shadowy, sunken patch shook furiously, as if in seizure—something struggling, being taken down. While she spoke, he kept staring out there, trying to glimpse the animals involved, but only seeing the green stalks shaking, grass and turf flying outward.

"The way he died?" Joanne said. "The way he died was, when Lana was eleven, he had her travel up into this high-rise office in Baton Rouge. She had to ride this elevator, and it was glass, she told me, and she told me she could look down at the pavilion in front of the building and see her dad standing there with his hands in his pockets. She didn't talk about it until she'd lived with us awhile."

She reached over and took his hand. He lost sight of the rustling grass as they passed over a waterway where islands scattered out in the sun.

"So she went up to this guy's office, high in the building, and she goes in and tells the receptionist to please tell this man that Burt Slaton's daughter is here. The guy comes out and Lana goes in his office and gives the man the note asking for money, and the man says, 'Your father shouldn't be doing this.' And he gets up and he wants to know where her father is. And Lana tells him her dad is standing outside, so he goes to the window to check and he looks back at her like he's shocked or something. So she goes up to the window and looks down and sees a crowd of people standing around her father. Her dad's lying on the sidewalk, just like that. Dead. And she's looking down on him from way up in that building."

"Jesus," Sam said, feeling an inexplicable wave of hot guilt wash over him. He hadn't spoken to Lana in nearly two years. Now she had been dead for three weeks.

"Then she came to live with us," Joanne said. "We'll turn around soon, and on the way back we'll stop for dinner at a rib place I know."

As they rolled on into the sunken plains of overgrown swamp, Sam considered it all being taken up by ocean, the life covered over and wiped away. He'd learned a lot about Louisiana in the two weeks he'd been seeing Joanne. She liked to explain things.

Louisiana's coast is a skirt of islands and swamps double the size of the Everglades. Over eight thousand miles of canals crisscross these wetlands, fragmenting them, allowing lethal saltwater to bleed into brackish and fresh water, boosting erosion. Computers that simulate land loss for the next fifty years show

the coast dissipating, and places like Shell Beach, Lacroix, and
Grand Isle vanishing under water. When Joanne explained that to
him—that the land they were on would one day be beneath the
ocean—Sam considered the possibility of beauty in this hostile,
subtropical place, that perhaps its transience lent it a different sort
of beauty. Sam was originally from the East Coast and now taught
composition at the junior college here.

Because of Joanne's story he began thinking about the question
Lana had asked him on their first night together, when she'd stood
in front of her mirror, staring at her own face. In memory she grew
more complex to him, acquiring subtext and implication.

The car slowed to turn at a red clay circle carved out of the
shoulder of the highway. "Hey," Joanne said, pulling at the wheel.
"What are you thinking about?"

"Nothing," he said. "Just how pretty it all is." They passed a
tribe of brown pelicans roosted on a group of cypress knees. "And
tragic."

"Tragic?"

"It's all disappearing, isn't it?"

"Oh."

*

SAM GALT WOULD HAVE NEVER MET JOANNE REAVER
if he had not found a letter in his mailbox. Two other men had
received the same. For the past year, self-pity and dread had
rubbed him raw, and the letter didn't help. It asked him to be at the
Crescent Moon Café at three o'clock on the twelfth, which was
today. The Crescent Moon Café was not a place he frequented,
but it was where he'd met Lana Slaton. He'd been new to the gulf
coast town of Port Salvador back then, more than a little baffled
how, at twenty-nine, published, a specialist in the Romantics, he'd
found himself riddled with student loan debt and marooned at a
junior college on the edge of the world. The people he saw around
town vaguely frightened him. Burly men with sloped brows and
thick arms, big-assed women in stretch pants and baggy shirts,
poofy hairdos, oversized religious jewelry. On his second week

in town, impossibly lonely, a little scared and drinking six beers every evening, Sam had come to the Crescent Moon with a volume of Keats and a pack of Camels. The café was a mile outside of town in a port village called Lacroix. Lana had been his waitress.

Now, almost eighteen months later, he'd received a letter from her, asking him to meet.

The letter said,

Sam, you may not remember me, but I guess you do. We met about a year and a half ago and went out a couple times. First, let me say that I am not writing because I want money or any other type of aid from you. I am writing simply because I have made changes in my life, and I am not the person you once knew, and I care very much about the truth and telling it, and I know that if nothing else I have to be able to give my child the truth. I am writing a letter like this to two other men. Please believe that I am not trying to take anything from you.

He'd slept with her exactly three times, and at first he'd taken meeting her as an indication that a young man could tumble into effortless sexual encounters a great deal in Port Salvador. But now, by the time he received her letter, she remained the only woman he'd been with since moving here.

The restaurant was a brick-and-wood diner set back from the road near the lip of a ravine. Tacked beside the door, a large plywood moon's flaking paint was the color of buttermilk. Some pines grew between the building and a small, oyster-shell parking lot, which held a few pickups and cars. Sam parked his Honda near the road and smoked a cigarette before going inside. The day was a mountain of light bearing down on the village, and the diner's roof blazed, two sheets of pure sun. To the west, sluggish barges slunk through shipping canals beyond the levee. In his head he rattled off his standard grievances: the heat, the moisture, the pollution, the phenomenally unhealthy, uneducated locals, the wealth of the churches. He tensed with the feeling of threat that had dogged him for the last year—a paranoia that he would be subject to imminent, irreparable harm if he stayed in Port Salvador. That fear had inspired Sam to attempt writing a novel, something he could try to publish that might provide credentials to spirit him out of here. The work kept him indoors, with his cigarettes and air conditioning.

A maroon Mercury pulled off the road and parked near the café's entrance. A man slightly older than Sam, wearing a gray suit, exited the car and walked into the diner. He didn't look like he lived in Lacroix. Sam pegged him as a lawyer. This part of the country was flush with them, venal meatheads who went to Tulane or LSU and dispersed along the coast to feed on tragedy and divorce. They all had commercials on the local stations and low billboards along even the most rural roads. He wondered if he was going to have to talk to a lawyer in the near future.

What I mean to say is that I have a child. He is nine months old and named Aidan. I am certain that his father is one of three men, of which you are one. Again, I do not want anything from you, even if it is the case that you are his father. I want only to be able to tell my son who his father is, on the day when he might ask. To that end, I only want to meet and talk with you regarding the methods of testing available to us. I was kind of a mess when we knew each other and please don't think I am putting you on in some way. I have made many changes in my life since then, and I am a person dedicated to honesty and living clean.

He still didn't know how he felt. He couldn't help an initial sense of persecution at the idea that he might have a child with this girl, whom he truly didn't know, with whom he'd only shared certain bad habits. After their third encounter, she never called again, and he never felt a strong urge to call her. All in all, he had considered the affair a bit confusing, but exceptionally neat and undramatic. Now he'd decided to wait and see what the proper tests revealed before allowing his emotions to spin him around. It wasn't as if she'd written to inform him that she might have passed a lethal virus into him, a shadow in the blood.

Enough, he thought. Walk in the goddamned door.

The cowbell above the screen door rang and the door cracked shut behind him. The dining area was shaped like a squared W with its middle prong replaced by a counter and kitchen. Hearty, fried smells thickened the air. Many of the tables were empty, but at a few, rough-skinned men in work clothes chewed their meals. The café thrived on stevedores, fishermen, and the refinery workers who passed through at lunchtime with dozens of orders to go. An older woman with broad shoulders and a wide, crinkled neck called to Sam from behind the counter.

She wore a long white apron over her T-shirt, and said, "Just one?"

He stepped forward. "I'm supposed to meet someone. Actually, do you know her? She worked here. Her name's Lana."

The woman studied him from her hard, flat face. She nodded, pointed to the counter, "Have a seat." Sam noticed that the man in the gray suit, the one he'd seen in the parking lot, was sitting at the counter.

He sat next to the man and asked for some coffee, which the older woman delivered without comment. Sam blew into his mug, determined not to look at the man beside him, possibly a fellow candidate for fatherhood. But would she do that? Would Lana gather all three of them together at the same time? Why? He kept his head down, stirring sugar into his cup and staring into the inky whirl.

Sam didn't hear the phone ringing, and he didn't notice the old woman leaving the counter to answer it.

"So," a low voice said to him. Sam turned to the man on his right, whose face was shiny as polished leather. "You know Lana, huh?"

Stunned a moment, Sam started to answer, but just then the old woman returned to the counter and began gathering things from underneath it. She moved quickly, almost frantically, and rose up with her bag. Her lips pursed and her jaw worked side to side, as if she were grinding her teeth. When she spoke her creased cheeks shivered.

"All right fellas—everybody's got to go! You just take it with you. I got to close down. We'll settle later."

Every man in the diner stopped and turned to watch the counter. The old woman tried to hold their stares for a second. Then her face broke like a sandcastle in a rain.

"What happened?" Sam asked. "Are you all right?"

"That was the sheriff. There's been an accident." She caught her face in her hands. "Lana's not coming."

She lifted her purse over her shoulder and walked around the counter and clattered out the door, covering her face as she rushed behind the café. They all heard her car start and watched it kick up dust that settled in a red-brown patina across the café windows.

Sam and the other man looked at each other with the same dumbfounded expression, then turned to the rest of the café. The suntanned laborers faced Sam and the man in the gray suit with accusatory glares. One of them, a young, rangy stevedore in his orange dockworker's vest, seemed to watch with a face more curious than indicting. His eyes met Sam's, and Sam looked away.

Abruptly, the man in the suit rose off his stool, smoothed down his jacket, and walked out the door. The cowbell clanged and the screen door slammed shut.

*

BECAUSE HE WAS WRITING A NOVEL ABOUT YOUNG people and love, Sam had planned to have a funeral somewhere in his book, and at Lana's he found himself paying attention to the details of ceremony, the expressions of mourners, the placement of flower arrangements—material. He was slightly ashamed that his mind worked this way, but he didn't know anyone at the funeral, and it was a good method to avoid eye contact. He'd noted a similar distance when attending his parents' services, his mother's within a year of his father's.

A low front of gray clouds squatted over the cemetery. The old woman from the café stood beside a younger woman who held her arm throughout the services. This girl had brown hair and a petite figure in black.

There were a couple more women, older, but the rest in attendance were men, patrons of the café, Sam deduced. There were about thirty of them total, but no one Sam recognized, which is to say no one from the Department of Languages at Port Salvador Junior College. The priest lowered his hands above the two coffins, and the old woman choked out a sob. Lana's car had crashed through the guardrail on the 2-10 bridge. She and her child were being buried in adjacent graves.

The woman tossed a clump of dirt down as the coffin descended. The priest made the sign of the cross and the men began to drift off.

Attempting to personalize his perceptions, Sam tried to remember sex with Lana, but he'd been drunk at the time and the images that came to him were inexact and distorted. Nothing stirred his heart. There were only clinical observations, or else the words of other men who wrote of other feelings.

As the small crowd thinned, Sam noticed a man in a navy sport coat and black shirt, a thin beard shading his jaw. This was the stevedore he'd marked at the café three days ago. Now the man locked eyes with Sam and started walking over.

Sam looked around until it became apparent the stevedore was walking toward him specifically. He appeared to be younger than Sam, though his face was already burnished by the sun, fissures begun around his cheekbones. He stared bluntly out of deep-set eyes.

"Hi," the man said, offering his hand. "I'm Lee Robicheaux."

Sam shook. "Sam Galt." A damp breeze sloughed between them.

Lee spoke in a high, twangy timber, a voice born to hustle livestock. "I saw you at the Crescent Moon. You knew Lana?"

"Yeah. For a little while."

"Right." He nodded. "Me too."

They were the only ones near the grave, though the woman from the café and her friend had only just begun to walk away.

Lee's eyes darted back and forth and he pinched his nose before leaning so close that Sam smelled brine and oil. His tone hushed to a throaty whisper, he said, "You got a letter. Right?"

Sam looked at him. "That's right."

Lee nodded and hunched, suggesting his harmlessness. He turned back to face the graves where two men in blue jumpsuits were shoveling dirt. "Me too, brother." Lee drew a cigarette from a pack in his jacket and offered one to Sam. He took it and silently bristled at being called brother.

"You remember that other fella sitting by you at the Crescent Moon that day?" Lee asked. "That one in the suit?"

"Yeah."

Lee lit their cigarettes. "I think he got a letter too."

"I wondered about that myself, when we were waiting there." Sam caught himself nodding, replicating Lee's body language. Lee was the sort of man who made Sam ashamed of his education and compelled to act simple, agreeable. Without intention, his manner would become friendly and imitative, and after he would hate himself for such performances.

Watching the grave diggers, Lee's eyes squinted as though taking the measure of something. His lips twisted around his cigarette. "I didn't like how that one ole boy just got up and left when Miss Claire told you about the accident. Like he didn't care at all."

Sam nodded.

Branching smoke slunk from between Lee's teeth. A few wet leaves stirred among the small stones ahead of them. The old woman—Miss Claire, Sam now knew—still stood on the main grounds, having stopped walking halfway to the parking lot. She and the younger woman were talking while they watched the workers continue the burial. Sam's eyes fixed on the girl's face, small-featured and open. Her hair danced around her shoulders as she comforted Miss Claire.

"Hey," Lee said, and waited for Sam to look at him. He stepped closer and once again his pitch sunk to signify its seriousness. "Did you think about asking them for a test?"

"What?"

"Asking the police or somebody. For the baby. A DNA test."

"Oh, I don't—I think it crossed my mind, but I didn't think so. What would be the point, I thought. Would I really want to know?"

"Yeah. Right." Lee dropped his cigarette on the ground and stepped on it. "That's about the same thing as I thought." He looked out at the two men lifting the dirt, dropping it, repeating. "I didn't like the way that ole boy just left though. You stuck around and called and found out what happened. That other seemed kind of suspicious to me."

"Suspicious?"

"I don't know, man. I just didn't like it." He checked his watch, a digital rubber device. "See you, man," he said. "I gotta get back." He began walking away, to the parking lot on the other side of the grave.

"Sure," Sam said. He watched Lee's thin form trudge toward the grave workers, wind tossing his hair and flapping his coat. He was actually the kind of man it seemed like Lana should have been with, a native, born to the land's customs and predilections. And now Sam and he were bonded in a singular way, though he had no desire to see Lee again and in fact hoped he didn't. Their bond was too sordid, the intimacy negative. He felt a little violated by Lee's probing, fraternal manner.

Sam made his way back to his car, trying to order his thoughts about the gravestone and the two coffins. He couldn't locate a true feeling, not even relief, which he'd feared might be all he was capable of. He walked into the parking lot at the same time as the brown-haired girl who'd stood by Miss Claire all day. They glanced at each other and offered polite smiles. She was cute, he thought, in a small black dress, her round eyes flush with grief. Their strides seemed to be drawing them together, and he couldn't help glimpsing her from the corner of his eye.

The girl suddenly stumbled to her knee. She knelt in the parking lot, reaching behind her and bending a leg up in what looked like a painful contortion, a dancer's gesture. She slipped the shoe off in a graceful, smooth pose that he thought should be a sculpture somewhere.

"Are you okay?" he asked.

"I broke my heel." She sat back on her calves and sighed. This distraught air made her more real to him, drawing him to her face and the hand holding the black shoe. She looked beleaguered but strong, the fringes of her hair undulating on the wind.

She stared up at him and he found his mind suddenly blank. He smiled and reached out and took her shoe with inappropriate joy, given their surroundings. He grinned as if he could already see that in a couple short weeks he'd be describing this woman, Joanne Reaver, as someone he loved.

*

IT WAS ON THEIR THIRD WEEKEND TOGETHER THAT
Joanne took Sam on a drive along the Creole Nature Trail, and
she told him about Lana's father. Sam was still thinking about that
story when they got home from the trip, and he found the police
had left him a message.

The police, apparently, had not known that on the day she died,
Lana Slaton was on her way to meet three men to whom she'd sent
letters. Nor were they aware of the contents of that letter. This
information wasn't secret, but they hadn't asked, and Miss Claire
only mentioned it in passing one day when two deputies came in
for breakfast. Since then they'd taken another look at Lana's car
and found that the brake lines had been tampered with.

So they'd asked to talk to Sam in person. After he'd answered
their questions, two hours' worth, they'd let him go, not because
he had alibis (he didn't; he'd been cloistered back then, still
fooling himself about writing a novel), but because the officers
were sufficiently convinced that he wouldn't have any idea how to
tamper with brake lines, which was the truth.

For weeks after that, Joanne seemed wary of him while
pretending not to be.

She'd ask, "What are you doing?" sharply, with suspicion—
though she wouldn't mean to—when she caught him doing
something that for unclear reasons upset her, like staring at a wall.

They had been talking about moving in together, but that
stopped. She still demanded he be present, though, usually at her
house, and their sex life didn't suffer much. For his part, Sam was
glad for the silence, the long reflective spaces which more and
more were filled with thoughts of Lana. He thought of the story
Joanne had told him, imagined the little girl taking all those long
walks into unfamiliar places, forced to pass strangers shameful
notes. Alone. And he thought about her baby.

Later that month, Lee Robicheaux was arrested for the murder
of Lana Slaton and her child, Aidan Jefferson Slaton. The trial date
had yet to be announced. Sam kept smelling the briny, petroleum
odors that Lee had given off. The way he'd called Sam "brother"

now made him shiver with self-disgust. And these thoughts were juxtaposed with what Joanne had told him about Lana's childhood. Wordsworth slipped into his thoughts, "Lucy Gray."

> *She wandered up and down*
> *And many a hill did Lucy climb*
> *But never reached the town.*

Sam reread the letter she'd written and noticed the voice of that letter, the hope in it. *I am a person dedicated to honesty and living clean.* Each time he read her words, he felt more certain that he'd committed a great transgression, that he had failed in some essential way.

After Lee's arrest was announced, Joanne seemed to relax a little, tried conversing again, her voice always tinged with relief and guilt over that relief, the idea that she could have suspected he'd do something like that. But when she tried to move back to him, she found Sam still withdrawn, distracted, always paying attention to something else.

They would sit side by side on the couch, and it would be as though they were each afraid of something the other might do. So they looked forward, faces pointed at the TV. Sometimes he wouldn't come to bed.

One day he asked her which hospital Lana had used to deliver her baby. She told him she didn't remember, but he was persistent and they were still talking about it while she prepared dinner.

Joanne moved the skillet over a low blue stove flame and brushed her hair back, finally pulling it into a ponytail frayed from the steam. "And I don't, I really don't, see why you would want to bring this into our lives. Why would you want to know?" She took a few cloves of garlic off a hanging string, began picking them apart and mincing them with a gleaming butcher's knife. Hunks of catfish sizzled in the pan.

"It's just something I feel like I have to know."

"I don't see why now." She put down the knife and talked with antic desperation, her round eyes wide and forlorn. "I mean, things are going so well with us now. I was telling my mom the other day, you know, that I...the way I've been thinking

about you. You know, I've been saying this looks like—what
we have—it looks, you know, good. And I don't know what you
even want to know for, if you're the father. I don't know why
you want to do this at all."

Sam stared across her small breakfast table at the salt and
pepper shakers that stood atop a few envelopes, bills.

Joanne turned off the stove and nudged the fish with a spatula.
Her tone dropped. "You're obsessed with her, I say. The way you're
always asking about what she was like when we were growing up.
Why would you even want to know?"

"I'm not sure," he said. "It has to do with the truth."

His voice sounded crisp and clear, which frightened her.
Softly, she almost pleaded, "But it's a truth that can't do anything
for you."

"I know that. That's not why it's important."

"Then why is it?"

He turned to her wearing no expression, but his jaw clenched
in what she took for contempt. "Because it's the truth."

When she made herself cry he remained unmoved, and she
kept saying she didn't know why he was doing this to her. Hadn't
they talked about moving in together? Now they barely spoke and
he didn't seem to care.

She talked through dinner, and the dispute ended only when they
settled on a date for him to move in, after which Joanne told him
the name of the hospital. It was a women's hospital called Humana,
in Lake Charles, a riverboat town two hours west of Port Salvador.

*

NEARLY TWO YEARS AGO, WHEN HE'D JUST ARRIVED
in Port Salvador, Sam had brought a copy of *Endymion* to the
Crescent Moon Café. He was a little drunk and wanted some
coffee. The diner was empty except for a waitress sitting at the
counter, talking to an old woman behind it. The waitress, a long-
boned, slender girl, brought his coffee and some water. Her name
tag read "Lana."

She pointed to the unopened book on his table. "Is that good?"

He poured sugar into his cup and shrugged. "It's poetry." He put his spoon down and saw her face again. "It's pretty good."

"I like poetry. I used to read those Silverstein books when I was a kid." She had high cheekbones and a searching quality in her eyes.

"Oh, yeah. *The Giving Tree?*"

Her eyes rolled up and to the right. "I think it was something about an attic." She smiled a brief, pleasant grin, as if to properly close their conversation, and turned away.

He revolved in his chair, trying to think of something to ask her, and his elbow slipped and knocked the steaming coffee into his lap. He yelped, leapt up, grabbed his glass of ice water and dumped it on his jeans.

Lana was standing above him, looking concerned. She handed him a thick, terry-cloth towel.

"That was pretty smart," she said. "Quick thinking to grab the water."

Abruptly sober, Sam said, "I've thought about the situation before. What I'd do." He wasn't sure why he'd confessed this, but it was true.

Lana stood beside him while he toweled off and asked, warily, "Did you want more coffee? Or is your night ruined?"

"No, thanks. That woke me right up." They smiled at each other while he patted himself with the cloth. "How about your night? When do you get out of here?"

She cocked her head as if he'd posed a riddle. "Another hour."

He handed her the towel and his fingertips brushed her wrist. "Why don't you let me go home and change and I can come back to get you and we can go for a drink?" He wasn't typically this bold. The combination of loneliness, sudden sobriety, and the coffee's hot shock placed him momentarily beyond concerns of pride or fear.

Lana shook her head. "You're a mess."

Later that night they'd gone to one of the more-benign taverns in Port Salvador, a sports bar next door to a seafood shack, both buildings resembling large toolsheds. She ordered them two double whiskeys. A jukebox played some of the new country-pop that Sam hated, but with Lana laughing beside him, the music seemed in its right sphere, like everything in the bar, from the names scratched into the stools, to the stuffed alligator perched on the hood of a defunct pinball machine and wrapped in Christmas lights. She mostly grew up in New Orleans, but came to Lacroix to live with relatives when she was younger. She asked him where he was from.

"I was at school in Missouri last year," he said. "But Connecticut originally."

"Are your parents there?"

He shook his head. "They both passed in the last couple years. Cancer."

She apologized but he shrugged it away. She told him that both of her parents were dead too. He lifted his drink and lit a cigarette. When he spoke again, he told her he'd come here to teach. The market was bad because he hadn't completed his PhD work, but he'd thought his publications would be more helpful than they had been. She asked about his classes, and though he taught five composition courses, he told her instead about Wordsworth and Keats, Coleridge and Blake, Byron, Shelley. They ordered more drinks. He quoted *Endymion* randomly while running his fingers over hers.

"'Dead as she was I clung about her waist.'"
"That's like he couldn't let go? Like that movie?"

He was drunk and laughed.

At one, they bought a bottle of Jameson to go and left the bar. Sam was still amused at the lenient alcohol laws in Louisiana: drive-through daiquiri shops, bars that never closed, liquor available at every type of store. When he would eventually live here with wife and children the prevalence of such spirits would play a major role in maintaining his stability. But back then, he was still in the phase where he was ready to regard Port Salvador as an adventure, a temporary excursion.

Lana lived in a one-bedroom apartment near the junior college, one of the newer complexes that housed mostly students and middle-aged bachelors. She lit the living room with only a black light perched atop the cabinet that held her TV and stereo. Sam was dizzy and taken with her ass—high, firm and narrow— her jeans hanging low, and he'd been delighted to see that she hadn't marred her sacrum with one of the idiotic tattoos so many girls got there nowadays. He remembered that Leonard Cohen's low, grating voice had seemed to scrape along the dark edges of the room, like a cat rubbing itself against a wall. She sat on the couch with a mirror and began cutting cocaine while he poured their whiskey.

A number of matted collages decorated her walls, pictures constructed from magazine photographs of faces that had been cut into strips and rearranged. "Those are my pictures," she said, calling over her shoulder to him. The lines on the mirror were incandescent. The room was an eclipsed world, a place beneath a black sun with deep-voiced monks moaning in the hills.

Of the actual sex, he never remembered much, except the givens of clutching limbs, tentative movements, reading the signs in her eyes. But later, after that had happened, he did always remember that she stood naked before the mirror in her bedroom, staring. Her ass was round and undimpled. She patted her cheeks with her fingertips, lifted her hair up and creased her brow. She made a face. Then another. She stuck her jaw out and grimaced. Then she only stared, fixing on her own eyes in the reflection.

"Do you think…" She spoke in a quiet, dry voice. "Do you think there are places we can only get to by imagining them first? Or does it all have to be a surprise?" She turned to him. "Do you understand? If I imagine a place, does that mean I can't ever get to it?"

He never answered her. He'd thought she was trying to sound deep.

*

SAM DROVE TO LAKE CHARLES ON A FRIDAY, IN THE morning, without telling Joanne. He'd made an appointment with the chief resident of the maternity ward at Humana Hospital.

Humana was a series of staggered red slabs, at the center of which ran driveways in every direction. Women in wheelchairs held babies, baffled men shuffled about. He followed directions from a receiving nurse, and eventually he was seated in a large office with a high ceiling and a picture window looking out over the pastoral section of lawn to the east of the hospital. The chief resident of the maternity ward was a healthy pink man whose nameplate said "Alan Richert, MD." His clipped white hair still covered his head, and his large, square face had a fresh-scrubbed quality. Stacks of paper cluttered his heavy desk, which he sat behind in a white physician's coat over a shirt and tie. Sam sunk into one of the two plush leather chairs that faced the desk. The wall opposite the window was covered with diplomas. On the other, a hanging clock with a swinging pendulum ticked the seconds like a metronome.

Dr. Richert in fact remembered Lana. He remembered admiring her attitude. When she was waiting for one examination, he saw her reading a book about child-rearing, her stomach gracefully swollen. He'd asked her what the book's title referred to and she gave him a long explanation about the necessity of ingraining certain qualities of self-worth in children.

"I remember Lana," the doctor told Sam. "I don't deal directly with many patients anymore, and I was very sorry to hear about her." He tugged his eyeglasses up, then folded his hands on his desk. The office smelled faintly of detergent and pine. "My secretary, Maggie, told me what this was about. But I have to say—"

"I just want to know if you have a sample of the baby's blood somewhere. You must, right?"

He nodded. "We have readings that show, among other things, the child's DNA."

"Thank you. That's what I want." Sam leaned closer, propping elbows on his knees. His eyes, bloodshot and dry, quivered atop his unshaven face.

"I understand, Mr. Galt. It isn't typically our policy to do that. But—"

"But they're dead," Sam said. "They're dead. See? It doesn't matter to them."

"I was going to say, but there are unusual circumstances here."

"Yes. Thank you. When can we do this?"

The doctor sat forward and removed his glasses. He seemed mild and harmless to Sam, a slave of sad duties. "Mr. Galt, I'd like you to consider, just for a moment—" He held his hand up as if to stop Sam from rising. "Consider if this is in fact what you want. Maggie said this wasn't a religious matter."

"No. I'm not. I mean, it's not religious. It's what I want."

The doctor frowned. "Technically, you'll need a court order. A lawyer can get that for you, if you really want it. But you'll have to go through all that. Ask yourself what this will get you. How will it make you feel, if you learned the child was yours?"

"I don't—see, Doctor, the whole point—I feel, I don't know, I don't know why no one wants me to find out if this baby was mine."

"Perhaps," the doctor mused, "they're wondering why, if you care so much, you weren't here for Lana when the child was born."

"What? What is that supposed—you have no idea. I mean, why shouldn't I know, why should I have to—and then explain myself? Explain myself, to you, when she wrote me a letter?"

The doctor watched Sam pull the crumpled paper from his pocket and shake it in front of him. This was Lana's letter, which Sam had begun carrying over the past few days. "I spoke to this man. Who killed her? He stood—Why should it—I am not allowed to care? Is that what I'm being told?"

The doctor's face leveled polite indulgence. He slid a box of tissues across his desk, and Sam didn't know why until he realized there were tears coming from his eyes.

"I'm sorry," he said, wiping his cheeks. "This is ridiculous. I'm sorry. I don't—"

"It's all right. Just try to settle down."

"I mean—I never behave like…I don't know."

The doctor looked to the side while Sam pulled more tissues from the box.

"I don't see—" Sam paused, inhaled deeply. "Maybe it's—my parents died? Not long ago? And I never really—or—then I came down here. I'm sorry for this."

The doctor rose. "Would you like a prescription for something? A small scrip for Xanax or Valium?"

"No. No, I'm okay. It's just—could you let me stay a second?" The sincerity of his plea struck the doctor. "I just need to think a minute. I can't—"

Sam became aware of the ticking clock. It took several seconds before he could speak again. "I can't tell—you think you understand how you feel, or, your motivations? But everything's always changing? And those things change, in, you know, a moment, and it's just… difficult to get a handle on."

"Oh," the doctor said, not understanding what Sam meant, though thinking that he'd been wrong in his assumption—it appeared to him now that this young man had loved the dead girl. The doctor sat back behind his desk and said, "Yes, of course Mr. Galt. I didn't mean that you had to go right now. Take some time. And think about what I've said, and if you come back to me, if you come back and this test is what you want to do, I'll help put it through for you. But you can't think straight like this."

"No," Sam said. "I can't."

"No. So I want you to relax, Mr. Galt. Talk to a friend."

Sam shook his head and laughed.

"I'm sorry," Sam said. He bundled all the crushed yellow tissues together, shaking his head. "I just don't know."

Standing to offer him the wastebasket, the doctor nodded and put a hand on his shoulder. He patted him there. "It's all right. Take a breath."

They stood like that and didn't move until the ticking clock had settled the room back to its natural, ordered tranquility.

When Sam got home that night he was still confused, but he told Joanne where he'd been.

"You went there? Why didn't you tell me? What did they say?"

"They told me to think about it first."

"See?" she said, her voice climbing higher and higher. "And, so, you're going to—I can't believe you did this without telling me." She waited for him to answer, and when he didn't she started crying. "I don't even know you nowadays."

He didn't speak while she continued to voice protests and beg him to talk to her. She talked and cried for almost an hour, and he never said anything. When he was getting into bed she was still talking.

She turned on a lamp. "You've never stopped thinking about her," she said. "You love her, don't you? Just tell me."

Sam sat up, reached across her face and turned off the light.

The emotions of his hospital visit faded quickly, and Sam already felt embarrassed at the way he'd behaved in front the doctor. What remained in the wake of his tears was an acute sense of his own lack of feeling, a realization of how far his distances ran. He thought about black smoke dispersing into blood, the mingling of blood. Some time after, he lost the letter Lana had written.

He never returned to the hospital, or pursued the testing, but silence persisted between him and Joanne. She understood his withdrawal as intimation that his thoughts were not on her, and he never attempted to dissuade her of that notion. But the more withdrawn he became, the more adamantly she pursued their future. He was passive, stoic, without strong feelings for any of his choices.

They were married early the next summer.

.

BETWEEN HERE AND THE YELLOW SEA

INTERSTATE 10 AFTER MIDNIGHT, WESTBOUND. EL Paso now. Coach Duprene says he can drive till morning. Blank asphalt rolls ahead, but I'm seeing Amanda, picturing the way she looked in high school: small-chested in a cheerleading uniform, auburn hair, green eyes, freckles. Grasslands give way to desert with purple and orange barely visible, hallucinated colors. Then such immensity of night over flat, featureless land, I can see how certain people could fear open spaces.

"You see that?" Coach asks.

"What?"

He uses a bottle of Cuervo to trace an arc across the windshield. "All the stars are gone. It got pitch black."

I stick my head out the window, into explosive air, and he's right. Around us is nothing but darkness, and even though the sky's invisible, I know a storm is coming. "It's going to rain."

He passes the tequila. "How you know?"

I tap a scar under my chin. "Broken jaw."

The metal in my lower jaw twitches, something that happens when the air is charged with electromagnetism. Steel stitches an X in my mandible because when I was fourteen, convinced of my own possibilities, I tried out for the football team. That was seven years ago. Coach still coached the Port Arthur Toreadors back then. I never made it past tryouts, but I went to a lot of games. I'd be the boy sitting quiet, peeking between loud fathers in front to watch red and blue cheerleaders kick and clap. My favorite cheerleader was Coach Duprene's daughter, Amanda. Honey-skinned, her eyes closed when she smiled. The kind of cheerleader who paid attention, actually cared about the score. She'd follow the game while the rest of her squad twisted their hair or discussed what to wear to the after party.

"You said it," Coach says, and I wonder if I was thinking out loud. He nods to the windshield, where rain spatters. I'm used to thinking out loud, especially in a moving truck. At this time, I still work for Alamo Sewer Treatment in Port Arthur, and my days are spent driving backroads with a clipboard, noting phosphorous and ammonia levels in the watershed, making sure farmers aren't spreading chicken shit over their fields. In the evening you might catch me at Petro Bowl or Chili's, trying to buy drinks for grade school teachers and secretaries, but at work I drive alone, five to seven hours, and on those days I tend to narrate my thoughts, turning observations into stories. Rilke writes, "Love your solitude, for solitude is difficult." I remind myself not to think out loud.

Rain builds, and before we reach Las Cruces a torrent lets loose, hiding the road under a curtain of water. Metal writhes in my jawbone. The wipers don't do much, and Coach leans close, squinting. He takes a pill from a brown plastic bottle.

"It's late enough," he swallows. We pull over on the shoulder, rain drumming. He slouches against a window and tugs his baseball cap down. Coach doesn't coach anymore, but he receives a generous stipend from Port Arthur High and the honorary title of athletic coordinator, which is what eight district championships and two state titles gets you in East Texas. I watch him breathe, softened, rain making the windows look like creeks, and I try to connect this man sleeping so calmly with the man I used to see, the steaming, granite-faced commander on the edges of hallways, on the sidelines of a game. I try to figure how he got from there to here. I do that because at this age one of my essential habits is to look for causal links, find stories, and I spend a great deal of time combing through the past, as if answers were there. I'm at an age where I drive in circles, and I take the words of poets and famous men at face value. I'm four years out of high school, living in the house my grandmother left me, and it won't be until some time after Coach and I reach Los Angeles that I stop looking for answers.

My cheek rests against the window because it's cold and dulls my jaw's throbbing. Coach starts to snore.

I was there the day she left. I mowed lawns back then, and on that Sunday I worked the yard next to Coach Duprene's house. A red Chevy Blazer parked in their driveway. Four boys I knew from school were in that truck. The back end sagged with boxes and bags, a surfboard. High school was over, and they were all moving to California. Coach Duprene watched from the porch and didn't wave as the truck rolled away.

Someone, we can now say, should have stopped that Chevy. It's no secret. She makes movies under the name Mandy LeRock. I've only seen one.

Lightning flashes over a plain, lights my reflection in the rainy window, and I realize I'm not telling the whole story. There are two stories here. In the first I am sitting beside Coach Duprene in his truck. We are driving to Los Angeles to kidnap his daughter.

In the second story, the reflection in the glass, I'm a teenager named Bobby who lives with two generations of women, a mother and her mother, on empty stretches of grazing land. This boy sleeps in a room with no air conditioner and mows lawns for spending money. He's a student athlete, but only runs track. His grades are good, and he draws the same picture over and over again in his notebooks, from every angle: a Naval Destroyer taking counterfire off the coast of South Vietnam.

And what joins both stories, their causal link, is Amanda Duprene. We're lab partners freshman year and biology class is after lunch. I can't stomach dissection exercises, but Amanda handles the cutting. I build refuge from ammonia and formaldehyde in the scent of her hair and neck: shampoo, lotion, sweat. On Fridays she wears her cheerleading uniform. A lot of these long days are eased by watching autumn sun move over the back of Amanda's legs, from one o'clock till two, and this is the girl I'm searching for.

Later, a second search will occur.

It will be undertaken after we get back home, by an investigative firm in Houston whose specialty is locating people. They're called "Reunions Inc.," charge me three hundred dollars and take two months to produce results. Their report is mailed to me in a big white envelope with the company logo printed on it: two open palms cradling three people, who all hold hands under a shining yellow sun.

For now, though, outside Las Cruces, it's like we're parked under a waterfall. Coach sleeps and grinds out each breath. I should have brought something to read. This is the snug, familiar isolation I experience at work, when I'm eating my lunch in a truck cab and reading, say, a Saint-Exupéry book about desert pilots. Then I steer the company truck over dirt roads that go on for miles and miles without passing a house, hazy gold cordgrass and grain fields yawning into horizon; checking groundwater for ammonia spikes and algae blooms; turning to the empty seat beside me, telling my stories.

The countryside ripples with superheated colors. Surfaces look like they were cleared with explosives. We cleaned up at a truck stop in Tucson, and I'm labeling things with brochures we got there. Cholla cactus and greasewood. Sagebrush, saltbush. All the clouds stack up over one particular peak of the Maricopa Mountains, like a volcano's portrait. Near Theba we decide to fish for our dinner. Late afternoon, a tiny branch of the Gila River splits high green meadow grass.

Coach starts going through a pile of tarp and tools in the bed of his truck. "Can you cast open-face?" he asks.

"No. I don't know anything about fishing."

"Really?"

"No."

"Well. What do you know?"

"Nothing."

"I think I got a closed reel in here. How'd you grow up in Port Arthur and not learn to fish?"

I shrug and let Coach shake his head while he digs for a pole. How should I answer him? Should I tell stories about growing up hearing guys tell fishing stories? Terminology like secret passwords to me: leaders, streamers, spinners, D-lines. The grass is tall and soft. The creek makes watery noise, gathers light.

Coach finds a pole and says, "I'll set the line for you."

He shows me how to attach a stone sinker. He demonstrates the best way to get a neon rubber salamander on the hook. The push-button cast is simple. I flick my wrist and the salamander flies, trailing shimmery filament. Then here we are, Coach Andre Duprene and Robert Corresi, fishing—illegally, I guess—among Joshua trees and painted stones. I watch Coach's wrists, the way his hand starts to call the line back almost as soon as it's cast, and I mimic his movements.

Any coach will tell you that mimicry and repetition are the fundamental learning tools. But what could you mimic if, imagine, you're a boy waking up for seventeen years to rooms choked by perfumes and powders? Say, for instance, every time your clothes get hung on the line, bras and billowing panties flank them— the mother's skimpy things with lace, the grandmother's wide- bottomed and big as sails. Say certain things are always on the periphery of your senses: smell of wet stockings, reds of lipstick, tampon wrappers. You burn yourself countless times on untended curling irons.

A lot of the time you're nervous and don't know why. Biology class is the highlight of your days. Time waiting for the bus after school, cheerleaders watching athletes, these graceful hunks of movement on sunburnt fields.

In the spring of your fourteenth year, two weeks after you've read *In Our Time*, you try out for the football team, and Eric Dempsey breaks your jaw. Next fall, Amanda's mother will die.

I'm so lost in reverie that the pole almost flies out of my hand. "Whoa, whoa," I say and Coach is calling for me to pull up, jerk the rod, reel him in. The line flashes, stirs the water, stops. It goes slack and comes back with the salamander shredded. Coach holds the hook up.

"He got a piece of you. When you feel the tug, give it a jerk, make the hook catch. Then work him awhile. Let him wrestle and get the hook dug in worse." Coach puts another salamander on and returns to his spot, about fifty feet away. That tug on the line exhilarates me. For the rest of the evening I've got the pole in my hands, smiling like a goon. Coach catches two trout and I lose two more.

We cook them over a fire that Coach builds in a clearing. He found hot sauce under some clothes in his truck. The sun is almost down. Nine o'clock now. Blue hues.

"Smells good," I say.

"These're fine." Coach has a new pint of Cuervo. The fish pop and crackle. "Well," he says, "I guess we'd better get straight on how we're going to do it."

I nod. Fire makes our faces orange and jumpy.

What we come up with is to locate the address taken from a videotape I have. The address is for American XXXtacy, the company that makes Amanda's movies. We start there. Find her. Coach stole chloroform from the chemistry lab. From there, he says he hires a deprogrammer. Apparently, a lot of people had to be deprogrammed in the seventies, and Coach has much faith in this idea.

We sit around a waning fire, now sharing the night's second pint of Cuervo. I'm not used to drinking hard stuff. Usually, it's just Lone Star while trying to talk to secretaries at Petro Bowl amid the banging racket of tenpins. "Where do these bottles keep coming from?"

"I went shopping before we left." He lights a cigarette. Coach wears good cowboy boots, maroon eel-skins, and a denim shirt he got when he was thinner. He's retained a full head of sandy-gray hair, still kept in its boxy crew cut. He passes the bottle. "You said your dad was military?"

"Navy." I swig the tequila.

"I flew jets, you know."

"I know."

He takes a long drag. "And what happened to him?"

"The USS *Mullinnix*. Took counter-battery while retaking Quang Tri. My dad was a sergeant. I never met him." This is the story I believed most of my life, and I'm still comfortable telling it. "Travis Corresi was one of five men lost."

"Goddamn," Coach says wistfully, upturning the bottle.

Only five months ago, dying of pancreatic cancer, my grandmother explained that Travis Corresi never served on the USS *Mullinnix*. He was just a merchant seaman stationed in Port Arthur for one week in 1973, when my mother was fifteen. They went out only once.

Coach taps ash into the fire. His eyes glisten from a web of wrinkles, and I can imagine an event for each line drawn: flying in Vietnam, coaching the Port Arthur Toreadors for fifteen years, losing a wife named Marguerite to encephalitis, losing his only child to the state of California. Skin around his eyes is a catalog of gouged disappointments. He takes Vicodin every couple hours. I think things would be better for him if he had a son.

We get around to discussing the day I broke my jaw.

"I remember that," he says, grinning. "That was you? Boy, Dempsey laid you out, huh?"

I steer the conversation to Amanda. We start drinking faster.

His cigarette trembles in his mouth. "You know, she had real joy in her. Maggie used to say—" he takes a long drag, exhales, "that's a happy kid."

I nod. "She was always in a good mood."

"Well." His face puckers. "But she did have a temper. She did have to have things just so." Coach makes a mincing motion with his fingers. Our fire is smoldering ash, red glow dying like the battery light on my mineral tester. We're silent until he tosses his smoke and speaks with grim, exhaling effort. "No court would convict us."

"Nope." I remember saying the same thing two nights ago, during the conversation that started all this. We were both drinking alone at Petro Bowl, and I saw a tall boy in a letterman jacket leave a group of teenagers to approach Coach at the end of the bar. These snickering kids watch their friend ask Coach a question. Coach grabs the boy's throat and throws him over a table. I pull him off, and he bucks in my arms until I say into his ear, "Coach. Coach. I loved her too." We ended up getting a bottle and sitting in his truck, remembering her loudly.

Now Coach's head lowers in the firelight. His knuckles fall in his lap and he sighs. "When did you say you went out?"

"We didn't. We were just friends."

He nods. Hoists himself up by holding onto a tire. He opens the tailgate and climbs in, metal squeaks, junk rattles. He calls out, "Hey—is it kidnapping if you don't ask for a ransom?"

"Yes."

More rattling, and then the steady rasp of his snores. I stir embers with a stick. I want to believe we're doing the right thing— that the girl out west is the same one I knew in high school, and all she really needs is to be reminded of who she is. Rilke says to "raise the submerged sensations of the ample past," but later I'll understand that's slippery advice, because memory can be interpretive. Later I'll realize that the synaptic fields where it lives are the same spaces where longing and desire exist, and sometimes memory is only a vehicle for those things.

But even now, beside the cooling ash of our campfire, I don't trust my motivations. That's one of my most basic traits, and it's mostly rooted in a broken jaw—the small metal cross in my chin reminding me that what I want and what I'm entitled to are traditionally separate things. To understand what I mean, you have to imagine me at fourteen: five foot six, a hundred and thirty pounds in oversized shoulder pads and a helmet I can remove without unbuckling it.

April sun smothers the field. Cheerleaders sit in the bleachers, evaluating the world and hiding cigarettes. I chew my mouthpiece compulsively. I've been reading about Nick Adams and going to war and getting shot. I meet derisive stares knowing I have my ethos, imagining theories about pain and honor. When we move to open-field tackling, I'm first to volunteer.

Coach Duprene sets me against Eric Dempsey, a monster-sized senior who's an all-district linebacker. On the one hand, this might be cruel. To me, though, at the time, I think, He's taking me seriously. He's giving me a chance.

When the whistle blows, Coach tosses Eric the ball. I don't hesitate. I get my center of gravity low and straighten my spine by sinking my head into my shoulders and looking upward. I don't swerve or go for his knees.

A sudden gust and I actually hear myself break. Red, shocking pain. I roll over on the ground, sun stabbing my eyes, grass in my mouth, warm copper tastes, dirt. Before I black out, I glimpse the girls in the bleachers, little dots of color all in a line.

So at twenty-one, I imagine life's chief lesson is that you have to limit your longing, or it can fester until, say, it gets your jaw broken. And it's that twitching metal cross that stains my expectations with dread. My eyes dart around in the dark. A log, a moon, noise of wind over rock. Coach cutting Z's. Imagined sounds echo in my ears: the clatter of bowling pins falling, artillery booming into a Destroyer's foredeck. My jaw sleeps. No rain.

Telephone poles resemble crosses in the sun. A large green sign says, "Welcome to California." Coach's head dips and rises. I think he's taking more Vicodin.

"This is the farthest west I've ever been," I say.

Coach stares silent and bleary at the road. He fiddles with the radio and finds Merle Haggard singing "Mama Tried." The day Amanda's mother died, the intercom called her out of biology class. The way she removed her plastic goggles and undid her smock, I knew she was expecting this. I watched her leave from the window, wanting to reach through it and touch her sadness as she crossed the concrete walkway.

At San Diego we take Highway 15 north. Later we rise into an elevated space of signs: slogans and bold, primary colors. Vehicles swarm us. I wonder if my own mother made it this far. Her initial postcards all came from Nevada. I have five postcards altogether, kept in a shoebox on the floor of my closet. Suppose one day near the end of senior year, you came home and your mother was gone. Your grandmother explained that your mom would be away for a while. A cryptic note began, "Now that you're seventeen," and talked about each person having to "follow their own heart." Phone calls came once a week for the next two months. I don't look at the postcards anymore. The shoebox stays closed.

Cars pull us and we merge, rising higher on the concrete slope. Below us, parking lots are everywhere, as if we're flying over a city of parking lots. The air becomes a radiant gloom, a bleached fog. Enormous buildings vanish into this haze. Something burning—a stale, decomposing odor.

Coach's face crinkles. "Smells terrible." His words slur. A Volvo honks as we drift into the wrong lane. In February of senior year, a story was told in the track team's locker room. They said Amanda had gotten wild. She rode back from a basketball game on a team bus, and something crazy happened. Howls and laughter. I dressed in a hurry, trying not to believe this.

The truck squeals onto the shoulder. Coach slams it into park. "We need to figure out where the hell we are." His pupils float in bloody murk. "You—you gotta drive."

I sink into the driver's seat. The engine rumbles and Coach slumps against the window. With my hands on the wheel, I feel new and worthy. This is what we see: dry concrete reservoirs, asphalt everywhere, heat-warped air. Mexicans. People wearing sunglasses that make them look like insects. Convenience stores and billboards—pictures of bronze, muscled flesh, cleavage. I glance at my own slight, pale biceps.

Once, I saw Amanda crossing a flooded football field, kicking up water with her bare feet, and I devised a yearlong muscle-building program. Self-improvement notes still decorate my house: *A fragment of sacred duty saves you from great fear. All pain is the result of desire. People are generally as happy as they choose to be.* But some time after Los Angeles I take those notes down. Papers crackle as I crush them and my footsteps boom on hardwood floors throughout my house.

At a gas station, Coach waits in the truck while a Persian helps me with the map. He says the zip code, 91411, is "in the valley." We have to go farther west. Coach pops two Vicodin. Streets and sidewalks radiate heat like a skillet.

American XXXtacy is part of a strip mall in what's known as the San Fernando Valley. Their sign is a simple red-letter job on smoky glass doors, tinted so you can't see inside. A few cars in the parking lot. Dusk. A hillock rises at the far end of the mall and on top sits a TGI Friday's. Coach has been staring out the window.

His fingernails rap against the door and he rubs the brown bottle of chloroform. He hasn't spoken since I got directions.

"Stay here, why don't you?" I say. "Let me go see what I can find out."

He stumbles out, head down. "I'm going in."

"Look, Coach. Let me talk to them—I'll make up a story. Trust me, I sort of got a plan." I ask him for his driver's license and tell him to trust me again. I leave him leaning against the truck.

The office has lime green carpeting, stamped down and gouged with cigarette burns. It smells vaguely like rubbing alcohol and Vaseline. A door behind the front desk is closed. Posters decorate the walls: The Goddaughter Part II, Back-Ended to the Future, and one of Mandy LeRock wearing a transparent raincoat and standing under an umbrella—Rainwoman 5: Eye of the Storm. Those aren't her breasts. A receptionist greets me, an older woman with overcooked skin—orange, papery. She wears flared eyeglasses.

"Can I help you?"

Smiling, I show our driver's licenses. "We're both from Port Arthur. We drove a long, long way."

"What is it you want?"

"Do you see that man out there?" Beyond the window Coach slumps on his tailgate, puffing out wafts of smoke. "His daughter is an actress." I point to the Rainwoman poster. "Her real name is Amanda Duprene. She's from Texas. We're looking for her."

"I'm sorry, we're not allowed to—"

"Ma'am. We don't want to make trouble. But, it's, the thing is…he's dying. He's dying and he just wants to see his only daughter before he goes."

She looks past me, out the window. In the parking lot Coach appears folded. His back is bowed and he coughs into his hand, smoke blanketing him and dissolving into dusklight. He really does look sick.

"We're trying to find her. That's all. We're not making trouble for anybody."

For some reason, she whispers. "What is it?"

"What?"

"What does he have?"

"Pancreatic cancer."

"Oh, Lord." She puts her hand to her mouth. "Just a minute. Okay? I'll be right back." She takes our licenses and walks to the back room, opening the door only wide enough to step through. A moment later, she reappears. "Sir? You can come in." My heart skips, but through the door is just another desk with a young, thin man behind it. A bag from McDonald's spills French fries across his desk.

His face is acne-scarred, scanning our licenses. "Are you for real?" he says, sucking his fingertips. The receptionist clasps her hands in the doorway.

I tell the story of Coach's cancer while eyeing stacks of videotapes on the desk, explain how difficult it was to drive the old man here from Port Arthur. The man chews fries as I talk. At the end, he asks me for a contact number and says the most he can do is pass the message along to Amanda. He's sorry, they can't just give out addresses, especially to family.

The woman catches me at the outer door. She passes me a slip of yellow paper. "You don't know where this came from," she says. Pats my arm. On the paper is an address.

Coach nods and falls into his seat. Back on the highway, he stares at the chloroform and says, "I don't know. I don't know about this."

It takes us another two hours to find the address.

A ranch-style house in Van Nuys. Palmetto and ferns, palm trees with ridged skin and no foliage. A yellow Corvette in the driveway. From bay windows, pale lemon-colored light lies in three wavering rectangles on the trim green lawn. Around are similar houses, warm air. We park across the street and turn out the lights.

"So what do you want to do?"

His head, reclined, turns slowly. "Go home."

"C'mon. Do we go to the door? Do we wait to see if she comes out?"

His eyes are lacquered dots, absorbed by wrinkles and folds.

"Coach?"

He closes his eyes. Laborious breaths. "Go see."

"Me?"

"Go see." He brandishes the chloroform in some gesture of reassurance.

The porch light is off, and a dim peach glow emits from the doorbell. I walk toward it, through darkness between windows, the doorbell's glow like the end of a tunnel.

I would watch her green eyes, the smile that always closed them. I remember things like her face lit by a Bunsen burner's quivering flame, laughter bursting from her like confetti. Once, I saw her slap Junior Wendell's hand away from her skirt, and I felt the confinement of a teenage girl. The way her mind was full of longings—a knot of emotions constantly rising to the surface, like a tumbleweed rolling downhill, carrying her over a harrowed suburban field, past the shopping mall and long acres of bluestem grass, to backseats of cars, truckbeds.

I knock. Again. "Who is it?" from behind the heavy wood.

"Amanda Duprene?"

"Who is it?" the voice repeats.

"Um…Robert Corresi? From Port Arthur?" A porch light ignites and brightness blinds me. The door opens the length of a chain lock, and a dog's black nose sniffs the gap. A pair of female eyes, brown and bloodshot, glide over me. The door closes and metal slides loose.

In the second it takes for the door to swing wide, I become conscious of my looks, until I remember that I don't have acne anymore, and my haircut is better than it was in high school. She has dark skin, and her reddish hair is pulled back. She holds a large brown Rottweiler by its collar. Light from inside silhouettes her, making her robe almost translucent blue. Her voice is familiar, but rawer, deep—"I know you."

She manifests from the light, becoming solid, as if stepping from the place where I keep her in my mind.

Her eyebrows are plucked into precise waves; her cheeks and chest shine. She stares, eyes fractured with red, tilts her head, "I know you."

"Robert. From high school? We were lab partners?"

The dog whines and she crouches to scratch its ears. "Hush, Pete." She looks up. "Bobby? Bobby Corresi?"

"Robert. Nobody calls me Bobby anymore."

"What are you doing here?"

"I wanted to see you. We've been driving."

She glances over my shoulder. "Who's we?"

"Me and your father. Your dad's here. We drove to see you—"

"What?" Amanda moves past me, and I see Coach standing in the dark behind his truck, only bare hints of him visible. She points furiously in his direction. "What did you bring him here for?! What do you want?! Get him out of here!"

Before I can reply, a man steps into the foyer. He's about my height, but with hard muscles and toasted skin. He wears a white tank top, jogging pants and lots of earrings. His short glossy hair stands straight up. He puts an arm around Amanda's waist and stares at me. "What's going on, babe?"

She barely regards him. "Nothing." Back to me, she asks, "What did you bring him here for?" She yells over my shoulder. "Stay over there! You don't come near this house!" Her dog keeps hopping up, lunging and choking himself on his own collar, barking from the frenzy in her voice. The man next to her shifts his eyes from me to Coach and back again. Through all this I notice with somber clarity how sweet she smells.

She looks at me, accusing. "What?"

"Amanda. Can I talk to you? Please—just for a second. We really drove a long way. I just want to talk."

Her eyes narrow suspiciously, and her dog sniffs my crotch.

"Please."

She huffs loud. "Hold on." And she shuts the door and leaves me standing in a cone of dull light on her porch. Murmurs come from inside the house. Coach's cigarette smoke plumes up on the far side of his truck like a phantom tulip.

When the door opens again, Amanda points over my shoulder, "He can't come in. He stays outside." The man beside her walks out the doorway and bumps hard into my shoulder, passing.

"Tony's going to wait out here too." He positions himself behind me with his arms crossed.

She and the dog step to one side and I move into a foyer with a dried flower arrangement standing on a nice marble table, then into diffused light and the scent of incense, jasmine maybe, a television's flickering blue in a living room of brown, thick-cushioned furniture. Maroon walls and photographs of landscapes, some odor lingering from the kitchen. I can't believe we made it, that I am standing here.

Amanda mutes the TV. She motions me to the couch and curls her legs beneath her, covers them with the robe. Pete the dog lies on a cushion between us. I feel my chest tightening. Her lips look bee-stung, and I suppose it's collagen or something. Her breasts are too round and firm under the robe. Her eyes are brown.

"Okay," she says. "I'll give you five minutes."

"We just—I mean, I came here to help you, I guess. We want to bring you home."

She rolls her eyes and laughs. "Right. Whatever. Perfect."

"Look—"

"You look. What do you think—are you judging me? You bring my dad out here, and, and what—" She rubs her nose and talks fast. Even though it's cool in here, beads of sweat have broken across her brow. "I mean, what do you know? We're like lab partners freshman year? So you know me or something?" Her laughter is bitter, nothing like it used to be. She has gray rings under her eyes. I can't get over her eyes.

"Do you wear contacts now?"

"No." The question confuses her. "Look." She makes an encompassing gesture over the entire room. "Do I look like I need help?" She scratches the dog. "I mean, I haven't done drugs in almost a year." Stares at her toenails, painted purple. On her ankle is a small cuneiform tattoo. "I haven't made a movie in four months. I mean, I don't think I'm even going to again. Probably. I've got offers for, like TV and stuff." She tugs her hair and brushes something off a sofa cushion. I remember the hair-tugging. She always did do that. There's so little I recognize here.

"But you're not happy. You're better—"

She throws up her hands. "See? This is what I'm talking about. You come out here and what, because you don't like the way I live my life?"

"Come on—"

"No. You come on. Really, Bobby. I have news for you. The world's a lot bigger than Port Arthur, Texas. Okay? A lot bigger. How I make my living isn't your business, and it sure as hell isn't that asshole out there's."

"Tony?"

She frowns sarcastically. "My dad." Rubs her nose. "But it's my life. Mine. You need to worry about your life, right? Do I tell you how to live your life? What do you do anyway?"

A moment of hesitation. "I work for Alamo Sewer Treatment. I monitor groundwater."

She claps. "Wow. Super. Never left town, right? Never went to college, right?"

"I don't know, not yet, but—"

She puts her head in a hand and laughs. "I cannot believe you actually came all the way out here. I cannot believe you brought my father here." She stares hard at me. "You've got a lot of fucking nerve."

I look at pictures on her wall, black-and-white photos of empty vistas and lonesome shorelines, and all I can think of is to try and convince her of what I still know, a speech I've rehearsed since we entered California. "I saw you once. It was sophomore year. Early sophomore year. I guess you didn't have eighth hour back then, but it had just rained, and I'm waiting for the bell to ring, you know? Bored, the sky's that weird gray where there's sunshine, but no blue, and I just want to go home."

She picks at her thumbnail.

I keep my eyes on the landscapes while I talk. "And I look out the window, and I saw you. You were walking across the football field in your uniform, and you'd taken your shoes off—and you were taking your time, kicking up water with your toes. I could see little splashes of it, and you would spin around now and then, you were looking up at the sky, and in the glass I'd lose you in the sun.

And you'd step out of the light, kicking water, in your skirt, looking really distracted. And, it wasn't that you were beautiful, and you were, but it wasn't that." All my stored years cohere into language, and I believe she can yet be reclaimed. "I remember thinking: I knew what was distracting you. You know? Even though I couldn't name it, or put words to it, I had this sense, this real calm feeling, and I used to be pretty nervous I guess, but a feeling—like the world was a good place, because I could see it with your eyes."

The dog seeks my leg and whines a faint, choked sob. A newscaster tells a silent story on TV.

She closes her robe some and touches my cheek. "Bobby. Look, you're a sweetheart. I mean it." She wipes her eyes with a tiny laugh that almost echoes the one I remember. "I'm sure I was just high, though. I was taking a lot of acid back then."

Her fingers trace my jawline, stopping under my chin. "You're sweet. But you need to leave."

Because there's nowhere to look but at her, I close my eyes.

This is where all my stories converge. Every lost moment between experience and memory meets at a crossroads: at the metal X in my jaw, where her fingers sit like a shotgun barrel.

"...Can I have five more minutes?"

"No."

Someone shouts, and I open my eyes.

We move outside, where the voice came from. In the near distance, just beyond the porch's light, Coach sits on the lawn, holding his face. Tony looms over him, fists clenched.

Tony sticks out his jaw. "He said he was going inside. I told him no."

It's hard to not pity Coach crumbled on the lawn that way, struggling with a palm over his eye, but I manage. I walk over and Tony steps in front of me. "You want some?"

"Tony—" Amanda calls behind me. "Come on. It's all right. Come inside."

Coach sprawls at my feet, holds the chloroform out like some impotent offering. The front door shuts and we are left alone on the lawn.

I tell Coach to get in the truck.

In the driver's seat, I toss the chloroform out the window. He slumps against his door with a bruise swelling over his left eye. "This really worked out great," he snaps.

I study him, trace the lines on his face with my eyes and keep staring after he meets my look. He turns to the window and I watch him for a few moments before twisting the key.

The engine turns over, stuttering, and we move forward.

Later, a second search will occur.

Back in Port Arthur, I see an advertisement for a firm in Houston called Reunions Inc. Because there is still one question to answer, one piece of unknowing I will not abide, I contact them. What follows are two months where I continue to work for Alamo, letting the vacuous fields and long empty skies pass by like frames of an overexposed film, telling no stories, taking soil samples and testing air with my nose for signs of contamination. Only occasionally during this period, I'll reflect on Coach Duprene.

We made the drive back in silence. I drove and Coach kept his face to the window. Red-clay mesas and purple skylines. Half-conceived mountains in distant mist. His guilt as certain as the road beneath our wheels.

I will not see him again.

Reunions Inc. returns a report that costs me $300. The envelope spends an entire day sitting on my kitchen table. The company's logo feels like it's trying to stare me down. After five beers, I open the envelope and remove two sheets of paper. This is what they say:

Travis Corresi is a missing person. His last known whereabouts was on the *Leslie Charles*, a cargo ship out of Shanghai, lost in the Yellow Sea in 1989. But I'd always known that. All my life, my father died at sea.

Tearing down every bit of philosophy, every maxim in the house, I crushed the notes, making a single bundle, and decided there was only one story. Everything that's gone before is one story, the same long one, and if it doesn't end then the next decade might be like the last one, a period of anxious stillness that sees you crouched nervous like a mouse in a corner, leaves you mourning a life you never really had.

That life is fragmented into scenes you barely recall, their significance due only to their lack of competition, until these moments, this life, become like a pair of green eyes you're convinced you once saw, blinking at you in the sky of a long wandering night, when you wondered what you were doing driving this late, and how you'd make it home. Years you can't remember, because you were too busy disguising true sadness as trumped-up nostalgia.

So the house is up for sale. Last night you decided not to pack anything, and spent time staring at the long, fenced prairie across the street.

Now you might picture your next story, your second one, but don't be too definite, don't make a vision you might cling to, or create an idea you lose yourself in. Don't look at a map and ponder the depth of the Yellow Sea, don't imagine the shapes of its waves. Don't contemplate lost parents or lost girls. Resist the urge to explain their stories, because eventually you've got to understand that an answer isn't the same thing as a solution, and a story is sometimes only an excuse.

If you have to, let yourself imagine the mood of this story, the places it might happen, what the weather will be like. Tell yourself it will be a world, at least, where you're less abandoned, and sustained by more than illusion. If you have to.

Just leave before you change your mind.

THE GUILD OF THIEVES, LOST WOMEN, AND SUNRISE PALMS

THE RV PARK WAS BASICALLY SIX TRAILERS surrounding a grassy mound. On the mound old concrete foundations shot up from the grass like broken teeth. Hoyt's glasses steamed up on the ride over, sweat soaked his back. He leaned his bicycle against CB's silver Airstream. He pulled his shirt down over his large stomach with a pang of self-loathing, walked up the two steps and paused because he heard voices on the other side of the thin doorway. CB never had visitors, and Hoyt guessed it might be cops.

The night before, CB had used his good hand to spread out jewelry stolen from the Tronke home: many rings, a silver Rolex and gold Tag Heuer, a choker lined in diamonds, a pearl necklace, and other precious things. The back office of CB's pawnshop smelled like dust and rat poison. To one side of the jewels had sat a DVD player, a fifty-capacity CD changer, and two shotguns, also from the Tronkes' house. CB always said to get guns whenever you can: guns moved easier than jewelry. Guns were the easiest thing to sell.

CB has told Hoyt that CB used to mean Charles Bailey, but now it meant Coffin Boat. CB used to be enormous. He used to hold the state triple-A division record in the shot put. He has a composite plastic plate in his hip and a note that excuses him from metal detectors. He's always refused to tell Hoyt stories about Iraq. CB's skin is dark brown and hard like wood, and he has a thick face, a flat nose, black eyes. He is full Choctaw. Great pink scars engulf his left arm—a gnarled arm seeded with shrapnel, always bent in a way that reminds Hoyt of the tiny, useless claw of a T-Rex. Hoyt met CB two years ago, pawning the first thing he ever stole, a neighbor's shiny .45 Magnum.

At the RV park Hoyt decided the voices he heard were too quiet to be the police, so he knocked on the door. From the other side of the door CB said "hello" like it was a question.

Hoyt opened the door and saw CB kneeling on the floor. His bad leg was stretched out. His thick black hair fell around his big face. The hair covered an arc of scar Hoyt knew existed above CB's left ear. A woman was lying on CB's couch. CB nodded to Hoyt and returned to the woman.

He'd propped a small bowl of water between his knee and bad arm. He was washing the woman's feet with a purple sponge. The girl looked at Hoyt once, then ignored him. She had short red hair and moon-white skin. She was slim in a muddied green dress, her white legs dangled off the arm of the couch. She looked like she had just run through the forest. Her top lip and right eye were bruised, swollen. Blood trickled from her feet and into the bowl. A few pebbles and pine needles stirred in the water.

CB looked up and his eyes were trembling. "Can you give me ten minutes here man?" Then he wobbled on his knee and the bowl tumbled, splashing pink water over the all-weather carpet. The girl moved off the couch to help him gather the bowl. Before he left, Hoyt saw them both kneeling in front of one another.

Across from CB's Airstream was a larger, brown trailer. A wooden sign leaned against it: an opened pink hand with a blue eye at its palm hovered above the words "Mother Divine—Palmistry Tarot Spiritual Guidance Your Future." The words were written in a peeling red with a bleached-out shadow of each letter beneath the cracking paint.

After Hoyt had sold the .45 Magnum to CB two years ago, he started hanging around and asking to hear war stories. The most CB ever said was, once, "I's nineteen when I went and it only took me four weeks to get blown up and I came back." CB showed Hoyt how to crosshatch strips of duct tape for windows, so when the glass shatters you can pull the tape away and the whole window comes with it. He showed Hoyt how to use a thin blanket to muffle the single strike of a ball-peen hammer. There had been many rules. Don't mess with storm windows or dead bolts. A back entrance is good, a garage entrance is ideal. Partners divide search time and police pursuit. If you have to make a noise, make it once, and decisively. CB had told him, "I never met anyone who could disarm a good electronic alarm." CB put all his faith in the unobstructed entrance. The unobstructed entrance is something people forgot, a wood chute or crawlspace, a third-story attic window. A point of safe penetration. The parts of an average door lock include the escutcheon, the faceplate, the latch bolt, and the rose. CB showed him how to use Freon to freeze the bolt, then break it with a tap. Then he told Hoyt to forget all that stuff. He said to find the unobstructed entrance.

CB said he learned everything from two uncles in the thieves' guild. He said, *If you're caught, no one is going to help you.* And, *Whatever you say, don't say anything.*

By the time CB came outside, the pines around the park were practically glowing in sunset, a burning green. CB dragged his left leg down the steps and lit a cigarette. He cocked a big thumb toward the trailer. "She's asleep or I'd let you in." He'd put on blue jeans and sneakers, a black rodeo shirt with orange-yellow flames stitched over it, the left sleeve knotted and tied off to cover his arm. He'd said once that doctors tried to remove his arm but he wouldn't let them.

Hoyt said, "What's going on? How'd you find a girl that would talk to you?" He felt a little jittery.

Smoke eased out of CB's stony face. "That's Robin. I used to know her a long time ago. She showed up here this morning."

Hoyt wiped the sweat off his glasses. "And then you beat the crap out of her?"

"Shut up. That's how she was when she got here. I hadn't thought I'd see her again."

"How'd she get hurt?"

The muscles in CB's face tensed. He looked annoyed. "She'd married some punk in Westlake." That was a neighbor town, a swampy place of oil refineries and meth labs. "Anyway, what do you care man? Go eat something, fat boy."

"Maybe I'll just blow up half my body." Hoyt kicked at pebbles. "I need that stuff I asked you about. By Friday."

"The yak?"

Hoyt nodded. CB told him he'd have it by Thursday. Sometimes CB gave Hoyt drugs to sell as a kind of cash advance against one of their scores. Over the past year, his senior year, Hoyt had traded drugs for academic work several times.

A light breeze blew CB's long hair across his cheeks. Where the wind lifted the hair you could see the bald curve of scar. Hoyt asked, "So what's up with you and that girl, man? Who did that to her?"

CB threw a stone at Hoyt, hollering that it wasn't anyone else's business. Just before riding away Hoyt yelled, "Hey! Does this have anything to do with the war?"

The next morning Hoyt woke to the sound of loud whooping. The wall thumped. His dad had been sleeping with a woman named Miss Tilly for the past few weeks. She danced at T-Back's over in Westlake. The week before, they'd been eating pancakes and Miss Tilly had popped open her robe, flashed one breast at Hoyt and winked. He thought about that as he finally got out of bed. He waited until he heard the sound of her Jeep leaving before exiting his room. He heard his father grunting through his morning push-ups. He poured a bowl of cornflakes and ate. His father appeared a few minutes later wearing a blue jogging suit. Where Hoyt's body was soft, sloping and round, his father's was tight, muscled. He told Hoyt, "Good morning," drank the rest of the orange juice, and went for a run.

Strange things had been happening in their house. Hoyt heard late-night phone conversations, his father's voice raised in anger. He found his father home at noon, drinking whiskey and smoking cigarettes in silence. His father had started to bring home boxes, something he'd never done before, boxes labeled Sunrise Palms.

The week before Hoyt had found three thick rolls of hundred-dollar bills in his father's sock drawer.

After two home invasions in their neighborhood, Hoyt's father had installed an American Security 9000 alarm system. It had motion detectors. If you crossed an invisible barrier, high electric wailing commenced. Hoyt knew there were voids in the radio waves that caged their house. He couldn't know where they were, though. The unobstructed entrance to his home eluded him.

Inside, there were no pictures decorating the house. Walls were empty and bookshelves bare. There used to be many photos of Hoyt's mother, but they had gradually disappeared, and finally, one day years ago, his father had told Hoyt that it was time they both moved on. Then all the pictures came down. Hoyt remembered a couple times with his mother that had terrified him as a child. They told him that she was a danger to herself and others, that she wouldn't want to hurt him, not really, but she might.

When he was six she was delivered to a gated white building that stood alone in green and open country. Ever since then, Hoyt had felt the house was locked into a certain moment. Shortly after the pictures came down Hoyt's father began exercising relentlessly, devoting long hours to his real estate agency. He was tan. His teeth got whiter.

His father hadn't mentioned the new rug in the dining room. Hoyt looked at it. Blue and white with a muted bird pattern, the rug lay in a column of sun. The rug appeared to Hoyt in Wal-Mart, and he'd felt the familiar impulse to possess something. This was a constant impulse and unpredictably particular. The things he shoplifted often seemed random and useless. During his quieter moments he was conscious of a thousand vague desires tugging at him, yet the objects of these wants were always changing. He could possess things, but often once he acquired something he lost all desire for it. He couldn't find whatever had attracted him about the rug now, but at the time, he'd thought it must remind him of his mother. The rug was so big that he simply walked out of the store with it rolled on his shoulder. It wasn't the kind of thing the store expected to be shoplifted.

Hoyt had known the thrill of burglary before CB. But what he liked was the air of a strange house, its furnishings and photographs, its smells. Two houses never had the same air. His feet padding silently, his flashlight's beam might find a pair of shoes or half-drunken soda can, a family portrait, and in a hundred ways he could feel human essences filling the house.

Bored, alone, Hoyt walked to the slough at the end of their block and smoked a cigarette. He smoked True menthols, CB's brand. Along the bank of the slough, there were so many white egrets roosting that they obscured the trees. A three-story waterfront home stood across the water on stilts. Hoyt had discussed the potential burglary of that house with CB, but a plan was never formulated. He swirled smoke in his mouth and got the idea to enter the home from the water, through the boathouse. If he could keep coming up with jobs for him and CB, then the future was secured, and things didn't really need to change.

Later in the week, one of the football players that wanted the cocaine gave Hoyt two hundred and fifty dollars. The player's name was Lucas George. He had long blond hair and looked like somebody's hero. Lucas was having a party at his parents' house later in the week. He hadn't really invited Hoyt to the party when he asked for the coke. It was suggested that Hoyt could just "drop it by." His girlfriend picked her lip while she waited for Lucas to count out the money. She had a long waist and pert chest, and her body made Hoyt want to steal something.

He felt excited biking to CB's to deliver the money. He figured CB would offer him a drink, maybe they'd watch television, or maybe CB would let Hoyt fire his .380 as he'd done in the past. He could explain that girl who'd been there last time. Why, after all his stories about women, had CB never told him about one with red hair and skin like a Greek statue? At the RV park, a different CB stood in the doorway.

His black hair was cut short and choppy, the sickle of scar tissue banding the left side of his head. He wore a plaid button-down shirt, with one sleeve rolled up and the other tied over his bad arm. "Hey man," he said. His big head constantly leaned toward his right shoulder.

"Hey." Hoyt craned his neck trying to see around CB. The aroma of cooking meat blew through the door. "I got the money for that stuff."

"Right. Oh, right. Cool." CB stepped back from the door and it opened wider. "I'll get it." He walked toward the small loft area at the trailer's rear. He didn't indicate if Hoyt should follow or not. Hoyt stepped inside the trailer.

Things had been put on shelves. Beneath the smell of cooking there was the sharp hint of Lysol in the air. CB's car magazines were stacked neatly beside a row of records that before had been sprawled around the stereo. Hoyt looked at the woman in the kitchen area. She stood before a skillet of hamburger meat and noodles. The meat sizzled and popped while she stirred it, and tiny beads of sweat were broken over her forehead. Her red hair was pulled behind her face, and her bruises had faded some. She was almost beautiful. Her eyes met Hoyt's and he immediately looked away.

When CB reappeared he passed Hoyt the small baggy in a handshake. CB's stiff leg dragged toward the door. He said, "You still owe me two for that nine."

"I know." Two weeks before, Hoyt had purchased a nine-millimeter semiautomatic from CB on credit. Hoyt stopped walking and asked, "What's for dinner?"

The girl, Robin, answered from the kitchen. "It's just Hamburger Helper."

"I love Hamburger Helper." Hoyt moved toward the couch. He sat down. "I think I figured something out about that house on the water. We should talk about it, you know, come up with some plans."

"Not right now." CB rubbed the short hair on the back of his head.

"What'd you cut all that off for? You look retarded now."

"Ah, it's too hot."

"There's not much to eat," Robin interjected. She turned the stove off and lifted the skillet above two bowls on the counter. "It don't make much." The counter was clean and shiny.

Hoyt felt mean all of a sudden, insulted. "Hey, I forgot your name, lady," he said.

She served the meat and noodles into the bowls. "Robin."

"Hey, Robin, do you know what CB stands for? You probably think it stands for Charles Bailey, don't you?"

She put spoons in the bowls and gave CB an impatient expression.

He put a thick hand on Hoyt's shoulder and said, sternly, "Hey man, what're you doing?"

"Tell her about Coffin Boat. Give her the score."

"Come outside. I want to show you something." He guided Hoyt off the couch and out the door.

Sun sparkled in broken glass on the ground. Hoyt said, "What I was thinking was we could paddle into the boathouse from the lake."

CB's dead foot scraped loose bits of glass and gravel. "Look dude, the thing is, she's having a kid, okay?"

"She's pregnant?"

CB nodded. A trace of happiness in his features alarmed Hoyt.

"So what? Where's her husband?"

"She's with me now."

"How do you know her?"

"We go back. This's how it is with me."

Hoyt held out his hands. "Don't you think somebody's looking for her?"

"Man, get out of here." CB turned with his stiff gait. "You're a negative mother, you know that?"

He went inside and closed the door. Hoyt saw the sign across the way. Palmistry Tarot Spiritual Guidance Your Future. He had three scenarios for his future. In one, he worked his way into the full-time position of drug dealer and fence. In another, unlikely, he was employed, with a family, sitting down for dinner. In the third scenario, he pictured himself going crazy, just like his mother. They'd put him in a white room where he'd sing to himself.

When he got home he could hear music from his father's room. The door was shut, and Zydeco played loudly. This was the music his father grew up with as a boy in Morgan City, a gulf port where the first Tarzan movie was filmed. Hoyt knocked softly, but no one answered. A moment later, the music raised in volume.

The next afternoon Hoyt's father said he wanted to talk to him. Hoyt had seen his father folding clothes into a suitcase earlier that morning. His father came into the living room carrying a large gray suitcase and a red duffel bag. He sat down next to Hoyt and turned the television off.

"How you doing?" His father had the same friendly expression he used when showing someone a house. He put his hands on his knees and said, "Listen, if I had to go away for a little while, just a trip for a few weeks, you'd be okay, huh? I mean, you're out of school and everything."

"Yeah." Hoyt shrugged. The back of his neck became hot. "Where you going?"

His father's few wrinkles had been hardened by exercise, making sharp creases. "Well, I'm not sure yet. It could be a few places right now. It depends on some things." His blue eyes glanced at Hoyt then darted away. "Don't worry about it. Best thing I should do is call you when I get there. It might be better."

"Why?"

His father scratched his forehead and smiled at Hoyt. "Listen, I might not be going anywhere. It might not even happen. If I—I mean, we'll see. But I'm going to leave you some money."

"I got money."

"You do?" His father rose on heavy, flexing thighs. "It doesn't matter." His father dug in the duffel bag and produced twenty hundred-dollar bills. "This is just in case, okay?" He handed it to Hoyt and for just a moment, a brief instant, his voice seemed to crack and reveal something else. "Be careful with this. It might have to last you awhile. Okay? You want to stretch this out."

He touched Hoyt's shoulder, then hoisted the suitcase and duffel bag. He walked to the driveway and loaded the bags into the trunk of his car, a red early-nineties Cadillac he'd bought at an auction the summer before.

He came back in the house and said, "Like I'm saying, I don't even know if I'm going to have to leave. It's all just in case." He made another trip to the bedroom, this time moving the cardboard file boxes to the DeVille.

Shortly after, his father said he had a date, and left wearing a brown suit and gray silk shirt. Hoyt explored his father's room.

The drawers were empty except for bits of odd change, matches and scraps of paper. Slippers were under the bed, but many hanging clothes were gone. The closet was nearly bare, but at its back, in the top right, was a shelf Hoyt had never noticed when there had been clothes hanging. A paper bag sat up there in the shadows, and he took it down. Things inside rattled. Hoyt's own closet was filled with unopened CDs, stolen clothes he never wore, books he never read. He wondered what his father had been hoarding, feeling for the first time that they had a common quality.

He sat on the floor and unfolded the bag. All the pictures of his mother that his father had taken down were in the bag and he touched their frames.

He put them back in the bag, and put the bag back in the closet.

He didn't see his father the next day. By nightfall he was supposed to deliver the cocaine to Lucas George's party. Hoyt walked his bicycle past cars that started filling the curb about fifty yards away from Lucas's house. The entire neighborhood was large homes with nice lawns. The Georges had two stories of brick and brown siding, two gables, and a long porch. A plank fence with open sides surrounded their acre. Hoyt had done a few bumps of the coke Lucas ordered, and his vision felt clear and his head hummed with purpose. He was aware that he would be nineteen in a few months. The same age CB was when he got blown up and lived, when he became Coffin Boat.

Young voices carried down the street. Hoyt's heart quickened as he moved toward them. Ahead, lights in the house were on, and a few teenage silhouettes meandered in the yard. He could hear faintly the music as he walked. He felt his jacket. In one pocket was the gram of cocaine, in the other, the nine millimeter. He thought he'd really like to shoot someone in the foot. Maybe they would put him in the gated white building in the green and open land.

He was late. Hoyt began circling the perimeter of the party. He recognized many of the people as faces that didn't know him and stayed in the dark, the way a prowler might. Through French doors, young people could be seen, the girls laughing, boys wearing ball caps, clutching cans of beer and talking too loud. People in the backyard surrounded a keg, and the girl Hoyt recognized as Lucas's girlfriend was walking around with a garbage bag, picking up discarded beer cans and removing drinks from the lacquered tables and shelves.

Hoyt paused and wondered why he was not one of those voices, why he had never been. The answer felt obvious, but was broken up across eighteen years. His thumb brushed the trigger guard of the gun in his pocket. Then his thoughts were impeded by a girl's voice.

"Oh, hey, I know you. Luke was looking for you."

Hoyt saw Lucas's girlfriend. She was small and smiling pleasantly, holding a garbage bag full of cans and cigarette butts.

"What are you doing out here? There's beer in the back."

"Oh, yeah. I just got here."

She put one hand on her hip and cocked her head backward. "Luke was waiting on you. I've almost had enough, but you should go in." She lifted the garbage bag. "This is bullshit."

Hoyt watched the party while the girl began to pick up the stray bits of trash on the ground, tossing them into her bag. The way she moved and smelled made him swoon with want, and he was so tired of that feeling, and felt the gun in his hand, knew she was so close. He took a long breath. He had a clear thought, in a voice different than his own. *No one is going to help you.* The phrase for unknown reasons seemed to lift his spirits.

He walked up to the girl. "Hey, it's Mary, right?"

"Mm-hm." She nodded in the manner of a gracious hostess.

"Mary, could you tell Lucas that Hoyt said forget it. Also that he's not getting his money back. I spent it. I'm not dealing to some shitbird that can't invite me to his party."

At first she laughed a little. "What?"

"Seriously. Not this minute, though. Give me about ten to hit the road." He winked at her and walked away, fading back into the shadows. She had a very small smile on her face. Was that the first time he'd ever winked to anyone? he asked himself. Yes.

His father had never come home. A small shed behind their house contained rusted garden tools and beach toys, an inflatable child's raft. The raft was gray rubber and took some time to inflate. He squatted in the dark, puffing hard. Its nozzle tasted moldy and plastic in the total dark of the shed.

On the water the raft sank in its middle while its front and back ends jutted upward. Hoyt's legs hung over its sides. His legs disappeared into black water that covered his lap, drenched the paper bag lying on it. He paddled across the slough in the liquid silence, sliding toward the house on the other side of the water, its shape looming, blocks of shadow on stilts, something like the future there, a shape waiting to be mapped. Hoyt rubbed his nose, which stung. Dripping echoed as he drifted into the boathouse out of curiousity. He could see the outline of a door that seemed connected to the main building. It probably would have worked, he told himself.

He paddled back toward his side of the slough. Some gray clouds unveiled a moon like the glowing print of a boot's heel in black mud. At the center of the slough he dropped the paper bag with his mother's pictures into the black water, and he watched them sink. In the water the pictures ripped through the wet bag. Momentarily the brown paper floated back up, torn and empty, sitting on the surface of the water like a scab.

A week passed. Rain on a few days. His father never came back.

He got beaten up by three football players, but he felt good.

One of the men in a black suit pointed to the bruises on Hoyt's cheek and forehead. "Did your dad do that to you?"

Half his forehead was swollen, and his left cheek was purple and maroon. "No. Some kids jumped me."

Hoyt sat on the couch. Two deputies stood by the front door, and a second man in a suit was strolling around the house casually, inspecting bookshelves, opening cabinets. They'd come early in the morning. He'd seen two cruisers pull into the driveway, and he knew they'd caught him. He rose from bed in a hurry, expecting questions about a series of home invasions, or maybe to just be arrested. Of course just to be arrested. They don't come get you to have a chat. To prepare him, his fears had anticipated this, and the event had the feel of something he'd been seeking.

The deputies wore brown, short-sleeved uniforms with wide-brimmed hats. The two men in suits held a search warrant. The deputies stayed by the front door while one of the other men walked back and forth in front of Hoyt. Hoyt was waiting to be charged when they saw the contents of his closet. But when the questions started, all they talked about was his father.

"You sure he didn't hit you? A guy who'd do that, he's not too good." The man paced, shaking his head slowly.

"He didn't."

The other man in the suit walked out the hallway. "This's in the bedroom." He held up a fold of bills.

"What's that?"

The man in the hall thumbed through the bills. "It's two thousand dollars."

"Two thousand dollars."

Hoyt didn't look at them. "He said he was leaving and that had to last me awhile."

The man sat on the couch next to Hoyt, resting his wrists on his knees. He had a deep, mumbly voice. "And he didn't say anything to you about where he was going? You got no idea where he is?"

"He wouldn't say. Just said he's leaving for a while."

The two men in suits looked back and forth at one another. One dropped the money on the couch. "Your dad ever talk about something called Sunrise Palms?" He squatted down to look Hoyt in the eyes. "He ever say anything about Florida? Come on, kid."

"I don't know."

"You don't know. You don't think it's a little weird your dad lays two G on you and leaves all of a sudden? You don't ask about that?"

Hoyt lifted his head. His eyes were wet. "I did ask. I did ask."

"And?"

He put his head down again. The two men exchanged looks. One of the deputies idly examined a fingernail.

The one on the couch spoke. "And you got a mother in Charter House. That right?"

Hoyt nodded.

"You see her much?"

He shook his head.

The man stood and walked over to his partner. "So what are you going to do?"

"I don't know."

"How old are you?"

"Eighteen."

The men stood still, communicating wordlessly, tilts of their heads. They handed Hoyt a card and instructed him to contact them if he heard from his father. The card said Securities and Exchange Commission. They told him they would be watching. They said, "Keep your nose clean."

On the way out, one of the men turned around and said, "Is there something you want from us? Something we can do if you help out?"

Hoyt thought a moment, then stepped back into the doorway. "I don't want anything." He closed the door.

*

CB SMACKED HIS LIPS AND RUBBED HIS EYES, GROGGY in the doorway. He was shirtless. Half his big chest was collapsed scar tissue that flowed horrifically into his left arm. His eyes were bloodshot and murky. "What happened to you?" he said. "Look at you, dog."

Hoyt shrugged. "Got jumped."

CB turned back inside, opening the door for Hoyt to follow. A box of cereal and several empty beer bottles were strewn around the living room, some broken glass, disarray. CB put on a T-shirt and came back in the room with two bottles of Old Style. One of the plaster walls had a fist-sized hole in it.

"Where's that girl?"

CB handed him a beer and shook his head. He turned the bottle up, drawing almost half of its contents.

"Gone?" Hoyt said.

"She wasn't ever here, man." CB kicked an empty bottle over with his dead leg. He moved to a pile of records on the couch, sorted through them and found his box of cigarettes. "Stupid, man. Look at me."

Hoyt watched CB fall into the couch and suck hard on a cigarette. "What're you up to?"

"Nothing." Hoyt set down the beer and turned to the doorway. He sat down on the steps outside, looking at the park, the concrete slabs that broke through the ground. Mother Divine's big open palm faced him across the way. CB came and stood next to him, leaning against the doorway.

"You want something else to drink?"

Hoyt shook his head.

"You all right?"

"I think I am."

They stayed there for several minutes, and neither spoke. The shadows in the grass stretched, and the lights between the pines became orange and red. CB flicked his cigarette and cleared his throat. "I's thinking about what you said. About paddling up to that lake house? That might work. We should get on the water and check it out."

"That's okay."

"No?"

He watched the high grass wave against the concrete. "Never mind about it."

"You don't want to?"

"No."

CB bent down and studied Hoyt's cuts and bruises. He stood up and turned away. "You know, you always ask, but I wasn't even in the fight. We were playing football around mines. We didn't know."

Hoyt said, "Don't tell me about it." He tossed a rock. "You took out fifteen enemy troops with your bare hands before they got you with a grenade."

"I was swatting them off me like ants."

"They thought you were a giant."

"Yes they did." CB threw his bottle into the trees. A sunset haze overlaid the clearing. "You want to get high?"

"No," Hoyt said. "I don't want anything." And he didn't.

But on the way home he saw two pretty girls walking the street outside the mall, laughing and eating ice cream, a glittering 4x4 Jeep with chrome package. He pedaled toward deep recesses of cypress and sumac, and he saw the egrets in white ascension and the moon on the water. There he recognized the old ropes of want, desire, tugging, and gradually it was clear to him that he had no choice, that the world would never let him go.

A Cryptographer

ADAM LEFT ONE NIGHT IN APRIL, AND SHARON FOUND a paint-dusted stencil under his bed. Everything else in his room was as he kept it—the computer, the television, CDs, most of his clothes, his high school pictures, yearbooks. She sat on his mattress after taking the stencil from its place under the bed. She scrutinized it like a note she was meant to find. A cardboard sheet, no bigger than a file folder. The picture of a military tank had been cut out of it, with the words Police State cut below. Orange spray paint lined the edges of these voids. She tried to remember if she'd ever seen this picture sprayed anywhere in town.

It was September now, and she'd begun carrying the stencil in her purse. She was walking more, foregoing the bus in the mornings, taking odd routes into the city, searching alley walls and the sides of Dumpsters for the orange silhouette of a tank. Her legs began acting up, and her back ached. When she got to school in the mornings she was often hunched, too tired to properly control the children before noon. She taught fourth grade at a public school largely composed of low-income kids, most black, some Hispanic. What the state referred to as "at-risk" children. Lately she'd let them do whatever they wanted until lunch.

It was the stencil's fault. Among the trappings of adolescence her son had left behind, the stencil was the only one that possessed this hypnotic gloom. The other objects in his room had their place; though abandoned, sad, they were understandable, they belonged. The mystery of the stencil became the mystery of her son himself, his incomprehensible desertion, his anger. She never understood his anger.

"Why you gone paint stuff?"

Sharon looked down. Eaton Slavin was beside her desk, staring into her purse where the cardboard stencil stood out among the tissue, prayer books, cosmetics, and wallet. The rest of the kids were at their desks, trying to complete a coloring project.

"Excuse me?"

His shirt, crusted with stains, rose up over a small brown belly. He lifted the cardboard sheet with a tiny hand. "You paint the telephone pole?"

"That? That's not mine. What are you doing out of your desk, Eaton?"

He held the stencil and looked at its picture. "I seen you paintings on the phone poles."

She snatched the stencil from his hand.

He jumped at her gesture, but his surprise immediately vanished, his face returning to its placid, slack-jawed expression of inquiry. "Can I go th'bathroom?"

"Yes, go." Sharon felt bad at the hardness with which she'd grabbed the stencil, felt that she'd frightened the boy. But she recalled his reaction—shock, followed by instant reconciliation. She'd seen that before, and many times, the bovine acceptance these children had for sudden, violent gestures.

She'd never hit Adam, not once. Even when his ranting took the Blessed Mother and the Holy Church as its targets, Sharon had never struck him, only listened quietly, her mind reciting prayers that his anger might be relieved. Adam would talk about the church or the government as if some ravenous creature were standing right out in the street, waiting for them to leave the house so it could chew their bodies with razor-toothed jaws. He was six feet by age fifteen, with thick blond hair and an improbably attractive face, gaunt, projecting. This compounded her bafflement. Adam could have been the type of effortless youth that devastates the people around him. He'd let his hair grow long and stayed skinny as he grew, but she encouraged him to lift weights to correct that. The sounds of his harangues had become the jumbled noise of the children in her classroom.

Mo'Nique and Yolanda were struggling over some scissors. Looking out at the classroom, Sharon marked two of the three— Lester Tuttle, DeRay Fauk, Eaton Slavin—almost surely headed for jail in a few short years. Sometimes they all stood on the front steps when school let out, watching their classmates depart and eyeing each backpack, trying to determine who had money on them, no doubt. She'd seen the boys chase a limping dog with rocks. Locked in her bottom drawer, she kept the stack of comic books she'd taken from the three boys a couple weeks ago. Behind her desk, she discretely slid off her shoes, her feet swollen from walking.

She'd been teaching here for six years, after a professional absence of fifteen. Sharon had given up teaching once David's dental practice was established, but she had to start again after the divorce. Coleman PHS was the only school that notified her of an opening, and it had had three. She was forty-six. In early October, Adam would be seventeen, if he were still alive. But of course he was, she knew, because someone would find his body, and because she did not feel he was dead, not at all. She felt him living so strongly that she'd wondered whether she could simply set out, with her heart's thumping as a kind of homing device, and eventually locate him.

When Adam had first disappeared, Sharon called David to see if the boy had run to him, but David said he hadn't. He reminded her that she was to contact him through his lawyer. She remembered when she'd learned about his assistant. How unmoved David's face had been when he packed the suitcase. That had been hard to endure, his face. It had shown no anger or regret, just a stoic determination to get away from her. Now he had another son.

The stencil sat flat on her desk, the wood surface filling its inscription. She read it again. A tank. Police State.

She did not like puzzles, never had. The door opened and Eaton strolled back in, picking at his nose on the way to his desk.

"Eaton?" Sharon said, leaving the stencil on her desk.

He paused, looked up with dull, bored eyes. The other children stopped what they were doing to watch. Mo'Nique had won the scissors. "Huh?"

"Don't 'huh' me. Come up here, please."

The children were quiet. They observed Eaton walk languidly to the front of the class, running his fingertips over the edges of desks.

He stood before her twisting on his heel. She tapped the sheet of cardboard.

"Eaton, did you say you've seen this painted somewhere?"

He nodded his head, pulled his arm behind his back. His navel protruded like the tip of a brown thumb.

"Where?"

"I seen that on the poles at my house. An on the walls." His eyes were wet, deep black, like the onyx in the class's rock collection.

"Where do you live?"

He pointed behind himself. "Timpan'ca."

"All right. Thank you. You may sit down, now. Finish coloring your picture."

He almost sashayed back to his desk, giving one little foot a limp. His sneakers were too big for his feet. Timpanica Gardens was a housing project near the school, about eight blocks east. Many of the children lived there, and Sharon knew it from the day she had bus duty. The building itself was a large cube of apartments with a hollow center. Gray brick, paint stains on the plaque at the end of the sidewalk, a tall wall around it, she remembered. It had been raining that day. The neighborhood had looked broken. Everything from the walls of buildings to people's legs seemed in the process of buckling, slowly, toward the ground. Her own street, Aster, had seen its better days. And the house was now coming into question.

She hadn't known about David's loans until the actual divorce. Rather than the house being hers, it had liens against several outstanding loans, half of which were now hers to pay. She'd worked it so they took something out of her paycheck every month. Her fingernails slowly moved around the sides of the stencil.

The stencil had creases down its middle, as though it had been folded around something. The children were all talking, a rumble of noise and movement in front of her desk. They were laughing and arguing, making a racket.

Without considering her own intentions, Sharon reached into her desk and produced a sheet of white typing paper. She slid it beneath the stencil, took a Sharpie pen and began shading in the picture. She didn't notice that the children all stopped, briefly and as one, to watch her. Then they were making noise again.

When she'd finished, she stared at the black sketch and the two words below it, and her eyes seemed to fall into those spaces, to descend into the ink, the bottomless shapes of letters. A few of the children were running in circles now. Someone pulled a reading poster off the wall.

Gray buildings fenced her. This area of the city did not feel safe, though she saw several other, older women hobbling about on the streets. There was a block-long line of Arab vendors, and a few black men stood in front of a corner store and didn't acknowledge her. Children, home from school, were tumbling into the streets shouting. To maintain her calm, she prayed a rosary silently, extending her prayers to the denizens of the chipped and patched buildings around her. Boards over those windows. Big slabs of metal warehouses in line toward the river. She saw the walls of Timpanica ahead, and had to rest at a crosswalk before going the rest of the way. The air was warm and damp, heavy in her lungs.

She saw one almost immediately, a blur of orange on a telephone pole that also had dozens of tattered flyers stapled to it. She peeled off some of the papers until the mark of the tank and the words were clear.

She spread her hand over the graffiti, pressing into the splintery wood. There was such a pitiful homecoming in this gesture, she wanted to weep at her own stupidity. But she never cried anymore. All her life, she had been easily moved to tears, but for many months she'd been unable to cry, even when she was most willing, even when Adam left.

She moved to the next pole and saw another tank. They were both at about the same height, a couple inches above her head. She took a deep breath and began walking around the wall that surrounded Timpanica.

Another tank, this one in green, had five copies painted side by side along the gray brick wall. The stencil she'd found showed the residue of no colors but orange. Maybe that was only the most recent color he'd used. Maybe somebody else painted these things. If that were true, someone might know where he'd gone. She wanted to move outward, to search the sides of alleys and the overpasses, but the sun was setting, new life rising into the dimming light. She waited for the next bus and noticed that across the street, about thirty yards away, three figures were sitting on the outer wall of the housing project.

They were her students, Eaton, DeRay and Lester. Their feet dangled down the side of the wall. She couldn't be sure that they recognized her, but they all sat, unmoving, staring in her direction.

When the bus came she hurried on, feeling gratitude she couldn't account for. Body odor filled the bus, passengers close together. She stood holding one of the handles to her right. This caused her to stretch over a young man who was sitting, and he gave her a look of disdain as her arm reached above his head.

Those children that spray-painted things almost surely did so at night, and she would be unable to walk these streets at such times, so Sharon realized there was little chance of ever catching someone else using the stencil. But that feeling of recognition was still with her, and when she got home she looked in on Adam's room, studying the empty bed, the inert computer, dusty desk. For the first time in years she felt an authority over the room.

The following day at school she again showed Eaton the stencil and asked if he'd ever seen anyone spraying it. He told her no, but she knew that he might be lying. She asked him if he'd seen her yesterday. He shook his head no, very slowly, the moist black of his eyes unblinking.

Today she'd tried to instigate a reading lesson, but too many of the children had become restless, refusing to follow along, and now she had them assembling animals out of construction paper and glue. It was nearly time for lunch, anyway.

When the children had gone to recess, she found herself thinking about the graffiti she'd seen the day before, wanting to revisit the picture as though in its markings she saw Adam. He was nine when David left her. She'd worried that David would fight for custody, but he didn't have any such wishes. Adam became quiet. He had grown into a sullen reader.

She'd look up and he'd be on the couch, then across the room, then gone.

As the children ran across the grass, leapt on the climbing equipment, she remembered Adam's athleticism as a child, his speed and grace when running. It was already an old trick that she did not think of him in the present tense. She did not think of where he might be at that moment, or what he might be doing, but kept her emotions firmly tied to their past life, and she would cast those emotions as far back as she needed in order to remember a boy who was not angry, who did not see injustice in every human endeavor.

That was his most aggressive quality, his sense of justice, and it permitted no shades of gray. In his early teens, he'd begun asking questions when they went to breakfast after mass. Soon she saw him reading histories of Catholicism, then Christianity in general. She became afraid to sit down with him at dinner, stressed at the thought of what he might want to tell her.

Once, he'd insisted on her staying put while he recited the history of the Crusades. He hadn't stopped until she wept, and then he scolded her for that. He asked if she knew her church's position during World War II. By the time the new war started, he was inconsolable on matters of church or state.

The last night, he'd been dusting his roast with red pepper. "But you can't be telling me, honestly Mom, that you actually believe that, like, hell is a place, or even heaven. Like these are real places where people live and it's good or bad depending on how well you followed one interpretation of the Bible." He was cutting his food with hard, brief strokes.

"Well, I do," she said. "Of course I do."

Chewing, his mouth full, he said, "Look around, would you? Think about reality for a second, the expanse of matter, the shape of the universe, and you really think that folklore developed by a completely savage, uneducated people somehow explains all that?" He bit off his words, and the scowl he summoned indicated an alarming disgust. "And you're going to vote with this as your criteria?"

She'd kept her head to the roast. Why wouldn't he talk about things like other teenagers did? Why? Couldn't he look at the roof over their heads, the food on their table, and admit the essential goodness of life? Lord knew she had enough reasons to be soured, but she persisted. She persisted out of faith—nothing more.

"So how do you justify voting for an idiot, spendthrift warmonger in the name of your pacifist, nonmaterialist God?"

She placed her fork down calmly. "You know, you have made it very clear that you do not share my beliefs. I believe we should support our leaders and their decisions. You do not. But since I am the one providing us with food and shelter, I'd think that you might have the grace not to attack me because we disagree about politics."

He leapt upon her participation the way a cat would a mouse. "And that's it! It's not just a difference in opinion!" He leaned over his plate, blond hair falling in front his face a little. "It's not just a disagreement. I'm talking about fundamental issues of good and evil."

"Ah!" she said. "But you said heaven and hell don't exist. So how's there good and evil?"

He paused. She thought that was because she had him. "I'm sorry, what's that mean?"

"If you say there's no heaven and hell, then what's good and evil? Why be good at all?"

He seemed genuinely aghast. "Are you saying, Mom, that if there's no heaven, there's no reason to be good?"

She shrugged. She hadn't thought that was what she said, but maybe she had. It sounded dumber when he said it.

"Being good means doing so without thought of reward, Mom. You're the one who's supposed to teach me that."

He was silent then, appeared satisfied. He ate the food she'd prepared, silverware clinking against the plate. The dark house settled around them once again. But she, for once, nursed a silent fury. As if he'd smashed something dear to her for no other reason than to see it break. It was the smugness she couldn't stand, his amusement with her as he chewed the roast she'd cooked. Why should she tolerate this disregard?

"If you're so smart, I wonder why you don't have any friends? Hm?"

He put his knife down and looked at her.

"You know everything, Mister Informed, so can you tell me why you never go to any dances? Tell me why you don't have a girlfriend? Because you're so much smarter than everybody else, you must know."

He stood from the table. She saw the shadow fall around her plate, but wouldn't look up. Sharon was nearly trembling from what he might say.

His voice shivered with disgust. "You can't even see how diseased you are." He walked away.

How could someone say that to their mother? What cure was there for a boy given every blessing, except perhaps a good father, who still insisted on seeing darkness in everything? She thought he was actually begging for Christ's light, and part of what upset him was his inability to see it. So she prayed that night that Christ's light would find him.

Two days later he was gone, a brief note explaining that he would not be coming back.

Over the playground, a thundercloud broke, and the children screamed and ran to the pavilion's cover. The rain grew heavy quickly, and she saw the three boys, Eaton, Lester and DeRay, standing out in it. They were watching her.

Coach Phelps began yelling at the boys, and he scattered them under the awning.

Sharon would not go searching the avenues for graffiti today.

That night she ate some leftovers and went to bed early. As she was drifting to sleep, the words of the Our Father in her head, she kept seeing the three boys as she'd seen them the afternoon they'd been chasing the small dog.

The dog was thin, with clumpy fur, and its right front leg was held just above the ground, unable to bear any weight. They were chasing the creature down the empty lot across from the school, around old chairs and a refrigerator left in the grass. The dog swerved like a rabbit trying to lose them. White teeth spread out on the boys' dark faces, and they broke stride only to hurl a stone at the fleeing animal.

She'd screamed at them. Told them to stop immediately.

From across the street they'd looked at her, not talking, not moving. They'd seemed to be judging their own distance from the schoolhouse, gauging the weight of her power. Almost as one, they turned around and continued after the dog, who'd slowed a little, stunned by a rock Lester had thrown. She'd watched the dog and the boys disappear into a web of buildings. The next day she'd taken a stack of comic books from them.

Now, in her sleep, what she saw most clearly was the face of the dog, worn, fatigued by the chase and unable to understand why it was being pursued. Whom had it offended? In her dream she could see its tongue flopping as it ran, a pink flag, the small head, the black eyes.

Three days passed. She was in the part of town where Timpanica Gardens could be seen. She left her hand inside her purse, lightly touching the metal cannister, remembering it was there for her. She walked close to walls, moved discreetly around corners, and she allowed her back to hunch. She'd thought she saw Eaton Slavin a few blocks back, but kept to herself. She tried hard to disappear.

A few people sat on stoops, smoking, a mother yelling to her two small children who were in the street. Behind them was the Timpanica compound, absorbing an entire square block. When Sharon passed the tenement she turned into an alley that cut left at its end, and she stopped in front of an overturned plastic garbage bin. She stared at a red brick wall.

The most distressing thing during Adam's disappearance was her powerlessness. There was no action for her to take, nothing she could enact that would bring him back or even allow her to know where he'd gone. Until this morning. Her idea this morning had been a communion, a sharing, a sympathetic fellowship. Perhaps in a bad moment he might see one of her symbols and come home. That was the part that kept returning to her mind. She imagined him destitute, sick, perhaps robbed, and in his moment of greatest doubt he might chance to look up and see her mark, like a divine sign, and know that she was still here, still loved him, and he would return. The bottom line was that she had to do something.

She looked over both shoulders and slid the stencil from her purse. She stepped close to the bricks and laid the stencil flat, holding its edge. She turned her back to the street, to block any view of what she was doing. Then she pulled the metal can out of her purse, fixed her finger on the nozzle. She'd chosen red.

She'd hardly had to move her hand, and it was done. She lifted the stencil and now the tank and the words were hers, her mystery glowing red on an alley wall. Sharon had used an X-Acto knife to add the word Mom into the cardboard, below its original message. She wiped the stencil with a tissue, turned around to the street and saw him at the mouth of the alley. Eaton Slavin stood directly in front of her, blocking the street, his yellow shirt risen above the tiny gut.

"Oh," she said. "Eaton?"

The boy walked toward her, slowly, dragging his hand along the side of the wall.

She fought an urge to retreat. He kicked at the ground with his oversized sneakers. Sharon moved her purse to the crook of her arm and clutched it tightly. Behind Eaton a tall strip of daylight hung beyond the alley.

"Eaton?"

He didn't answer, and didn't seem to really be looking at her. His eyes lolled down to the corners behind her feet.

When he was a few yards away he stopped, twisting a heel, and looked up at the wall. He reached out and touched the red paint, came away with a wet finger. Finally he looked up at Sharon, who didn't know what to expect in this confrontation.

Eaton said, "You was one of them?"

His voice was so childlike, she exhaled relief. "One of who, Eaton?"

"Them in camouflage."

"I don't know—are you saying the people that paint these wear camouflage?"

He nodded his head vigorously.

Sharon winced as she bent toward him, her back full of needles. "Eaton? Do you know where these people are?"

He shook his head and stared at the ground.

"What are they called?"

He shrugged. "I can show where all they do this." He motioned to the paint on the wall. "Ain't you one of them?"

"No, dear," she said. "I'm looking for one of them."

She turned him gently toward the street, and kept her hand on his back as they walked out of the alley. Their forms were as insignificant against the buildings as insects in a canyon.

She stayed close to him as he led her up the cracked sidewalk. Sharon could feel the people on stoops staring at her, but kept her eyes forward with stiff resolve. Her ankles were swelling, she could tell, and worried what her feet would look like when she got home.

They walked less than two blocks. Eaton led her through a maze of interconnecting alleys. She could see the boy playing here, searching and mapping each strange new road in the warren of brick and glass, entire summers spent alone, navigating these inner channels. She knew that he might only have seen one person in camouflage spray-painting something, once. Adam had a camouflage shirt, but she couldn't remember if it was among the clothes he'd taken.

They came out near a Thai grocer's, and Eaton pointed up to the wall beside him. At least twenty copies of the stencil had been painted in close succession along this wall. Blue.

The first tank was a bit runny, blue tears stretching down from its treads, flowing into the words Police State. The next two were lighter, fading at their edges, created with quick bursts of the nozzle. Eaton stood beside her, kicking the wall with his toes. The entire front half of his shoe now appeared to be empty. The last two tanks were the clearest and best defined. All of them had been set on a fairly straight line. He always could draw a straight line.

She turned around. The street was more narrow over here, a few tiny houses set beside quiet stone buildings, fewer people around. She looked left and right, the lean sidewalk empty, a dusky white sky set low over the roofs. She took the can and stencil up and moved close to the wall, laid the first stencil under the blue graffiti.

Eaton said, "What you doing?"

She'd almost forgotten about him. "I'm looking for someone. You wouldn't understand, Eaton. But it's very important. Go play."

"Who you looking for?"

"Eaton, please! Be quiet. I'm trying to find someone, and I need you to be quiet. This is very, very important. Go play. Run home."

She turned back to the wall and touched the nozzle lightly twice, two poofs of paint dusting the wall through the stencil, a little freckling her hand. Her sign sat just below the blue ones.

She moved back to Eaton, who was standing near her, still watching.

She was bending forward again, her shoulders tight now, to insist the boy promise to keep her secret. She was going to offer him all the comic books she'd taken from him and his two friends. But as her face lowered, over Eaton's shoulder she saw a policeman exit the alley. In five steps he was next to them.

The policeman was short and stocky, his dark blue uniform tight across his chest, red hair visible below his cap. He nodded to her and stood close behind Eaton, who'd been staring at Sharon. Then Eaton turned around and saw the cop.

"So what's this? You're tagging again, Eat?" The policeman pointed to the can and stencil in Sharon's hands. He shook his head with disappointment. "I don't think your mom's gonna like this. I don't think your case officer's gonna like that."

For the first time she could remember, Eaton showed a dramatic emotion, his eyes wide like lanterns, head shaking furiously. "I didn't! I didn't do anything!"

The policeman looked at the fresh paint on the wall and back to the can in Sharon's hand. "Then what's all that?"

"She did it! She was doing it!"

The policeman surveyed Sharon, her lumpy form. Her glasses inflated the appearance of her eyes, and the brown dye she used on her hair made it dry, so she kept it in a short, feathered style. She herself thought that with age her face resembled a softball. Her cardigan was clean and her big purse was a yellow quilted bag she'd made over three decades before.

"Who are you?" the policeman asked. The uniform, its authority, caused a panic she'd never felt before.

She could feel her eyes welling up, her voice choked. "I'm his schoolteacher."

The cop looked back and forth at Eaton and the can in her hand. He adjusted his hat, seemed to understand something.

He took Eaton by the arm.

"She did it!"

"Uh-huh. Let's go talk to your mom, Eaton." The cop nodded to her. "Don't worry. I'll get him home." He reached out and took the paint can from her hand, and took the stencil. She let it pass out of her fingers without resistance, her open mouth offering no voice.

The policeman showed the objects to Eaton. "Think your mom might want to see these."

Eaton was almost howling now. "Tell him! Tell him! It wasn't me!"

A few people had opened their doors and were looking out on the scene. Their faces stayed hidden in the doorways, the barest glint of eyes. Out on the street a gray light prevailed. Eaton pleaded as the policeman guided him down the sidewalk. She felt terrified, needing so badly to take action that she was stuck with only the need. Her feet had not moved from the spot, and her mouth only gaped a little. The policeman turned a corner with Eaton, and the two of them disappeared. She looked down at her spotted, knotty hands, flecks of orange along the fingertips, and she heard him once more. "She did it! She did it!"

She realized, again, that the stencil was gone.

School became strange after that. Eaton was absent for two days, and when he returned he was quiet and didn't speak in class.

She'd seen him talking to Lester and DeRay, but that was the only evidence that he was not mute.

She returned the stack of comic books she'd taken from the boys, placing them on Eaton's desk. He didn't touch them, and he didn't look her in the eyes. He just stared around her, toward the chalkboard in the front of the room. His two friends raided the comics and Eaton did not complain.

Her hair had been thinning lately, and her feet became numb and tingly during the day. The boys stared at her during recess, from across the soccer field, and she felt that now when they saw her, they knew her, knew her in a way she didn't yet understand. Above all, she could not abide the idea of an unearned fate.

She'd closed the door to Adam's room and left it that way, feeling the space had become accusatory, and she felt guilty when she passed it, as if she'd lost something that had been entrusted to her.

Fall arrived. The leaves on the scant trees became a luxuriant, glossy collage of intense color. The streets became wet. Flyers were pulled down, walls were repainted. Eaton did not come back to class after Christmas break.

The final trial happened in early February.

She'd been sitting in front the television, next to an electric heater, eating a bowl of soup. She now kept her hair in a shower cap whenever she could. Her feet were soaking in Epsom salt and baking soda.

The lead story on the news was about a bomb that went off in the city that day. The screen showed shaky footage of a department store, one she'd used to shop at, and its whole frontispiece had been obliterated, with small fires dancing in the wreckage of glass and brick. The video was fuzzy, people screaming, crying. She listened closely, already feeling a nearly imperceptible twinge at the base of her neck. She set her spoon in the bowl, and set the bowl down. She put on her glasses.

The reporter was a deeply tanned woman of that vague ethnicity Sharon was starting to see more and more. The reporter spoke about a message given to authorities, a message wherein a group of terrorists claimed responsibility for the explosion. The group called themselves The Freedomists. They alleged that this chain of department stores was owned by Saudi Arabian interests that had contributed significantly to the president's re-election campaign. Four people died in the explosion. Eleven more were injured. Sharon's face hovered in the green glow of the television.

The reporter's face gave way to three portraits, black and white drawings of men whom the police were trying to identify. The sketches were crude in some ways, but she still gasped in recognition. The third sketch depicted a young man with longish, light-colored hair, his eyes intense, his features familiar, gaunt, projecting.

No, she told herself. That was her imagination.

A phone number was posted at the bottom of the screen, telling viewers to call if they recognized any of the men. It was ridiculous, she thought, lifting her glasses off as she looked back at the screen. No, definitely not, she could see now. But still. Her heart was hurting its chamber, pounding away at its walls of tender bone. She turned off the television.

She took her bowl to the kitchen, rinsed it out, and set it aside. Through the window above the sink, the night was black, faintly whistling. Light rain pattering. She imagined the people in the explosion, the pockets of flame, the force of the blast.

Outside the window, she began to hear a dog barking. She thought of Eaton chasing the dog. She still saw the limping creature avoiding their rocks. She heard the barking again, different, higher, quickening as if in distress.

If there was an unearned fate, she nevertheless had to believe that somehow this had been deserved. A vague guilt had replaced certain parts of her will, but not, so far, her faith. Her faith she kept intact. She could not say why over the years things should flee her, why she should be allowed so little, but she practiced accepting this as part of a just and far-reaching plan. And her guilt was not the kind she could atone for; she wouldn't let herself understand it.

The dog outside continued to bark, and the wind tightened its soft whistle. In her thoughts, she could clearly see the dog resting beneath a tree, wounded, nestled beside a stone, a dry place. She could feel the animal curled somewhere with its injuries, waiting out the night, unable to recall how it had arrived at this shelter.

HAUNTED EARTH

MY FINGERS SLIP UNDER TSUNY'S BLOUSE AND pick at the clasp on her bra. She sinks under me, down in high cordgrass, and the stalks crackle beneath us as my hand maps her ribs, follows her smooth back to the dampness at the base of her spine. Outside this stand of tall grass is the open lawn where they say aliens landed two weeks ago. I'm trying to undress Tsuny during an autumn when our town, Big Lake, is buzzing with reports of demons and UFOs. One group in a Buick said they were chased by flying lights on the highway. A guy at my school has an aunt who moved to Houma because she saw a dark, hairy man-thing staring at her from the backyard, two nights in a row while she was washing dishes.

None of that matters, because it's all on the other side of the cordgrass, not down in here. Our breath is hot and my hands keep shifting, searching for an open pathway. She moves with me, blocking the waistline of her skirt. This is our conflict, and we repeat it with frustrated, fading spirit, like an argument we're tired of having.

Before she spread the black blanket today, Tsuny stood beside me and we saw past the tall grass, to the other end of the rice field. Over there a circle got scorched into the ground of Leon Arceneaux's farm, where he says a spaceship landed. Everybody's seen that. But today, before I tangled my hand in Tsuny's heavy black hair, we both saw that Mr. Arceneaux had gotten a couple boys to help him lay a banner across his roof that reads WELCOME in tall, red letters. Mr. Arceneaux doesn't work since City Services shut down the oil refinery in Big Lake. I know that because he used to work with my pop. I figure with the banner and the spaceship he's trying to get interested in something, which is good, because if you don't stay busy in the prairie slums, time and the sun will make you crazy.

I'm busy with Tsuny. I watch where our skins meet, my white arm against her rich brown. Her color mixes her mom's Vietnamese and her dad's black. She has plump lips from her father, a tiny nose and slivered eyes from her mom. Her skirt is from Our Lady of Lourdes, the Catholic school she goes to, and it bunches in my fist. The wool in my hand, its plaid pattern of navy and gray and yellow are a charged sensation to me, like her skin, and I want to be changed by it.

She goes to school with uniformed boys in khaki slacks and blue oxfords and I'm wearing the same jeans I always wear, today with my jungle fatigue OG 107 Utility Shirt from Army Surplus, where I spend a lot of the money I make recycling. My shoes are unissued FG combat boots, and I gave up taking them off when I'm with Tsuny. I've gotten afraid that the effort of unlacing them ruins the momentum, and if that happens she'll never get carried away by passion. Then, together, in shrinking motions we stop with no real advancement made into the disputed territories. We breathe rough. A silver dolphin gleams on Tsuny's neck, and under it rests the paper tag of her scapular.

"What are we doing?" she asks me.

I don't know how to tell her what we're doing. She might be asking me why we do these things down here in the grass, but we don't go to movies or hold hands in the mall.

It's 1983, and I have a map of Vietnam on my wall. I took it from a National Geographic when I was eight, and the sickle shape of its coast has become as familiar to me as sky. Pop got back from Vietnam when I was six, but I'd been seeing it on TV before that. Vietnam is fire and prehistory to me, the reason Pop isn't good at numbers and why my mom first got her job at the Shetler Insurance Agency. My name is Neal Lemoine and Vietnam is part of me in a way I can't understand, an inherited way, like a middle name. There's been lots of talk here lately about this movie, *Close*

Encounters, but I've never seen it. The new movies bore me, and everyone looks ugly. I don't play Pac-Man, Dungeons & Dragons, or sports. I have a good handshake.

I trace a finger across the brown shore of Tsuny's stomach, and she stops it at the top of her skirt. I picture her on my bed, where she's never been, under the mosquito netting that overhangs my mattress. Scraps of camouflage are scattered on this canopy, and at night I've imagined choppers breaking the stillness of marshes, big machines floating down weightless, blowing grass flat. This electric god voice speaking staticky, arcane words—Bravo, Echo, Alpha, Charlie.

We're fifteen, and I'm thinking Tsuny is on the verge of surrender, that soon this fight will end and the terms of ceasefire will mark an ultimate transformation in me.

We rise and straighten our clothes. We watch buttons and zippers and when our eyes meet, we look away.

"I can stay longer tomorrow," she says. "My parents have a party."

"Good."

We watch Mr. Arceneaux unspool cord for some spotlights the boys have installed on the roof, where his WELCOME sign is fixed.

*

Tsuny just has to walk over a hill to be back at her school, where her parents think she's trying out for the track team, but I walk three miles in the other direction, east of Parish Road 90 until turning up Ryan Street, along the lakeshore toward downtown. Downtown is rows of empty streets, soaped-over windows, broken streetlamps. The sign on the old Sears store is written in faded pink cursive and missing its last two letters, and when I look at the sign with my field binoculars I can see the gulf shore behind it and the word Sea becomes an advertisement. I have studied the town. Sometimes I skip school to do reconnaissance. I know when I pass the parking lot that covers the place where a skirmish was fought between bands of mercenaries in the Civil War. I know that the small, Masonic obelisk on the edge of the Civic Center is where a sailor

strangled his girlfriend in 1956, and I know that Jean Lafitte used
to have a hideout where a drive-through seafood store now stands
beside an enormous rock riddled with caves and wells. Across the
lake the closed refineries still rise, hunks of steel and metal piping
that look like a city made for robot insects. In the sinking sun
I imagine Cobra helicopters emerging, arclight bombers roaring
above and dropping conflagration, exploding those dead refineries
and clearing the lakeshore. An oily, fish-tinged breeze comes off
the water. Every fifteen years or so the lake and the gulf rise up
and I know that twice in its history, everything on this side of town
was washed over, uprooted and left stranded by the brown waves.
The people built walls of sandbags and the water carried them
away. In pictures of the flood these sandbags look like dozens of
teeth floating in coffee. I've been meeting Tsuny for two weeks,
but I met her before that when we were kids. She doesn't act like
she minds our secrecy.

I don't know how things will go with us.

Our neighborhood beyond downtown is called the "Charpentier
Historic District." Charpentiers were Acadian carpenters who
built strange swooping homes that might remind you of Dr. Seuss
drawings. Pop is trying to put macaroni and cheese into Lyla's
mouth while he stares at the news. His mouth is always a little
open and he's not really paying attention to where he shoves the
spoon. Lyla tries to bat it away but she can't move far because of
the high chair. I'm sitting at the kitchen table eating cold C-Rations
from the can. I ask Pop when Mom's going to be home.

He answers slow. "She's working late. They're busy getting
ready for the thing in Baton Rouge."

Mom is the only secretary they have at Shetler Insurance. She
comes home after nine most nights, and she has to go to a lot of
conferences on the weekends. She used to work there when I was
a kid, but quit when Dad came home. Since the refineries closed,
she got her job back and Pop stays home with Lyla. Lyla has a
noodle stuck in her tuft of black hair.

Pop has narrow, hunched shoulders and short blond hair. My
hair is brown and I'm five inches taller than him, about sixty pounds

heavier. It's because he's small that he had to go into so many VC tunnels, and I've seen the twisted white scar that runs from his shoulder blade to the small of his back. He is a hesitant man, as if he's always trying to make up his mind about something. We have a twenty-seven-inch Zenith with a new video movie player, and he sits in front of it with Lyla all the time. The TV's on wheels so he can roll it into the kitchen for dinner.

Right now the news is talking about a red van that's arrived in town recently, and the people in it. This group has come to interview us about the weird things being witnessed lately. And the news says that these people have put the idea to the city council that the way to revive the economy is to market Big Lake as a center for paranormal events, like Roswell, New Mexico. The light from the news is flickery and white on my father's face. He's put down the spoon and is not watching Lyla shove her hands in her bowl of macaroni. The rest of the house is dark behind the TV.

"What do you think about all that?" I ask him, nodding to the television.

He shrugs. "Well, I don't know, but, you can't really tell." He trails off a little, and his eyes look glazed in the white light, and I can tell he forgot he was saying something when the newscaster starts talking again.

He doesn't know that I've seen what he's been doing. The last few nights, my father has taken to standing in the backyard when it's really late and pointing an old ART scope at the sky. ART stands for Adjustable Ranging Telescope, an old sniper's model. He stands out there alone, searching the skies, and that rankles me. I'm not used to seeing him interested in anything. His silences don't bother me, because I still think of my father as an aftermath, a result, a tree whose leaves were peeled by Agent Orange. But seeing him use a tactical scope to watch the stars makes me feel nervous and worried for him. It maybe reminds me of myself, kicking my skateboard down the deserted streets, searching the roofs and windows with my binoculars. I skip school more than I should, but the rooms there have no windows and the desks are tight, and whenever I'm there I feel myself becoming more and more afraid.

There are piles of empty cola and beer cans in plastic bags stacked against one corner of the kitchen. I bring them to the recycling plant on every second Saturday. The pizza boxes have been on the counter since Tuesday, and after I brush my teeth I see we're out of toilet paper again.

Wood creaks and settles as I walk to my bedroom. Light through the window is thrown into an aquatic pattern by the mosquito netting, like light on the wall beside a pool. The map floats in the dark, and the spring handle I use to develop my grip sits on the dresser beneath it. I see the country's tan blur and think about Cam Ranh Bay, the Gulf of Tonkin above. At the bottom of my closet, in a padded green field case, I keep a Mac-Song combat knife, my binoculars, and a small, thin plastic box called a GI field pack that includes a box of waterproof matches, an ultrathin poncho, twine, a flat compass, antibiotics, and a condom in a plain olive-green wrapper. I don't know if the condom's still good.

From my window I can see my father in the backyard, pointing the scope skyward. His body is like five sticks and his face stays fixed to the stars. He walks real slow back and forth, and then stops in the moonlight and slowly revolves, never shifting his eyes. There is the feeling that I am watching a sort of weird ballet, where the movements are supposed to mean things, and it does something bleak to me.

Tsuny's father used to work at the plants with Pop, but he quit a long time ago and bought his own shrimp boat and now owns several of them. I was eight or nine when my parents and Tsuny's parents all got together at Contraband Days. A Ferris wheel drawn in light had been spinning and in the nearer distance waved flags atop tents, the sounds of bottles breaking at the shooting booth, an accordion and washboard playing over the speakers while a singer crooned in French. The lake was bursting with fireworks, men behind counters calling people to step up, laughter, all over the smells of frying meat and peppery spices. The neon bars on the Ferris wheel made Tsuny's hair scarlet and it had blown around my face while we both sat on the bench, rigid, and she didn't look at me or say anything while we rode up and down. All the lights below us moved across her eyes.

Headlights from Mom's car pass over my blinds and sweep across Pop in the backyard. He keeps facing up for a few seconds, then lowers the scope and trudges inside and Mom's car door slams shut. I hear her keys jangle and her footsteps around the house but no voices for the rest of the night.

Before I leave in the morning I eat an apple and the president, an old actor with real thick hair, reminds me not to be afraid, even though he says there is much to fear. Dad is sleeping on the recliner with Lyla on his chest, sucking her thumb and watching something with puppets. The sky shivers across its gray, wavy surface, and the damp air rumbles. Just then I realize I won't be going to school today.

Instead I get my Mac-Song knife and binoculars, and the poncho from my GI field pack and kick my skateboard past the bus stop, riding it downhill toward the lakeshore and the empty buildings that are being split by roots and smothered by kudzu. A warm drizzle starts and the poncho flaps behind me as I roll past some rusted stoves and refrigerators that all sit gutted among weeds, a nameless brick hut in the grass. I extend my arms and the poncho is like wings. An old black guy standing under an umbrella gives me a thumbs-up when I zip by.

Pop didn't start looking up at the sky until Mr. Arceneaux told his story. Mr. Arceneaux said a tiny thing, all in silver, walked out of the tiny spaceship that landed in his backyard, and this thing spoke to him with its mind and promised to return. On the news he said, "It was outer space."

His wife said it was true and there was the large circle burnt on his lawn, and then everybody started saying they saw things, objects in the sky, Bigfoot crouched in a shadow, a prehistoric monster swimming beneath the lake. I ride down to the lakeshore's fallen houses and sinking docks. I remember a party Mom and I went to when I was little, out at one of the houses here, and Mom danced on the dock. The water sizzles with rain, and somewhere at the bottom of it all a Plesiosaurus might be paddling. I could see the sea monster rearing its head from the water and smashing the I-10 bridge. Then the rain ends and bright, steaming sun comes out. Eventually I stop at the edge of downtown and climb a hill. I use my binoculars to look about a half mile away where Mr. Arceneaux's WELCOME sign shines white from his roof. There is a red van at his house that I recognize as the van on the news. His land sits in the basin between two hills and past the far one is Tsuny's school.

She asks me questions. She wanted to know why all the boys she knows are angry, and I guess that meant me. She sees guys freeze to stare at her legs when she crosses them or they lower their eyes to where her top button is unfastened, and they can't talk. She said we're all sad. She reads a lot. I like to stay moving too much to read the way she does.

I dig the high cordgrass and the marshy rice field to its south. My fingers move over wet stalks and I use the knife's blade to part bigger shafts, imagine using the barrel of an M16 to cut the brush. The rusted farm machinery that dots these places is heavy on the air, and it isn't hard to imagine the smell as coming from mortar shells or downed choppers.

By three Tsuny waves to me across the field's tan bristles.

We say hi and I kiss her. We look up to Mr. Arceneaux's house. The two boys from yesterday are dragging picnic tables into the yard. "Have you seen the people in the red van?" I say, and point to the van on the street in front Mr. Arceneaux's house.

"They just came to our school and spoke at an assembly. They want everybody to be excited by all this stuff." Her white blouse glows at a certain angle and her dark face and arms look held up by its light. I can smell her perfume and the way her skirt hangs makes me reach out. We set down our backpacks and she unrolls the black bedspread that smells like mothballs and sweat.

She tastes like she just ate candy, and her skin beneath my fingers almost makes me shake. I always get a little sad when we do this, but I couldn't say why, just that touching her can make me feel like I do when I pass the empty docks where I saw Mom dance, or I see the lots beside the lake where Contraband Days used to happen. My mind confuses me, so I hurry, and soon she is prying my hands off her skirt.

I get myself to act angry. "Are we going to do this forever?"

She rolls her eyes and sighs. Then she turns her head toward me and pieces of her hair blow across her eyes. "Tell me again why you dress like some crazy vet?"

"This stuff breathes better than what you wear. It's all made for this climate. It's comfortable."

"Whatever."

"Aren't you tired of fooling around? We never get anywhere."

"Shut up," she says, slapping my arm. We both lie on our backs with our hands touching, breathing hard. A cool breeze comes along the ground, rustling beads of rain off the stalks above us, and the shade is cool and quiet.

Later on my eyes are open and it's almost night. Tsuny wakes up next to me and asks what time it is. My field watch says seven. I start to tell her it's not too late, but I stop midway because we both realize that strong white lights are shining above the cordgrass, and for just a second I think that maybe something has come down to us from the sky, maybe the aliens or something else, and the fear runs hard over my back. But then I hear all the talking. Lots of people are talking. Somehow we are surrounded. Then, for just a second, with the voices and dark, the insects buzzing and chirping, with Tsuny at my side, I can't help thinking we're in country, dug deep into the jungle. We stay quiet as we gather up our stuff and move, close to the ground. I watch her legs and hips as we creep to the edge of the grass.

Mr. Arceneaux's field is circled by people. Three spotlights on his roof shoot into clouds and light up his WELCOME sign. The people meander, sitting on lawn chairs or at picnic tables. A lot of the men stand and talk and smoke cigarettes. One woman is crocheting in the bed of a pickup truck. A couple people are standing in front of the red van and talking to five or six others. I will learn later that tonight is when Mr. Arceneaux's alien visitor is supposed to come back.

"Morons." Tsuny rolls her eyes, and we start to move away from the lawn, back out the far side of the field. But then I see that one of the people standing around the van is Pop. She must see something happen in me because Tsuny asks, "What?"

"That's my father," I say.

She looks past me and stares a second. "He's tiny," she says. "That's your sister?"

Pop holds Lyla against his chest and he is the smallest guy in the crowd. He isn't really standing next to anyone, but keeps his eyes fixed on the man speaking in front of the van. The way his eyes squint I can tell he's really paying attention.

The speaker is a soft man dressed in black. He waves a book around and says they should buy this book, which he wrote, because it's all about the kinds of things people have been seeing here. The book is called *This Haunted Earth*, and he says, "There is deep magic in the world, y'all." He says that there are aliens and angels among us, secret wars in higher dimensions.

My pop raises his hand, shifting Lyla in his arms. I hear him ask, "Do you think they're come to help?"

Pop's voice never sounded so clear and loud, and the words of his question are still in my head, and I know I'll be thinking about them a lot. But while I'm trying to listen to what the man's answer is, Tsuny puts her hand under the back of my shirt. I stiffen, but then relax when I feel her kiss the back of my neck. Then we're both on all fours and kissing, and we lose our balance and fall over.

The people by the van all turn to see us fall out of the cordgrass, but shadows cover us and we jump back in before anybody can see the white boy and black girl with their clothes undone. I hear the people gasp and act shocked and Tsuny and I run into the field, with the poncho over my head and the black blanket flapping behind me, sailing over the tops of the stalks.

All that crowd can see is the black blanket waving as it disappears into the dark above the cordgrass, and people are hollering, acting surprised and scared. Tomorrow in the paper it will say that the man from the red van insists what they all saw in the cordgrass was a "massive psychic projection."

We come out the other side of the field and climb the hill. The acres under us are bright like a ballpark with light and noise. I show Tsuny my binoculars and we both look down at the people with them. People are spreading out into the high cord, looking for us I guess, and we both lean against a pine. Its bark is rough and sticky, and its needles quiver and straighten, like there was something on the wind.

"What?" she says.

"What?"

"You're crying."

"No I'm not." But she wipes my cheek and it's wet.

We move to each other again, in the forest scents, the dark, and the rustling of the pine needles I now know is the sound of memories, the sound of bare feet dancing on a wooden dock, of years moving backward and forward from this point. Tsuny feels me on her hip and she uses her hand for the first time and I help her with the button and zipper. She looks at me and her eyes go wide and curious, open, and I can tell that this is it.

She seems hungry and strong on the ground, tugging at my pants. Her hands are warm, and I exhale a breath I didn't know I was holding. I kiss behind her ears, and her hands leave me to unfasten her skirt. We huff and struggle together.

Past her head I can see the lights. The people moving. She puts me in and we both gasp. I think I can hear voices below in the field, wind rustling in my ear, Tsuny's breath. I'm thinking too much, then I'm gone, suddenly not thinking, not watching anything, only feeling her, where I'm going.

When I have to stop, I roll away and pull up my pants. I sit down by her but I don't want to be touched.

"What's wrong?" she says. "Aren't we having fun?"

"I don't know. I can't figure it."

We sit together and I don't understand why I'm sad. I want to leave but Tsuny makes me sit down and she puts her hand on my neck. Below us people have stopped combing the field and have gone back to drinking and talking. I notice Pop standing out there with Lyla, his face looking up. Something goes tight in my chest, but I can't figure if this is even the way I really feel.

I wonder if the lights and the tall brush at night remind Pop of being back in country, or if maybe it seems like that surgical hospital in Tan Son Nhat. The place with the big palms where it always rained. He'll describe all that down the road, when I get him to tell stories about the heat and insects and the biggest fears making him paralyzed in the night.

Right now I stand and let Tsuny's hand fall from mine. I see all the people and hear the voices and imagine the basin flooding, flushing them all away, and I know that they would come back, and this idea feels bigger to me than these particular people, this particular place. It feels like something new might be in me. Something less heavy, and I don't know how it got there.

"So are we having fun?" she asks.

"I'm going down there for a second," I tell her. "Will you wait for me?"

"Why?"

"I just want to go down there for a second." I pack my poncho with my skateboard in my backpack. "Stay a second. Please. I have to do something." I leave the backpack with Tsuny and start working my way down the hill, toward the people on the lawn.

Spotlights are yawning up, and I hear people talking and laughing, and as I round the high grass I see Pop standing alone, the baby curled up in his arm. I know that one day everything will end. I know my life and Pop's life will be washed away, and all the things I see and love will be wiped out, and the world will be all that is left. As if he knew I was near, just then Pop's face lowers from the clouds and he stares at me, a little cockeyed, like I'm someone he isn't sure he is seeing. We stand still, and we look at each other.

NEPAL

SEPTEMBER. THE WOODS DELAYED HIM. COLORS OF maples and elms distracted Thomas, white dandelions drifting airborne across his path, everything an invitation to linger. He walked from his home in Linn Creek, and other men passed him on the way—a migration of strangers riding or hiking to a point in southern Missouri where an unfinished castle stood. When he was four years old, his father told him about this castle, erected by a rich man, eastward in a place called Ha Ha Tonka. His father, Lars, a stonemason, came from Montreal in 1903, one among hundreds of workers imported from other countries to construct a European-style castle for Robert M. McRyder. At one dip in the road, wind eddied and maintained a small tornado of leaves in an otherwise still clearing, and he loitered there. He carried an old shaving mirror, a square of glass whose edges were rubbed enough as habit, hand in pocket, the corners were worn opaque and glossy as mother of pearl.

Six miles from Ha Ha Tonka, a truck bearing bushels of yellow squash gave him a ride. The trees curved toward the road and canopied the trail into town. He used his mirror to catch light through the foliage.

He was a glazier, and he had deep faith in surfaces. There was the known—surface—and the unknown. Surfaces were full of clues. He liked to read history and character into them. He was tall at nineteen, Scandinavian. In the circle of sunlight slowly nearing, at the end of the tree tunnel, he felt the place rise to meet him, dear, like a precious stranger.

Atop a steep hill the castle blocked daylight. Orange beams haloed its walls and he saw men lined up in front of a large tent.

At his turn in line he presented two stained-glass decorations to a man with a ledger. He said his full name, "Thomas Knut Koenig."

The man didn't look up. "What do you do?"

"Glass, sir. I make it. Fire it, set it. Anything."

This was in 1922. Robert M. McRyder, the rich man, had died in an automobile wreck in 1906, and his castle had been abandoned with only its outer walls built, a shell rustling through sixteen winters. Waiting, Thomas sensed, though when encountering new things, he usually felt they had somehow anticipated his arrival.

His father had settled in Linn Creek, found a wife, and died when Thomas was eight. His mother had remarried six years ago to a widowed, bookish minister with a wild daughter named Naomi. Now, in 1922, McRyder's three sons had pooled their resources to complete the castle's construction. While the man with the ledger eyed his glasswork, Thomas studied the castle: three stories of beige stone, ten gables, windows that stared with regal indifference, nine greenhouses and a tall water tower. He tried to be analytical, but its sudden actuality affected a quiet reverence in him. He was slightly stunned, like when he'd bolt awake in the middle of the night and have to systematically reassemble his world by reciting his name and the names of objects in his room.

He dreamed all the time back then, every time he fell asleep: vivid, intense dreams, "often exhausting in their richness and peril." So when he woke, he was tired, as if he'd ended a long journey, and some days it got to where he was always tired and always dreaming and couldn't tell the difference.

They gave him seven dollars a week, minus two for food and lodging, to set glass in the greenhouses. This was not really what he wanted.

He wanted to create a window that would cause people to stare and tilt their heads, that would create silence in its beholders. The glass for the greenhouses was already cut to specifications. The job required no skill, much less art; anybody could have done it. He found the land, however, stunning in its beauty and variety, "with that sacred quality in old, untouched places of stone and vine."

Ha Ha Tonka's centerpiece is a crack in the earth, shaped like a needle's eye. Long ago, groundwater and surface water ate away at bedrock, forming sinkholes, caves, springs, hills, and collapsing a huge cave passage, creating a broad chasm a half mile long. McRyder castle overlooked this chasm, and its charred ruins still stand there today.

Thomas walked the edges of the canyon. He took out his mirror and shined a shred of light on the opposite rock wall, bridging the gulf. He turned his hand and the light stretched into a rhomboid form, passing over the geography—dun-colored bluffs pocked with shadow like the face of the moon, fractured walls of slate-gray flint three hundred feet high, reefs of ancient fern and pine trunks. His teacher, an old Italian named Rossitto, once told him that the alchemy of glass was twofold: it transformed rough mineral into smooth surface, which was chaos to order, and it colored light, which was the illumination of the invisible. So much for that. He just enjoyed the light's revelation on the cliff face, an almost intimate gesture, as if the rock were confiding in him.

A Scotsman named Volta supervised him. They were the only ones working on the greenhouses, and Volta talked a lot. Despite disappointment with his task, Thomas remained thorough in his duties. He wanted to perform, minded his breaks, swiftly pieced in sections of clean glass—at times too fast for Volta. He told Thomas to ease off, pace the job, but was ignored.

In the improvised commissary, a tent with pine benches, Thomas noticed a serving girl. She was small and dark with large black eyes above a small chin, her face widest at its cheekbones. Sometimes, like now, he didn't realize he was staring.

She said, "Go on. There's others in line."

The tent housed peppery scents, aromas of garlic and butter. At a table with other men, Volta was telling a joke, his face resembling an inflamed grapefruit under a curly black wig.

"St. Louis women are better than any in Texas."

"Hell you say." A man nudged Thomas's arm. "Look. He knows."

He smiled, felt awake and close to life. They ate green beans and potatoes and rabbit and squirrel.

"I seen a magician in Kansas City could take off his head and walk around with it."

Another man said he'd climbed mountains on four continents and spoke about Nepal. "It's magic. Some snow there isn't white, it's pink or blue." He said in a temple he saw a holy man levitate for over an hour while chanting a word he couldn't repeat.

Thomas's eyes were drawn back to the girl. She wore an aloof expression, a definite distance between her mind and the job at hand, and didn't seem to speak. Her ladling was all wrist, automatic, and an essential thing revealed itself in her portrait, a fundamental distraction. He felt a tinge of recognition. The curve of her backside, in a blue dress, brought to mind his stepsister, Naomi, specifically Naomi's eyes on the occasions she'd walked in his room wearing an open-neck nightgown, fresh from a bath, her chestnut hair soaked and dripping, the loose nightgown transparent in moist patches. She would ask a perfunctory question, like if he'd seen her whalebone comb anywhere, but a wicked goading in her eyes and the way she strategically held the candle more truly colored the scene. Then fevered time after, alone in the dark, wishing she'd walk in and catch him.

Back at the greenhouses, Volta pointed out three men and four women strolling the perimeter of construction. "Thas the McRyders. Bill, Leroy, and Kenneth."

These men dressed in stiff bright clothes, hair slicked flat to their scalps. They lived with their families in a set of cabins a mile from the site.

"They're away often. Then Abberline's in charge."

Abberline rode a large roan and kept a long-barreled pistol strapped to his leg for everyone to see. Gray muttonchops framed his small, puckered mouth, and he rode in britches and a wool coat. Volta said he was English. He reminded Thomas of a falcon he'd once seen bound to someone's arm. When his head swiveled, it seemed the same smooth and locking motion as a revolver's cylinder aligning.

The McRyder party passed the greenhouses and nodded to Thomas and Volta. One of the women walked behind—a very thin blond following the couples, holding a flower in one hand. Rather urban in a green dress and black beret, she fingered pearls around her neck, seemingly with disappointment. As they passed below, she glanced up at Thomas but went back to staring at her flower, which he could now see was no flower but a dandelion.

The free hour before dinner, men played cards or rolled dice. Thomas crawled the chasm's edge on hands and knees, examining dust and powdered rock. The land was rich with silicates. Their grain sifted between his fingers, rough, brittle, and he imagined an annealing fire to unite them. Every day at this hour he noticed the Indian serving girl playing checkers with a hunched, gray-haired woman.

He followed the chasm until it reached a glade, one of many dotting this region, dry patches of the Southwest stalked by prairie spiders and scorpions. At a palmetto's base, he saw a tarantula being mobbed by a legion of fire ants. He crouched down and watched for several minutes until the spider was only a surface of squirming ants, and the structure began to softly collapse.

Most of them stayed in a long cedar bunkhouse where cots lined the walls, and a hearth occupied the entire back end, stale air full of smoke, laughter, curses, cheering. An enormous Indian with stony features betting on cards, slamming a booming fist against a wall in frustration.

He sketched pictures, wrote recipes for glass. He offered the mountaineer a cigarette and asked him to talk more about Nepal.

One day Volta sent him to the castle. "Y'tell Mr. Abberline we're gonna need more mix for the mortar. A'this rate we'll be out by the fifth house."

Inside the castle, men he recognized were installing paneling around one wall and two others hauled long stones being used as a staircase below a vertiginous ceiling of vaulted tin. On the floor spread an enormous chandelier, a gold-glass octopus. Grunts bounced off cold rock. Down a hallway voices dropped away and he could hear his own footfalls.

He came to a room empty except for a long, narrow window that ran the height of the wall. Light poured through it in an isosceles triangle, a soft, idle light. Standing it in was a woman with her back to him.

She wore a purple dress, a black shawl, and a bell-shaped hat. Outside the window a wall of cedars perched on the cliff's edge.

"Excuse me," he said. She turned and he saw the woman who had been walking behind the McRyders, the dandelion-holder. Her skin was pale, sharp features drawn above a long neck and she even seemed delicate enough to have hollow bones, this sense amplified by her large, disclike eyes, which were bloodshot at their corners. What his mother called "an artistic temperament" could reveal itself in the sustained, silent stare Thomas often leveled at people. In social interaction, a need to interpret and question created distance in him—something he recognized only as a kind of mental boundary, a window behind which he could watch. He often stood too close to people. He stood too close to the woman in the room. "I'm looking for Mr. Abberline. Do you know where he is?"

She wiped her eyes, took a step backward and shook her head no. As he turned she called, "Wait. I'm sorry. I think he might be at the water tower. I know they had a problem there." An English accent lilted and curled her speech.

"Thank you."

She kept watching his face in a discerning way. Her hand drew up suddenly, as if to touch his cheek, but she lowered it and took a step back.

"Are you all right?"

She turned to the window. "Yes. I'm a little out of sorts today, that's all. It's very beautiful here."

"You're English?" He had a way of talking, too, that dismissed formality. He spoke to people as if he knew them well. It may be that this illusion of familiarity contributed to what happened later.

She nodded. "Elizabeth McRyder is my aunt. I'm staying with her and Kenneth."

"It's nice country. Good mineral deposits."

She laughed and pursed her eyebrows, curious. "My name is Carmen Rogers."

"Thomas Koenig." He held up his hands to excuse himself from taking hers.

She tilted her head and fixed the green saucers of her eyes on his face. Her eyes skimmed over him, blatantly searching. "That's strange…It really is…"

Her flesh seemed especially thin, and it displayed the flushing at her ears and neck brightly. Another exchange was taking place behind things, and he felt the center of his back grow hot.

He spoke to break it off. "What is it?"

At his question she pulled her hands close and looked at the stone floor. "Thank you for asking about me. I don't want to keep you."

"Ma'am." He tipped his head, relieved, but disappointed also, abruptly wishing to change his last question. As she turned again to the window her shadow was drawn tall across the floor.

After talking to Abberline, he walked back to the greenhouses and saw this woman, Carmen, staring out the same window, hazed behind the dull glass like a doll displayed in stone.

*

HE USED A DEERSKIN POUCH TO GATHER SILICATES before dinner. Today the serving girl was alone.

She sat on a gray rock with the checkerboard flat and her blue dress draped over her legs, playing by herself. A pleasant frustration entered him, as if he'd heard a tune he could neither recall nor forget. He stood above her.

"Who's winning?"

She slid a piece and didn't look up. "How's your dirt?"

"This is glass."

She glanced up and back to the checkers.

"Really." He let the powder fall through his hand. "There's glass everywhere here." When she didn't look up he started talking about himself. "I make glass. That's what I do."

She brushed hair off her face. "Do you play checkers?"

Light mottled them through the cedars while she reset the board with short fingers, small palms. They were silent. When she'd taken three of his pieces, he asked, "What do you think about the castle?"

It was behind them, unassailable, somehow indignant in its stone mass. She tied her hair in a ponytail. "It's been there my whole life."

"You grew up here?"

She didn't answer, but bent forward and took one of his pieces.

"My father helped build it," he said.

"You make glass?"

"Yes." After a moment, he seized the question. "My stepfather's a preacher. One of his congregation taught me." It was the only thing he liked about church, the windows. "I grew up in Linn Creek."

"Do you know what Ha Ha Tonka means?" she asked.

"No."

"Laughing waters."

"What's your name?"

"Astra Monro." She was sixteen, Osage, and had a low, flinty voice, like warm iron filings. It touched something in him. In his limited experience, females seemed to be always either constructing or enacting secret plans. His stepsister, Naomi, was in the main petulant, chronically unreasonable, and lied like a child. She was engaging, though, actually fascinating. But Astra's benign indifference seemed without need or conniving.

If surfaces attracted him, then a mystery of great distance in hers, desolation even, drew him closer, a harsh and beautiful desolation, like pictures of the desert. He kept eyeing the center of her collarbone, where sunlight pooled in a lucent oval. At dinnertime he watched her walk into trees with the board under her arm and sunshine striping the slim taper of her back.

The castle grew, acquired itself. Tenacious elms and cedars crowded its borders. Sheep flooded the furrowed hills, hill light lambent and blue at morning. He played checkers with her twice more that week, but couldn't concoct a way to breach her distances. A partial solution came one night a few days later, when he left the bunkhouse.

All the noise and smoke had become stifling to him. Over the past weeks, the bunkhouse had developed a rank odor: sweat, tobacco, the myriad and pungent expulsions of grown men. He'd often sleep with his blanket pressed to his nose, smeared with musk oil, but one night around ten he simply left with the blanket and deerskin pouch, intending to explore and possibly sleep under a tree.

He wandered away beneath a white, muting moon, down to where mulberry and red maple spread apart onto a grove of bluestem.

Astra stood out in the tall grass, wearing her blue dress, apparently doing nothing but standing. The light made her skin brassy and her dress ash gray. She heard the grass rustle and turned to see him.

"What are you doing here?" he said.

"Are you looking for glass?"

"Not really."

"The white dust you like, it's all around the rocks back south."

She led him out of the grove, through heavy stands of pine that ended near a rock ridge bordering one of Ha Ha Tonka's hundred ponds. He watched the dress's canvas conform to her haunches as she walked. They arrived at a tall cliff face of opaque calcite and glimmering quartz edges. When he touched a finger to the ground he tasted a bitter wealth of alkalis. Astra helped him gather them.

On the way back he told her how to make glass, what a furnace consisted of, the minimum heat required, what minerals to add for color. He asked her why she was in the woods so late.

She said, "Look" and pointed up through a break in trees at a dull, yellowish star that was actually Saturn. She spoke about its ring and many moons. He was skeptical.

Then she pointed to the Great Square of Pegasus and to its northeast, an elongated patch of fuzzy light that was the Andromeda Galaxy.

"How do you know all this?"

"A teacher. She watched the stars, and knew about them. A lot of stars we see are dead. Their light's out. It just takes thousands of years to reach us."

"I don't understand."

She explained animatedly, using her hands to describe distance, and he realized this was the closest he'd seen to emotion in her. A loon cried out on the pond, and she stopped.

"Certain ghosts live at the bottom of the water," she confided. "They speak through loons. Cry through loons."

He pondered this scrap of character, rolling over in his mind his total knowledge of her, that she knew things about stars and believed in ghosts. He began assuring himself that she was intelligent, possessing a type of cautious imagination, that her lost eyes were romantic.

He spent the night in the woods, in a soft, shallow culvert between oak roots. Alone, he was compelled to picture her body in a nightshirt. When he finally closed his eyes, he tried to imagine seeing light that no longer existed.

Tin-colored clouds huddled over the castle and four men hammering out gutters refused to work for fear of lightning. The greenhouses stood on seven-foot foundations of river stone that supported four feet of wall and six of roof. Above the walls, empty frames awaited glass skin. Volta sat on a bucket, mixing mortar and whistling, while Thomas worked on the roof.

In mid-afternoon a woman called up to him. Below, Carmen Rogers shielded her eyes and tilted her head skyward. "Hello," she said. Yards behind her, Kenneth and Elizabeth McRyder stood together. They both waved.

Thomas slid down the ladder and waved back. Volta busied himself.

Carmen had brushed her cheeks with rouge. Her eyelashes were thickened black, a sheath of scarlet silk draping her thin frame. Strands of apricot hair hung errant around her face, and near her temple a black headband held a sharp black feather that trembled in the breeze.

She twisted her foot, looked back over her shoulder, tall, but under his six feet. "I'm sorry about my humor last week. I should have explained."

He didn't know why she was talking to him. "You don't need to."

"That's generous."

"I just work here, put glass in."

"They told me you work with glass."

He faced the greenhouses. "Anybody could do this."

When he turned back, she was staring patiently, as if he hadn't finished. "I make glass, though. I know how. And stain it. I made two church windows back home. That's what I wanted to do here."

"Where's home?"

"Linn Creek." He pointed northwest. "Thirty miles yonder."

"Yonder." She smiled. "I'm completely taken with the idiom here."

He just stared, confused. On a pine to her left, a woodpecker hopped and struck, precisely, as if its work were necessary and delicate. Her perfume wafted over him, strong and floral.

"You'd like to make windows here?" she asked.

"Yes."

"I once saw an entire building with broken windows, and they pushed the glass into piles. It looked like diamonds."

"Oh."

She stepped close to him behind a cloudy expression. The woodpecker flew away. "You know about the war?" she asked.

"Yes."

"If you lived in Europe you—every man your age I mean, is dead. Or worse." Her cheeks quivered, but then she laughed unreasonably, faced upward. "Right. My—I'm sorry, please— how stupid. I walk over here and start telling about the dead people I know." She laughed again. Behind her, Kenneth said something to his wife.

"I'm sorry," she said. He gave her his chamois and she wiped her eyes. "I don't know what's the matter with me now. You seemed polite, the one day, and I wanted to apologize, but, look."

She walked away, rejoining her aunt and uncle. Elizabeth took Carmen's hand and shouldered her head while they walked. They left him baffled and uncomfortable.

"Ey." Volta set down his trowel. "What was that then?"

"I don't know." He started back up the ladder. "I guess she's sad."

*

OCTOBER. AGAIN THE DRY, VACANT LIGHT OF OCTOBER.

Astra invited him to dinner one Friday. Her father was hunting all weekend, and she would cook for them. Thomas walked there with the two stained-glass pieces he'd carried from home.

The cabin was small, oak logs weathered and ill-fitted on a dusty yard over which several rattler and adder skins hung from a low pine branch. She was waiting outside for him. The snake skins were translucent, pallid sun through them the color of butterscotch.

A window in the cabin was broken. "I can fix that," he said.

Her eyes stayed on his shoes. "My father didn't go hunting. We can't have dinner." She wore the only dress he'd ever seen her in, old blue flannel.

"So? Let me meet him." He held out the stained glass. "I brought you these."

She looked briefly at his art. "Thank you. No, you should go."

It was like some regression had occurred and he knew her no better than the first day he saw her, and he panicked. "I want to meet your father."

She took the pictures and paused, remained still a moment, then opened the door and motioned for him to follow.

Inside, there were only two rooms in the house, stale and smoke-filled. Her father sat against a wall, next to an iron stove. Smoke leaked out its fractured chimney in dark threads that wove around his head. He had Astra's long hair, wore a heavy khaki shirt and was much larger than Thomas. This, he realized, was the big Indian he'd seen playing cards in the bunkhouse.

Astra said, "This is Thomas. He works at the castle."

"The castle," the man huffed, then leaned forward and squinted at Thomas. His voice creaked. "What do you want? I don't owe you anything." He lifted a tall clay pitcher and drank.

"I'm a friend of Astra's."

The man reached into a stove pot and pulled out something he began to eat. He chewed and watched Thomas suspiciously, as if trying to decide in what manner the young man had offended him. "You have money?"

"What?"

"Get out," he said.

Astra stepped away from them.

"Sir?"

The man nodded up, eyes glinting in the flat brick of his face. "If you don't get out of here, I'm going to stand up and kill you. I will break your neck."

Thomas turned to Astra.

"Don't look at her." The Indian lurched. "Get out!" His shout made them flinch.

Astra opened the door, calm, without complaint. She seemed to be a speck on the horizon.

The door closed before he could say anything. On his way back to camp he picked up a heavy branch and kept stopping to hit trees with it until it broke.

Because it was Friday, men arrived at the bunkhouse dragging burlap sacks containing Mason jars of grain alcohol. Peach or cherry, twenty cents. Volta bought three and gave one to Thomas. He asked Volta about the big Indian who played cards with the workers.

Volta shrugged. "Lives aroun here. Awful card player."

"He's a son of a bitch."

Volta grinned and belched. "Who isn't?" He began strumming an old guitar, singing something about a farm, a horse, a woman.

Eventually Volta's second jar rolled off his gut and banged empty on the floor. Little by little men retired and bearlike snoring rose in chorus. Lights extinguished. Thomas had to keep one foot on the ground to prevent a tumbling sensation.

Saturday they worked till noon. A red-shouldered hawk made a nest atop a basket oak, high above a cluster of bluish morning glories and pink ironweed. He watched the raptor circle and bob over crumbling treetops that trimmed the skyline.

Volta complained. "M'no good t'day. S'not right, that shite."

Late morning, Kenneth McRyder approached the greenhouses. In gray trousers and suspenders with a crisp white shirt, he lightly dragged a walking stick of dark wood. Volta greeted him. McRyder nodded and moved past him, looked up to Thomas.

"Hello."

"Hello."

"Coming along nicely."

"Thank you."

"May I talk to you? Koenig, right?"

"Yessir. Thomas."

"Will you walk with me?"

Volta sat back down and watched them leave.

Kenneth was thirty-five, trim. His mustache gleamed and his trousers sported razor creases as they walked along a dirt path bordering the castle, staying close to the trees. Thomas watched Kenneth's fingers pick at the grain of the walking stick. Now and then he pinched the tips of his mustache.

"You've built church windows before?"

"Yes. Just two. In Linn Creek. I can do anything with glass."

"We're thinking about installing a stained window on the eastern wall, where the tall clear one is now." He pointed his stick toward the castle and they stopped walking. "I was only sixteen when my father started building this." Men and simple machines moved around the castle at insect scale. "They spent an entire year harvesting materials before construction even started. Did you know that?"

"My father was one of the first people to work on it back then."

Kenneth struck his stick. "Wonderful! Where is he now?"

"Ten years ago. He was a stonemason. A wall collapsed."

After a respectful silence, he asked, "Where did he come from?"

"Canada. He settled in Linn Creek when the work stopped."

"Were you born here?"

"Yes."

Kenneth said proudly, as if it were his doing, "Then this castle is why you're American."

"I guess."

Kenneth dusted his shoe and perhaps pondered whether he found Thomas's directness charming or arrogant. "Would you like to work with glass here? Would you like to make a stained-glass window?"

"I'd like that."

"What would you need?"

"A furnace. I'd make all the glass here. Like everything else in the castle. Just tell me what you want."

"What if I told you to make whatever you wanted? What if you could design the picture?" He parted his hands like a conjurer, and two gold rings shined on his fingers.

The proposition needed some qualifier to make it realistic. As if sensing this, Kenneth added, "You know our niece, Carmen?"

"I've met her." Thomas couldn't understand why, in this situation, Kenneth was the one who appeared uncomfortable.

"A lot of people in St. Louis are uppity about money. I'd like to think the McRyders are not. My father began his career driving a cart for a grocer, and we've never looked down on the status of others."

"All right."

"I just want you to know that. My money came from my father, but then I say I don't know how to make church windows."

"All right."

"I'm not explaining this right." Kenneth leaned against an elm whose shadows sprinkled the two. Birds twittered invisibly. "Carmen's from England. I'm sure you knew that. She's been through a great deal. It wasn't so long ago, you know, they were in the war. So were we, but not like England. And there was the influenza."

"Yes."

"I'm saying that I would like you to be nice to her. My wife and I care about Carmen's happiness." He put his hands up as if pushing a wall. "I'm not talking about anything improper. Carmen has a life to return to, eventually, but, we feel, there is a sadness she must be eased out of."

"I'm not sure what you mean."

"I only want you to be affable toward her. We'll start your project, you'll be around the castle, making glass, and we'll come around from time to time. When we do, just talk to her. Visit. Chat. That's all."

Thomas watched parched leaves disperse across the path.

Kenneth's voice became final. "It would be a great favor to our family."

"I just don't—why me? I don't see why you'd want it to be me."

Kenneth looked up the rise at the castle. Cedars around it shook against a welter of blue-gold sky. He turned back to Thomas, with a face as though he were viewing some pure tragedy, like a burnt infant. "I believe you remind her of someone."

He only saw Astra days later, as she had not worked earlier in the week or played checkers before dinner. He worried vaguely for her, but he now had new concerns occupying him. He'd drawn plans for a furnace and studio—that was fun—but now came the difficulty of actually designing the window.

She stood outside the bunkhouse in a rose-colored dress and moccasins, a small red bundle dangling from her hand. "I brought you some food. Since we couldn't have dinner." Then, incredibly, she grinned.

"Let me get a blanket."

Astra walked quickly. With light steps she led him toward tall rocks riddled with lesions of shale. She kept smiling until he knew her mood as false, too insistent. "Hurry," she sang. Her voice sounded unnatural, like raindrops in the desert.

Without thunder or lightning, a warm drizzle began to fall. Combed ferns drooped and slapped at rocks with the wind's jostling and she laughed, a low sound. Fat drops pounded down as they ran, Astra moving quick, nimble. Her wet dress clung to her as she darted between moonshadows and lightning flashes.

At a wall of granite, glassy feldspar twinkled, pink as polished flesh, and she led him into a cave. The constricted dress took the color of her skin.

He used dried branches and moss to make a fire inside the cave. She unwrapped bread and jam while he laid the blanket by the fire. The wild caves secreted their own fluid and the weeping stone was slick as oiled glass and firelight leapt on the damp walls, snapping. A great horned owl landed in the cave, giant wings flustered, rain at its back. Astra's skin gleamed saffron in the light.

She stood and the dress stuck high up on her legs. He felt blood pounding the rims of his ears.

Her fingers touched his elbow, the bend in his arm.

She moved in determined ways, giving him no time. Then luxurious frenzy, where certain fantasies materialized, becoming real, alarming flesh in his hands. Her hair fell around their faces. She had wiped her lips with jam.

Fire hissed to shriveling embers. From the cave's entrance the owl watched them and lightning flashed behind the great bird.

*

HE CHOSE A SPACE FOR HIS STUDIO. AN AREA NORTH of the castle, about four hundred square feet on level ground, sectioned off under an awning with spaces for an oven, benches, a mixing and grinding station, and the furnace.

Six men were to build the furnace for him. They hauled cinder blocks and firebrick and arranged them with grim faces while he studied his own diagrams. A man named Jack Alden moved slow and carried light loads. Bearded, a pink scar ran across his forehead, and he watched Thomas with narrow eyes.

Every time he saw Jack watching, Thomas looked down at his plans.

This time he said, "Make sure the eighteen-inch go just above the base."

Alden dropped a firebrick on the ground. "No, sir. No thank you. I don't know that I feel like taking orders from a child anymore today." The other five stopped what they were doing.

"Just do your job," Thomas said.

Alden smiled, motioned with his hand as if dropping a dishrag.

Thomas took two steps back. "You'll take orders because it's all you can do."

Alden began closing the distance between them, and Thomas backed up, almost into Abberline's horse.

Abberline drew the animal around and looked at the two while his roan pawed the ground with a hoof. "How's it coming?"

"This one," he pointed to Alden, voice unsteady. "He's trouble. I don't want him here."

"You son of a bitch."

"Enough." The horse pranced in a small circle and Abberline's pistol flashed in the sun as he turned. "Come with me."

Alden didn't shift. He watched Thomas.

"If you value employment," said Abberline, "you come now with me. I will not ask again."

Alden moved, eyeing Thomas until Abberline directed him to walk in front of the horse. Abberline tipped his cap. "We'll get someone out to replace him."

"Thank you."

The others stood watching. Thomas put down his plans and lifted two firebricks, moving to stack them. Eventually, haughtily, the men followed.

Kenneth arrived at the studio site before noon, with his wife and Carmen.

Thomas nodded. "Hello," and, remembering, "Miss Rogers."

Kenneth said, "I wondered if you'd like to have lunch with us today?"

He'd hoped to see Astra at lunch. "All right. Thank you." They all walked away as clanging from the east announced the noon meal.

Inside the castle, a dining room contained several oak tables with strips of white linen draped across them. Two Negroes served stewed rabbit in a thick gravy with baked trout, garlic potatoes, and bread. He sat next to Carmen, who grinned demurely and kept her hands in her lap. He saw her stare from the corner of his eye, in the reflection on his silverware.

During the meal, Kenneth spoke. "Have you settled on a design yet?"

"Not yet. I've got some ideas." Nothing he sketched seemed worthy of the opportunity, and this was starting to worry him. He sensed the colors he wanted, but was missing his key element: theme and subject. The precise picture eluded him. A temptation to simply create a mosaic of abstract shapes was instantly dismissed. Using this kind of patronage to make an unremarkable composition would be worse than not doing anything, and he believed the opportunity required a subject of power and grace. He felt he had two points of leverage in his search. First, he trusted the processes of his art, that in the moment of creation the method itself would produce an essential discovery. Second, most important, he tried to use his eyes: use them like nets to snare the world, though his interest was in landscape, not human forms. He believed the subject of his window, the universe, resided only in the hills, trees, and water around him, the natural world.

Kenneth rose and pulled out his wife's chair. "Maybe you'll have some ideas, Carmen. But we've got to get back now. Keep me updated, Thomas." The two said their goodbyes and left the room, followed by their servants.

A window flanked Thomas and Carmen, laying a spire of light across the table, and they moved to the window.

"How are you?" he asked.

"May I call you Thomas?"

"Yes."

Her hair was crimped and bound into red-blond wavelets above her ears. Crystal hung from her earlobes. Her dress was diaphanous, ruffled at the calves, and now she slid into a brown fur coat.

"What are you thinking it will be?"

"The window?"

"Yes." Shadow nestled at her cheeks.

"I was thinking, something about the land, but I'm still not sure."

"Oh, something pastoral? Bucolic?"

"Sure." He didn't recognize her last word.

"Nothing religious, I hope?"

"No."

Thin eyebrows raised and she bit her bottom lip. "It's so boring, isn't it?"

Uncertain of his task, he stared determinedly out the window. When he hadn't said anything, she asked, "Do you have time to take a walk? I'm positive Kenneth won't mind."

"I'm supervising the studio they're building—"

"Please? Kenneth said I could have you all day if I wanted. Maybe you could tell me what some of these trees are. These men are building a castle here and they don't even know the plants on their own land." Her green eyes, lime, tinged with brass, again traversed his face. Her big eyes could flare, they could appear generous and encouraging.

On the way out, workers loading and hammering glared at him, Jack Alden among them, raising stones for a staircase. Alden whispered to the man next to him.

Leaves were vibrant, burning colors that crunched underfoot. He pointed out silver maples, white ash, post oak, and black oak. She kept asking questions.

They followed a creek beside which she walked with long, pointed steps on river stone, like a dancer. "Tell me about where you come from," she said. He told her about Linn Creek, its rock formations and the confluence of the Niangua and Osage rivers, his schooling, and his father.

She reached in back of her head, unfastened her hair and shook it behind her. Every time his talk slowed, she prodded him with questions. Her nature appeared extravagant, but part of something concealed.

"What about England?"

"It's gray." A few umber and scarlet leaves spun down. "We lost an entire generation." She had slender hands, white fingers that tapped her hip. *Kenneth said I could have you all day.*

Bluestem and Indian grass flourished in open forest of pine and blackjack. Carmen said that her mother was Elizabeth's older sister. Her father owned a factory that manufactured bridles and yokes. She mentioned his art collection.

"He has a Rembrandt. Do you know who Cézanne is?"

"No."

She rubbed an oak leaf between her fingers. "He's marvelous. He paints with light in his brush."

This excited him and he smiled, hearing her for the first time.

She placed a piece of blue sage behind her ear and brushed her hair off. "Bright, singing light." She took his arm on the walk back.

They parted by the greenhouses. Volta, now working alone, stood on a ladder next to a roof.

Thomas waved to him. "How's it coming?"

Volta squinted. "S'fine enough. But how do I get your job?"

To find his composition, he felt he had to rise above his everyday state, his sense of scale. But he didn't know if that meant thinking bigger or smaller. A simple landscape lacked the originality needed, and the closest he'd come was sketching an eruption of birds, but even that felt false, like he was forcing shapes to suit the colors he wanted.

He stayed at the studio, drawing, and missed dinner. Astra came for him after. "You missed lunch too."

"The McRyders wanted me to eat with them." He looked for traces of who she'd been in the cave, but her face was the familiar blank, a well-shaped void that only permitted the most cursory investigation.

She led him up an arched bluff, her form fluid, compact, and she built a fire. He watched her, muscles in her legs, remembering them. She'd brought a bearskin.

He moved into her.

She stopped him. "Not now." Her knees drew to her chin.

"What's wrong?"

"Nothing. I just want to sit here."

His hands moved, aroused by her refusal.

"Stop it, I said. Quit. Please."

"All right." Shame still lingered from the way he'd handled Alden, the persistent taste of cowardice, but what riled him became the overpowering feeling that everyone here was playing some game without his consent. He was tired of hidden intentions and things not said.

"Then why did you bring me up here?"

"Because it's nice. I wanted us to stay the night out here. Stop, please."

He threw his hands up. "I don't know what you mean. I never do. Why were you like that last night?"

She seemed to clench, betraying a kind of embarrassment. It made him want more.

"Well? Do you do that a lot? Take men out in the woods like that?"

"Be quiet," she said, nearly whispering as she watched the fire.

"You don't make any sense to me."

She stirred the fire and it leapt in her moist eyes.

"Say something. Who are you?"

She turned to him with an injured face, as if she'd been slapped. Her nose was short and flat on the tip, pert below black, wet eyes, and part of her hair always fell between her eyes. "That was something I did with you. I don't know why I do things."

He could see her reeling. The sudden control enervated him, her facades cracking. "How many men have you done that with?"

"Stop," she said, looking back to the fire. "Stop talking like that."

"Then say something."

"I just wanted you to sleep out here with me tonight."

He stood. "I'm sorry. I have important work to do. They've built me a studio, see?" He pointed down the bluff. "I need to get back to work."

"Nobody else is working."

"Nobody else can do what I can." As he said this, he realized he believed it, and figured that must be because it was true. Yes, he thought, what he was doing supplanted them all: Astra, Carmen, Alden, the McRyders, and whatever conspiracies shifted around him. It had always been true, he remembered. As a child, he'd learned to convince himself that he was alone due to an essential superiority. This was an extension of that rationale. He needn't be concerned about anything but the work, and that comforted him.

He wasn't even angry anymore, just felt large, appropriately brutal, flexing with ambition and talent.

"I'll see you later, sometime. Goodnight."

He started down the hill, forcing himself to think of the window he would make. Near the bottom he heard her call his name.

Had she even used his name before?

He looked up and saw her backlit by the fire. She motioned for him to return, an exhausted wave of her hand. He didn't move, but watched her, feeling more powerful the longer he made her wait.

He marched up the rise and when he reached her he became forceful. Her face turned away, grunts escaping rhythmically beside the crackling fire, and in the circle of warmth he felt his will had found itself. Everything here, people and land, seemed to need him.

He felt ecstatic in her, like a cruel king, above judgment. When he rolled off, he was already nursing a vague remorse. He stared into the fire, groggy, and let it carry him to sleep.

*

A DENSE FOG CLOTTED THE AIR IN THE MORNING, AND he woke alone. The campfire smoldered. Rising sun shined at his back and he rose, still satisfied with his sense of power. At the lip of the bluff he looked out on the valley and saw a shadow drawn impossibly tall, suspended in midair over the chasm. When he raised his arm and moved to the side, the giant shadow in the air moved with him. It was him: a mammoth gray spirit facing back from that void.

It was, in fact, the phenomenon scientists term the Brocken specter—brilliant light projected onto a thick mist that allows for several dimensions of shadow to overlap, occurring only at certain heights. To Thomas, though, it seemed like a miracle of his own doing: this manifestation of the land might as well have been a reality he'd willed. He turned and remembered Astra was gone, wondered for a moment if she'd left for work, but he didn't think about her long. He moved with the incredible shadow for some time, until the sun shifted and the specter disintegrated.

Firebrick stacked seven feet high and the furnace was four feet wide. A large, accordionlike billow grew out its side, and an iron clamp attached at the furnace door. From a bulky copper drum, a gas line entered the burner block at its top. The window was to be fifteen feet by four and a half, tapering up to a sword point.

He looked at his sketch: a single branching tree, meant to be a bare oak, formed the base of the composition. From that stage a fragmentation of color as birds ascended. Many birds: a falcon, a red-shouldered hawk, an owl, grackles, jays, and one woodpecker. A waterfall created the left-side border. Castle walls formed the right. Between those frames stood a pyramid of sun and a darkening shadow, shaped like a man, encompassing it all. Like a tune, its layers repeated in his mind, grains of sand cohering, becoming more solid and real with each refrain. The large masses of green would stabilize the throbbing reds, which bled into dull yellows, the yellows and golds embraced by subtle gradations of blue and brown, coupled with the soft shapes he'd use for the largest panes, the way those shapes dissipated to smaller and smaller fragments and shards, to greater color variation, the window should have the effect of a long, visual exhalation, an optical sigh.

Glass poured between his fingers, only dust. He debated ratios while plunging hands into the sacks of minerals. Sand 56, soda ash 20.3, feldspar 13.6, lime 9.2, zinc oxide 7, borax 5.5. If he increased the soda and reduced the feldspar, it would result in a cleaner finish. But didn't the subject necessitate a few bubbles and rough ridges in order to portray a more naturalistic climate? It should be more detailed the closer one got, but at a distance of even a few feet appear whole, each color existing for every other color with the precise divisions between them too subtle to locate. Two days later he moved his cot to the studio and began.

New black iron tools lay before him, beside silvery asbestos gloves. New paddles and sheet trays for flattening the glass. The firebrick was yet clean gray, but after today it would be properly scorched and soot-blackened. Tin pots of chromium, cobalt, copper, zinc, antimony, cadmium. Magic names. Thomas turned the valve and opened the gas line. He lit a kerosene-soaked rag wrapped around his shovel and stuck it into the furnace where air ignited with a growl and the fire roiled and twisted in a sinewy coil, disembodied and curling back on itself in the furnace. The furnace took all day to heat, and he had to constantly open and close the gas line, work the billow.

The burner port popped and sizzled and the edges of the firebrick turned a cherry color, then all the furnace walls were red inside and glowing. He shut the door and set the gas down by half. When the burner stopped popping he waited for a steady, continuous roar. By mid-afternoon, an inch of blue flame flickered outside the door frame and he didn't hear the lunch bell when it rang.

The McRyders walked nearby with Carmen. From a distance they watched Thomas work the shovel and move back and forth to his sand. His skin shined, shirtless and sootstreaked, his gloves glowed, hair knotted into a frizzy yellow nest. After a moment, they walked on without speaking to him. Some of the men who built his furnace meandered around the studio, pausing to watch. He didn't notice.

Days passed like that, and he did not see Astra.

The studio had a wooden bench where Thomas would sit to monitor the furnace and unlace his boots. His first batch was in the crucible. Glass was not a solid, he liked to inform people. Glass was a very cold liquid, inorganic compounds that on cooling form a random pattern rather than the set crystalline structure of a solid. He faced the castle and imagined its eighty-seven windows returned to their primal state, turning to liquid and streaming down the walls as if the structure wept.

Shortly before dinner Carmen approached the studio. She wore dark blue today, a white pelt across her shoulders. He stood up, filthy, unembarrassed.

"Did you skip lunch?"

He nodded, feeling himself to be radiating.

She looked bewildered. "Are you eating dinner?"

"I might."

She followed his materials strewn about the tent. "Will you come for lunch tomorrow?" He didn't answer and she turned back. "Kenneth was going to ask you the other day, but you looked busy. He told me to ask you."

"I'll try to clean up before then," he said.

Carmen blushed along her throat, started to say something, but departed.

By dark he sat on the bench, sipped from a bucket of water and watched the furnace in orange light. It rumbled and hissed, edges of the door sparked. Pulsing heat tightened his skin. In this place of purpose and security, he had time to think about Astra. She had stopped working in the kitchen, and he hadn't seen her. He remembered running behind her in the woods. What had he felt that split them the night on the bluff? In his memory of that night, she seemed sadder than he'd thought. The image of her at the top of the rise, having to wait for him, now created an aching sympathy, a protective sorrow underlined by the knowledge that he had failed her, had known he was failing her even as she stood above him. Why had he wanted to fail her? One day he'd acknowledge the part of his own confusion, a trapped sensation that caused him to act destructively, without specific intentions. At midnight his first batch was in the homogenous liquid phase.

Blue was first and he added cobalt to the melt. Colorants were tricky and governed by elusive rules. He no longer focused on rules like he had as an apprentice. He knew some colors depended on impurities in the mix and in that regard it was largely guesswork and instinct, at which he excelled. He hoisted the crucible from the fire and doused it in a stone tank filled with water. Steam erupted into the studio, spreading hot gray fog over him.

When the melt cooled he reheated it to produce a uniform temperature distribution, then removed it and poured the glass into large pans set on a marver. With the paddles he pressed the glass down, smoothed it like a mason with his trowel. He set down the heavy iron lids that would flatten the sheets and perfect their texture.

A few hours before sunrise he fell asleep, a half-formed wish for Astra sparking at the edges of his mind. At morning he bathed in a cold creek, scrubbing the cooked glaze off his body.

The group ate lunch at the McRyder's cabins. There were six cabins, long, made from polished logs. A small stable held four Quarter Horses. Two automobiles parked in a dirt semicircle in front of the homes. He paused beside them and admired their smooth metal, the precision lettering on their dials and gauges. Kenneth's wife, Elizabeth, showed him around. Antiques and kerosene lamps decorated the cabin, an old loom, plaid tapestries; a ten-point stag head stared above the fireplace. "It's not home, but we've tried to make it comfortable."

They ate steak with corn bisque. Carmen sat beside him. Unexpectedly, she reached out and brushed hair from his eyes.

"It's getting long, isn't it?"

It was. He hadn't trimmed it since July and it curled around his cheeks.

"Been working hard?" Kenneth asked, cutting his steak.

"I have. I'd like to discuss a couple changes in the design."

"I'm sure it's fine." Kenneth went back to his soup. He frequently engaged Thomas with questions, and always seemed oblivious to their answers.

Elizabeth paid more attention. She asked Thomas specific things about his education, family, and plans, and she would sometimes speak discreetly to her niece in front of other people. While watching Thomas and Carmen across the table, she pleasantly said, "Kenneth, why don't we see about getting Thomas his own room. I know there are extras in these cabins."

Kenneth chewed and nodded. "Good idea. You don't want to stay in that bunkhouse. I was told one of the men had been giving you trouble."

"It's nothing. I've been sleeping in the studio anyway."

"Well." Kenneth sipped his wine. "It's going to be too cold for that soon."

"The furnace keeps it warm."

When there was no reply, Thomas looked up from his plate and saw they were all staring at him with slightly confounded faces.

Then Carmen pushed his bangs behind his ear. "We must cut that hair. Do you use a treatment, Thomas? 'Murray's Hair Oil' I remember—"

Decisively, Elizabeth McRyder cleared her throat and glanced at Carmen, who quickly added, "I remember several boys used it, that's all. They carried it in their pockets with combs. That's all." She turned to Kenneth, as if in defense. "Lots of boys used it."

"You can cut it if you like," Thomas said.

She ran a hand over his head. "I will, I will. It's so thick!"

Kenneth and Elizabeth smiled at him, appreciative. Elizabeth whispered something and Kenneth dabbed his mouth with a napkin. "That's right. I nearly forgot. We're having a costume party. One week after Halloween, an anticlimax, but the ballroom isn't going to be ready till then. We'd love to have you."

Carmen remarked, "It's strange to have after Halloween, though."

"Well," said Elizabeth, "I don't think there's any point in having a castle with a ballroom if you don't throw a party."

"Thank you," Thomas stooped. "I don't know, though. I don't have a costume or anything. I mean, the type of folks—"

"Oh, stop it," Elizabeth said. "I'm sure we can come up with a costume. You're coming. You're invited." She spoke with closure and the conversation ceased, supplanted by the slow, congenial smiles between its participants. Everyone instinctively turned to Carmen. She was staring at her bisque and didn't notice.

"Carmen?" Elizabeth reached her hand across the table.

"What? Oh, I'm sorry." She laughed, slight. "I'm sorry. I don't know—drifted off a moment…"

"We were talking about the costume party."

"Thomas." Carmen turned to him. "Do you like horses? Do you like to ride?"

"I haven't done it much, tell the truth."

"We'll have to get you riding. You would love it. I bet you'd love a fox hunt. I'll cut your hair and teach you to ride. I know you would love that. It's just the kind of thing a man like you enjoys."

He inspected the distribution of color in a maroon sheet he'd created. The color boiled and left bubbles in the glass, faded from dark-rust to translucent brown. When he lowered the sheet, Astra was standing in front of the tent.

He set the sheet down and went to her. "Where have you been? You stopped working."

She touched his chest with her fingers and looked preoccupied, as if trying to solve a math problem in her head.

"Hey," he said.

She watched the furnace, dark eyes reflecting the flames at the furnace door. "I stopped working."

"Why?"

Astra didn't answer. She gently let her hands fall off him and kept looking at the furnace, as though mesmerized by the flames.

"Do you want to see what I'm doing? Look—" He swept his hand over the studio and showed her the blue pieces he'd already cut. She didn't move, placid as a sleeper.

"Astra?"

Orange sparks flittered in her eyes. "Would you leave with me?"

"What?" He turned her around by her shoulders, but she didn't look at him.

Her voice hushed, suddenly a quiet, intense whisper. "Could you do that? Could you leave here with me? Is there any way we could do that? I want to leave. Will you come?"

"What do you mean? I've got work to do. Here." He steered her toward the wooden bench. "Watch. I've got another batch about to go in."

She rose and flattened her dress.

"Wait. Don't go. Look at my design." He took his sketchbook out. She turned and began walking away. "Wait." He grabbed her arm. "What is it? What are you talking about?"

"Nothing." Their hands lingered until the fingers slipped away as she turned. He watched her retreat, her blue dress pulled by the breeze, and he thought of slim summer flowers in a high meadow wind.

*

NOVEMBER. COLORS FADE AND SCATTER ON BITING AIR.

Carmen dipped a porcelain comb in a bowl of cold water, tapped it against the rim and ran it through his hair. Her face was so close, he could see the slivers of brass in her eyes. The scissors made a soft crunching noise, whispers of hair falling into the water, where it lazily turned. She measured out small lengths between her fingers with a concentrated gaze. He understood she had very specific ideas about how his hair would look.

"It's just the right color," she said, not really to him.

She lay the scissors on an end table and told him not to move. "Wait," she said, walking to a back room. After a minute or two she returned with a tin of Beecham's Hair Wax. She opened the tin and dipped it in the bowl of water, stirred it with her fingers, and they came out stuck with soft yellow wax that she ran through his hair, smoothing the crown and sides. Then she combed it. Standing in front of him, the neck of her white dress drooped at his eyes, her pale chest dotted with earthy freckles.

"How's this?" She handed him a mirror and answered herself. "It's perfect."

In the mirror his hair shined and fit his head like a golden rubber cap. The pomade smelled like perfume. "Very nice." It would grow back.

Suddenly she dropped down and hugged him fiercely, gratefully, as if he were a dear friend she had not seen in a long time.

He had the issue of effective binding to consider. He could shear the glass into tiny degrees of color he would fuse and contain with copper bonding to make individual panes. Or he could try to make the color gradient even and use large, whole pieces for the panes. It was necessary to commit. He already had eight sheets— two blues that went from deep indigo to sapphire, two reds, a green with interesting patterns, two yellows, and one that started off as maroon and ended up brown.

He worried he was becoming confined by the limits of his imagination. When the window's concept first struck him, he felt the energy of genuine inspiration. But here he was, weeks now, engaged in the same familiar processes, the redundant techniques of craft that fairly doused the passion that brought about the initial idea. It was as if he'd started down a strange road with exotic flora and heaven's weather, a fragrant path through uncharted lands, and now he was walking in circles around a rock he'd passed several times.

Astra, asking him to leave, bothered him. It indicated the sorrow in her that he chose to ignore, and her desperate eyes made it hard not to take her request seriously.

He thought if he saw Astra he could come back and think clearly, an idea he wanted to fight, but didn't.

The woods murmured, black, moonless, constant frog croaks. The trail was a hint of light at points on the ground, but he remembered the way and pushed through branches and tall ferns he stumbled against. A wet odor on the air, plant rot, unseen piles of dead flower petals creating sweet bursts of fragrance as his feet slushed through compost.

Through the racket of frogs and his own movement, something like voices emerged. They startled him and he crouched for no good reason.

The voices came from a lower level, drifting up as loose, rhythmic talk of men. He moved toward it quietly. As he pressed through a kind of laurel shrub, he realized he'd been treading carelessly close to the edge of a drop which was at least fifteen feet above the forest floor.

The voices slurred together and traded comments, but he couldn't understand them. They grew louder, yet muffled, and below he made out the dark forms of two men walking a path. What he'd taken for muffling became a brogue. The squat, jaunty form was Volta. Laughter. Hushing. He moved along the ridge, trying to stay in the same direction as them, not having any definite goal.

Their path broke from the ridge and Thomas paused in a huddle of palmettos where the ridge curved. He could make out their passing by noise and subtle tremors that passed through the darkness when any part of it was disturbed. He cleared away brush to make out where they might be going, and saw that below revealed a flat, open area, somehow familiar.

Saw the two figures, small, away now, move out from the forest and cross the open area to a cabin, barely visible on the other side. At the cabin the door opened, filled with the big, solid form of Astra's father. The men entered, and the cabin door closed.

Thomas walked back to the studio.

He decided to shear the glass into small pieces for a mosaic structure. It would be much more complex, require firm commitment, but give him the greatest control and opportunity to impress people. Later in life he would denounce the composition, largely for that quality, approving of its destruction.

In his one reference to the window, he qualifies it as "the work of a young man, too eager to please, overcompensating for a clear lack of emotional weight by aesthetic innovation and uncomformity." However, these early experiments with fragmentary binding directly relate to certain of those three-dimensional sculptures that would bring him some fame in the early sixties, especially the celebrated Ascent of Sinai, which features at its center a decahedron made of such panes.

Carmen brought a package wrapped in brown paper to the studio, and she appeared jittery, moving her tongue behind her lips. Her hands pushed the package into his chest and pressed it there. It felt lumpy, light with cloth.

"What?"

"It's for the party. Oh! And this." From a handbag she withdrew a smaller package.

"You shouldn't give me things."

She squeezed his wrist, twisting her feet and moving too much. "It's for your own good. Go ahead," she nodded. He opened the small box. An ivory-handled straight razor, an envelope, a disc of Mickleson's shaving soap. She brushed the blond stubble on his face, and he felt her hand falter. "You have to shave."

Her upper teeth were arranged at crooked angles that somehow enhanced her smile as she waved the envelope. "Friday, you will need this. It's your invitation. Everyone's expecting us."

"All right."

"Eight o'clock, Thomas."

"Yeah."

She shot forward and kissed his cheek, hopped backward once, smiling, and walked down the field.

Inside the brown paper he found a British soldier's uniform of olive wool, with leather belt and holster, a soup bowl helmet, a pair of putties with brass buttons. A small note said: We expect you at eight o'clock.

Sunset Friday he shut off the furnace, its extinguishing hiss articulating his mood.

He brought his costume to the bunkhouse, where men were already donning clean pants or just shedding shirts and opening jars of liquor. Everyone happily accepted orders not to go near the castle until Monday. At the bunkhouse several men looked up from their cots and watched him with indefinite expressions. Volta sat at a card table with Jack Alden, another man, and Astra's father. Her father was in a chair, but his chin rested on his neck and hair fell over his face. He didn't move, and Alden and Volta looked at Thomas, then Volta said something and he and Alden began laughing. The men on their bunks watched Thomas gather his things. He walked out while Volta and Alden's laughter rose, one of them shouting something he pretended not to hear.

He bathed in a cold creek and shaved there, sat drying next to a fire. The soldier's costume was laid out on a log across from him, as if he were sharing camp with it. When he was dry he crossed over to the log and dressed, the uniform itchy, and the helmet kept sliding on his head. The castle loomed through the trees and tall brush, high dark walls guiding him.

Thomas parted a row of cutgrass and stepped onto the castle's lawn. To the attendants standing under gaslight at the door, in the soldier's costume he might have for a moment looked like a true ghost, wandered through the mist and explosions of a distant battle to materialize here, at the edge of the forest.

Several cars sat on the lawn, drivers in black suits smoking cigarettes. The doormen wore white tuxedoes and domino masks. They led him by candelabras down a stone hallway, kept dark because there was still work to do on it. The buckles on his costume clinked as they approached a space of light and noise at the end of the hallway.

The hall opened to an immense room where voices carried and people adorned in clothes from other eras mingled and waltzed. Torches perched up on all the rock walls. Four white men in formal wear and masks played music from a small, elevated stage. A bassist, two trumpeters, and a snare drummer. The music struck his heart as if announcing him.

Long buffet tables lined adjacent walls. More Negroes served refreshments from silver dishes. Most of the guests had not arrived, but the onslaught of sophistication overwhelmed him.

One man dressed as a brown bear. A couple baseball players. A bone-thin Cleopatra, complete with asps, smoked a cigarette in a slender holder. Others modeled in formal wear, with long capes, their only costume a porcelain mask covering the face.

Wearing a severe gray suit and a golden domino, Mr. Abberline walked erect with hands behind his back, nodding tight-lipped smiles to guests. A thin layer of smoke blanketed everyone's head.

Thomas had been standing in the same spot for a while when she grabbed his arm.

Carmen dressed in white and sky blue—a Red Cross nurse.

"Look!" she said, meaning at him. "I knew it would fit. Of course you're forty two tall. I knew it!" She revolved. "Do you like mine?"

He did. Especially the white stockings that covered her calves, something he'd never seen on a woman.

She took his arm and led him across the room where in the torchlight people looked theatrical, notorious. Carmen tapped the back of another couple. Kenneth McRyder was attired in the uniform of a Confederate general, with epaulets and a big hat. Elizabeth was a shepherdess, Bo Peep or something. Her hair was piled under a blue bonnet and she gasped, touched her gloves to her lips when she saw Thomas.

"Uncanny," she said.

Carmen put her head on Elizabeth's shoulder and they hugged. Kenneth nodded stiff approval while the women watched Thomas, and Elizabeth lifted Carmen's head up. "So lovely. We're going to have a wonderful time tonight." She turned to the men and repeated herself. "We're going to have a wonderful time."

Kenneth put his hand on Thomas's shoulder and asked if he'd like a drink. The punch was fruity, loaded with grain alcohol. Within an hour guests began spilling into the ballroom. Witches and sad clowns, kings wearing purple trains lined with fox fur. Among these outfits moved figures in black, their sole disguise white masks with no features except a long white nose. Bass thrummed as the trumpets rose dirgelike from nowhere and the snare kept slow, steady time. In the ballroom were three couches and several velvet divans where guests lounged and talked. Carmen flushed and they both kept filling their punch glasses and laughing. His laughter felt easy.

The man in a bear suit howled and used a ballerina to support himself. Kenneth and Elizabeth circled. Carmen led him to the dance floor, and she told him to move slowly back and forth as she rested one hand at his waist. He stared at a thin sprinkling of blond freckles around the bridge of her nose. The punch left pineapple and watermelon on his tongue.

Past her, he saw Kenneth and Elizabeth McRyder standing outside a circle of dancers. Elizabeth was speaking to Kenneth, who nodded in time with her words. When Thomas noticed Elizabeth watching him, she didn't look away.

Later saw guests dozing on couches, smoking long cigarettes with stunned expressions while others lay on the lawn and some engaged in games in various hallways. The frenzy of motion and drink distilled to quiet whispers and exhausted postures.

Carmen had taken off her hat, hair tussled around her face, and pale eyes widened, teasing, hopeful behind the apricot strands. She found a candelabra and grabbed Thomas's wrist, leading him away from the main ballroom. Stone steps ascended to darkness. The candles hung shadows down her face as she beckoned him up the stairs, an image of cottony light.

She brought him to a stone cloister where a large, old picture in a heavy frame leaned against a wall. She crouched down with the candelabra. "Look. They found this weeks ago." He squatted beside her. The photograph was sepia tone and the flames colored it orange and gold. In the picture, men swarmed a vast landscape of trees and rock, some near and some far. At a stand of grass in the center, two men stood wearing dark suits and sober expressions. Thomas studied it a moment before realizing it was the land where this castle stood.

Carmen rested a hand on his shoulders. "It's dated 1903. That man on the left is Robert McRyder. The other one's Adrian Van Brunt, the architect, but look—" She moved the candles across the picture with a gesture of summation. "All those men working in the background. Couldn't one of them be your father?"

He could hear the candles burning. Their light illuminated the slumped dust motes rising slowly around them. He leaned toward the picture until his face was nearly against its glass. The images blurred up close. One man pushed a wheelbarrow full of stone toward tiny train tracks that ran behind Van Brunt and McRyder. Another held a pickax at the apex of a swing. Thomas's own face reflected dimly in the glass. Up close the picture seemed remote and judgmental, and his eyes narrowed in defense; 1903, year of his birth. He understood that his father had merely labored here, one among hundreds, and rather than connection, he felt dislocation. Instead of imbuing the present with the past, the picture reinforced a belief in his own singularity, his unique, isolated stature—even the picture had only been waiting for him to view it. Carmen's hand slid down the back of his neck.

He stood, unbalanced, the candelabra between them. Her face became haunted in the candlelight and she smiled, her expression loosened and her mouth fallen slightly open. As he stepped to her, she backed against the wall. She blew the candles out one by one.

He walked her home late, leaving her standing in front of the cabin, with Kenneth and Elizabeth's silhouettes against the shades. Still in a soldier's uniform, he fell asleep easily at his studio, picturing further celebrations attended by a slightly older, more refined version of himself, an imperturbable man, someone other people admired and wanted to know.

Shortly after dawn he woke with sudden energy, as if he'd been in the middle of saying something. A clouded sky hushed the castle's hues and on the bluff it no longer appeared so formidable. He knew its halls, secret staircases, and its legacy had diminished. The weather cool and gray, the land felt deserted, not a figure stirring. After coming home, drunk, he'd laid his glass on the ground, and this morning the flat sheets looked triumphant, winking back by catching the damp daylight. Everything was near at hand.

But the sleeping quiet cast a dreamlike quality on the studio. He turned a paddle in his hand, letting the rough iron handle roll over his palm. Rossitto once said, "The easiest thing in the world is not to work." The silence, the lack even of birds, created an unreal presence—a mood that inspired wandering, and his feet began moving into the stillness. He put the paddle down and just started walking, still in his soldier's uniform.

He hadn't intended to follow the ridge through the forest, down to the bend where below bent a dilapidated cabin in a clearing of dust and bluestem, and snake skins fluttered from a pine branch. Astra's home still had the broken window. A wild turkey, lone and preposterous, waddled through the dusty yard. He was preparing to descend when the cabin door opened.

Volta exited. His nappy black hair stood on end and he relieved himself on a tree, moaning as he did. Behind enormous ferns, Thomas watched the man belch and shuffle down the path into the forest. He was thinking that maybe a card game had taken place.

He knocked on the door and Astra's father opened. He took up the entire doorway. "What? Who are you?"

"I want to see Astra."

The Indian eyed him. "I don't owe you anything."

He didn't understand the relevance. "Can I see Astra?" He tried to fit around her father but a stone hand shoved him back.

"You have money?" the man asked.

"What?"

"Ten dollars."

Thomas stammered. "I don't have anything with me."

The Indian nodded sympathetically. "Come back with ten dollars." He slammed the door. Thomas ran around the side of the cabin and peered through the only window on the other side.

A gray, grimy patina fogged the window, peppered with dust and loose hair. He could see into a dank-looking room with a small bed. The bed was covered with tangled sheets and, bound up in the sheets, a small bundle curled on one side. Black hair pouring from the open end of the sheets, he watched the blankets rise and fall with breath. He tapped at the glass.

The bundle on the bed shifted. From a part in the thick black hair, a single dark eye turned to the window. The eye was swallowed by bruise, indifferently regarding him within glossy purple swelling. The eye blinked slow, dully, at the face on the other side of the clouded window. A small brown hand brushed hair off the other eye. Then both eyes turned away and the bundle curled into itself and the gray mildew on the window seemed to swallow the whole picture.

He jogged through the woods, past groping branches and shrubs, to his studio, and the total quiet that defined the place that day.

Thick copper tape sat spooled for welding the panels into place. He began to reheat a blue sheet, intending to begin the shearing process, and he took out the shears and observed the strength of the blades. The shears were perhaps a little dull, salted with specks of rust. He wanted to start with a large panel and build around it. The blue had many gradients. The brown glass could look red in the light, and that was something he would have to consider when finalizing their placement.

He used a file to scrape rust and iron off the shears, crimson and silver flakes drifting to the ground. He'd scrape once across the blade, watch the particles fall and land, then scrape again. Falling slowly into a small pile, a tiny brown snow, the flakes began to embody something else to him, something he felt or used to feel, someone he once knew.

He moved in circles for an hour, picking something up and putting it down, rearranging materials. Then he walked to the bunkhouse.

When he entered the doorway, talk ceased. Most of the men were in there, sprawled in various states of recovery. A couple sat up in their bunks. They watched him walk toward one end of the hall, his footsteps sounding solitary. Jack Alden was cutting a plug of tobacco and he watched too.

Volta lay on his back, arms over eyes. He sat up when Thomas stood over him. "Hey, young son. Have a good time last night?" Volta rolled over to face the other men. "He's practically our boss now, y'know."

"Hey," Thomas said. Volta looked back at him. "What were you doing at Astra's?"

Volta eased off the bunk and stood close to Thomas, the top of his head barely reaching the younger man's chin. "Why don't you talk to the Indian, John Monro?" Volta smiled. "The man's awful at cards." He looked around the room. All of the men were sitting up, and he took a step toward Thomas.

He poked a finger at Thomas's chest. "Or you think any girl around's for you alone?" A few murmurs rippled through the bunkhouse. Volta glanced around again and spoke louder.

"You think you walk in here, among men who work fer a livin, men who sweat and exhaust themselves?" He spread his arms in an avuncular expression. "Well fuck you."

Thomas swung at Volta. He sidestepped it easily and threw Thomas into a bunk. The Scotsman hit him twice in the kidneys before he could recover, and when Volta moved over him, Thomas kicked up and back, striking the groin, giving him space to stand.

He charged forward, planted a foot, and hurled all his weight behind the fist. Volta's nose burst red—the blood splash hanging spiderlike in the air. Volta caught his next blow by the wrist, and he squeezed. His hand dug in a pocket, face lost in dark fluid, only the eyes and teeth visible. "Right. That's how you want it?" Volta pulled his hand out of his pocket. Brass knuckles wrapped his fist. "I do hate to be the one to teach you."

Volta drove the knuckles down, once, holding Thomas by the wrist. Thomas's legs went out and left him suspended like a punching bag. The knuckles fell again, ripped an eyebrow, split his lip up to a smashed nose. He could hear men shouting from an echoing place above him.

A haze of pain, blood in his eyes, he reached up and squeezed Volta's testicles, yanked down. Volta screamed and dropped him. Thomas tried to crawl backward, blind. Volta cursed, doubled over, clutching himself. His crotch was wet. "That's how it is? That's how it is?" Thomas tried to crawl, but Volta walked up and stomped his groin. He kicked his spine and ribs, then loped to his bunk and dug through his rucksack, saying over and over, "All right. All right."

The room hushed when Volta produced a Bowie knife from his bag. He crouched over Thomas. Hearth light glistened on the blade. Volta rolled him over.

Thomas couldn't see any of this. He only sensed that something bent over him, a noisy mass on the far shore of a murky lake in and out of which he bobbed. He felt something roll him over and he gurgled, realized his throat was filled with fluid that tasted like copper. He was drowning in a lake of copper.

His ears were ringing, so he didn't hear the gunshot, only felt the floorboards beneath him thump with weight. He understood that the dark mass was no longer on top of him, and as he sank under the surface of dark waters, a black bubble burst on his lips.

Silence echoed in the room. Abberline stood in the doorway, arm still outstretched. The pistol's smoke twisted upward and broke against the wooden rafters.

Two ribs, four fingers, his nose, and jaw were broken. A doctor came to the McRyder's cabins and set the bones, stitched his lip and scalp, splinted his nose and left the family with morphine and laudanum. The second morning, a fever rose that no one thought he would survive.

His face was bandaged and he slept in delirium. Carmen remained by his bed. She was sleeping on the fourth night, and Elizabeth McRyder was the only person to hear Thomas finally wake.

He started moving in jerks, mumbling. Elizabeth stood in the doorway holding a candle by her stomach, and watched his shadowy, swaddled form wrestle against the sheets, and heard him say "Astra" twice. The next morning, his fever broke.

Ambient light filtered through the bandages. Dull, sulfuric light. He could smell alcohol and balm on his face. He heard someone weeping, whispering. Gradually, through this slow sensory accumulation, he realized he was awake. Someone was crying close by. A girl's voice, familiar, English, said the name "Edward" between sobs.

Elizabeth McRyder was talking to Mr. Abberline in the front doorway, while from a window in the back of the cabin Kenneth watched the dissipating leaves being gathered on the wind, the short jabbing bursts of wind the jagged landscape created. One moment, a huge pile of ripe color would fly up, as if kicked by an invisible boot, then form a tight spiral that swept briefly in one direction before letting the leaves fall. As though for an instant they'd attained life, then lost it. The land touched his deepest appreciations.

After a week, they unwrapped the bandages. Harsh light blinded Thomas, and he did not see Carmen raise her hands and turn her face around. He heard her moan.

Strange, blue-capped angles composed his face, and one side of his gouged hairline sat higher than the other. Dark thread stitched along the high side of the scalp, and also stitched from his lip to his right nostril. Kenneth was near him and didn't speak. Elizabeth walked Carmen out of the room.

Later, he was alone, and heard them talking from somewhere in the house, but the room and adjoining hallway were empty, and he couldn't tell from where the voices traveled.

He didn't see Carmen as he gathered up his things. Kenneth gave him some superficial advice, "Rest for a while. Let us know if we can do anything."

Thomas wrote on a piece of newspaper: ILL FINISH WINDOW.

"Well." Kenneth scratched the back of his head, stopped, and smiled. "Well, just take things easy. That's not important now. After all, we already have a window there." Kenneth checked the hallway and took Thomas by the arm, a little too directly to be polite. "Listen, you know, you let me down."

"Why?"

With rigid jaw, he clearly communicated his disappointment. "This...brawling. Ridiculous. A real waste."

The silent woods anticipated winter. His path was damp, blued by evening, leaves disintegrating underfoot as he limped slowly into the forest, making stiff motions.

The one window was still broken at Astra's cabin. No lights burned inside and the door opened without resistance. The stove was gone, but its black iron chimney craned down from the roof, dripping thin flakes of soot above a small black pile. The two rooms were empty. Dust wafted across the floor.

He stood in the yard and in darkening light found two wheel tracks led by hoof prints. The tracks moved out of the dirt circle and into tall bluestem. The grass flattened in a direct line that led to a wide dirt road. Shortly down this road, the tracks were lost to wind and rain, buried under hard, chilled dirt.

*

FEW MEN REMAINED AT THE BUNKHOUSE. THE ONES there turned aside when seeing his stitches and dented cheek. Jack Alden was carving a block of balsa and he looked up, wood shavings and tobacco leaf hung in his beard.

Thomas spoke with difficulty, not moving his jaw and wincing. "Do you know where the big Indian is? Jack Monro is?"

Alden rested his eyes on Thomas's face, then turned down to his whittling. He shook his head no, and added, "You might talk to Abberline. They was talking a couple days ago. Last time I saw Monro around."

As Thomas walked out, Alden said to him, "A beard'll cover most of that."

He hammered on Abberline's door, and the supervisor opened, holding an unlit cigar between his teeth.

"Well," he said. "He did a job on you, didn't he boy?"

"Where's the Indian?" The words were slow and hurt.

"Excuse me?" He looked possibly amused by the amount of time it took Thomas to finish a sentence.

"Ind—Joe Monro. Where?"

Abberline lit his cigar methodically, held the smoke and released it above his head where it lingered in a gray halo. "I would like to suggest to you." He looked at Thomas and inhaled again. "I would like to suggest that you take this opportunity to reflect on your luck at being alive, and perhaps consider ways you might repay the McRyders for their friendship."

"Where's Monro?"

"And, I should add, you might show me some gratitude."

"For what?"

The smoke descended over his face like mountain fog. "For saving your life."

Carmen answered the door and he pushed past her, seeing only the back of her hair as she turned her face away.

He asked, "Do you know where they made her go?"

"I don't—who?" Carmen kept her eyes on a bureau. She adjusted a crystal figurine, a stampede of horses, with her long white fingers.

He saw Elizabeth McRyder standing in the hallway, her cold expression still and knowing. "Was it you?" he asked. "You sent her away?"

She said, precisely, "I can't understand a word you're saying."

"Hello. Is there a problem?" Kenneth's voice from behind.

Kenneth stood beside Abberline in the foyer, with the front door open behind them. Abberline eyed Thomas bemusedly and passed a thumb across the handle of his revolver. The five people stood as the points of a tense pentagram, and Carmen stared at the floor, traced the crystal manes of the stampeding horses. The horses were a single piece, individual forms wrestling through the lumpy crystalline welding of their base. She did not look up when he left.

Carmen returned to England shortly after Christmas. In 1930, she married a bank officer twenty years older than herself. She died in London, during a bombing, in 1944.

Due to financial troubles, in 1936 the McRyder brothers leased the castle as a hotel and vacation resort managed by an old matron named Josephine Raliegh. In 1942, sparks from a fireplace kindled a blaze among the mansion's wooden shingles, and the castle was soon gutted by fire.

A rain of white ash snowed all the next morning.

The Missouri Chamber of Commerce made Ha Ha Tonka a state park in 1978, and elected to leave the castle's remnants as they were, only the singed outer walls standing.

Thomas Koenig finished the window, his first privately commissioned work, in March of 1923. The stitches had come out months before, and his hair was long again. Unsure even if they would use it, he continued to work through Christmas, devoting all his time to the refining of surface, to facture and passage—the way pieces fit and their overlying textures.

At one point, he was going to insert a girl's face in the window. He spent days sketching it until he felt a workable portrait emerged. She would have brown skin and black hair, dark eyes. But even though he'd drawn her perfectly, he couldn't deny that the face intruded on the rest of the composition, and he abandoned the idea.

When the window was finished, the McRyders actually liking it a great deal, he supervised its insertion into the wall of the eastern gable, where it stayed until the fire of '42. In that blaze the window swelled with fierce light, it perspired, flames creating a kaleidoscope that danced, trembled, and shook. Then the glass burst in thousands of colored shards, as if spit from the rock, trailed by fire.

There is a long life. There are incoming decades, the twentieth-century wailing, rushing him through. There are sculptures in the fifties and sixties, a series of lectures, and a glass mural for the United Nations building.

But I want to picture him then, after just completing his window. I want to meet him in the place where he starts asking different questions.

They are hauling his window up with thick hemp rope and squeaking pulleys. He leans precariously far off a fiberboard ledge they've rigged. The heavy, fragile spire of glass twists and sways until one of the men reaches out, while another one pulls the rope, and the edge comes into his gloved hand. After the window is installed, Thomas stays two more days.

He sits below it and stares, free to be exhausted, but has to question it, the window: what it is, because it isn't what he envisioned in his mind. Not at all. Since it's not, he has to ask what, exactly, it is, and what it's worth.

He hikes around the chasm's edge to view it from a distance, sees that it contrasts the neutral stone like a sore bleeding light. He sleeps near it to see what moonlight will do.

The one certainty he concedes is that the window, simply, is not very good. Against the muted stone the colors now look gaudy, chosen for their bright strangeness, and missing the cohesion he'd wanted. The shapes and forms cause the composition to seem cluttered, noncommittal. The only thing he likes about it is the single, branching oak at its base—elegant, pleasing. It represents for him what the window could have been. But as for what it is—it becomes clear that he hasn't done a very good job.

Just what had he thought it would be, and had he ever even seen it clearly in his mind? Eventually, was it even worthwhile? Hard to say now. The more he ponders the piece, the more significant its errors become. He asks himself what one has to do to make such work worthwhile. This is a new question.

He walks down the bluff, canvas rucksack hoisted, turning down the same road he arrived on, and dragonflies fill the air between clawlike branches, knobby and brittle, the path matted with soggy leaves. Shadows pass over his face, a boy, the two new pink gouges and crooked nose.

He turns and disappears behind a bend of skeletal trees.

WANTED MAN

IN THE VILLAGE OF LATOURSE THAT EXISTS SOUTH between Port Salvador and Travis City in Louisiana, where decades ago the pine forests had been stripped and unable to regrow and the refineries now employed half of their original numbers, most of the eight hundred or so residents weren't aware of the Prater estate, and many who were, when asked, often just hung their faces and shook their heads back and forth in a pitying gesture, and some less sympathetic people curled their nostrils as if smelling something rancid. The place was out where the old Chenault air base used to be, a few acres of empty grassland south of the runway now overgrown and cracked with weeds, on the side of Lake Quelqueshue opposite the refineries, which at night reflect into the water the image of a future metropolis built of metal and fire. Once there'd been a family but the old man, Burris Prater, lived there now with only his youngest son, Wesley, who had been home for two months and still found himself missing vaguely the order and security and care of the hospital. Meals had been regimented, arrows painted on the floor told you where to walk, and people had asked how he was doing.

That morning, a shotgun severed his dreams. Wes Prater startled awake at the sound of firearms, the crash still echoing beyond the transparent yellow drapes. Another boom; it careened in his ears, blasted him into memories, and he saw TJ out in the field at dawn, how he must have kneeled and rested on the barrel as if praying to it. He never liked sleeping on the top part of the bunk bed but couldn't bring himself to fill the groove his older brother had worn in the bottom mattress.

Wes jumped down from the bed and pulled on a pair of jeans. His father sat on the porch, in a folding lawn chair, facing the broad sea of cordgrass around their house. The old man fit three more shells into the pump-action. Sweet-smelling smoke drifted from the breech and it was as though the smell reminded Wes of a memory he no longer possessed. His father's hair had gone thin and a sandy, metallic color, his face pressed inward and spattered with dark freckles. He wore a tattered pink terry-cloth robe that had belonged to his wife and Wes recalled his mother wearing that robe while smoking a cigarette above a pan of eggs and back-bacon. Beside his father's bare, veiny feet, shotgun shells were scattered around a half-empty bottle of Dickel. Two garbage bags filled with High Life cans slumped against the corner of the porch, near the weathered blue oxygen tank and its plastic mask. The old man kept his Dickel in a locked cabinet, the key hidden on him.

"They's something out there." His father used the shotgun to point into the vast fields of khaki grass while using his other hand to pull the pink robe shut over his chest. "Not sure what. A coyote. A bobcat. I could just glimpse it." He raised his glass off the porch and tipped it to his receded lips. "It's brown. Light brown."

"Pop…." The ends of the yellow ribbon tied around a live oak were frayed and stringy. A flaccid American flag drooped from a pole jutting out the single gable above the porch. Paint on the house had faded, cracked and peeled so that the small A-frame seemed to wear bark, and over Wes's left shoulder a deserted gray barn leaned westward as though trying to hear something. "We don't have nothing for a coyote anyway. It's not like we got chickens or something."

The old man's boxy head darted up. "What's that supposed to mean? That's a shot at me, isn't it?" He laid the shotgun across his knees and cinched the robe around his neck.

"No," said Wes. "I was just—" His father raised the gun and resumed scanning the field, which went unchanged, the color of dulled brass and spreading out from their home as though it had leaked or bled in every direction. The grass seemed cooked of all character by the sun and it gave the house a quality of being adrift, a skiff unmoored in a piss-colored sea. The moon was still visible like a cloud lathed in the morning sky. Beside the oak in the small dirt yard three signs leaned more or less in line. A breeze wobbled the one that read power of pride. A blast rang and Wes leapt back, heat and gritty residue of the gunshot crashing over his side. The old man ejected the smoking shell.

"I didn't see anything."

"Well I did."

Wes turned and looked through the front door toward the back of the living room, where the gun rack was visible. He could identify which gun was missing, his brother's Remington lying across the lap of the pink robe. His father raised his glass and drained it, smacked. Wes said, "You're using—?"

His father bristled, waited. "Am I using what?" He lifted the gun to his shoulder.

"Nothing."

"You gone to the store today? Or what. I need sausages and there's hardly any beer."

Wes nodded and beneath the gunpowder a stale, sharp scent like ammonia stung his eyes. The chair his father sat in had canvas straps criss-crossing an aluminum frame and beneath it a shiny puddle glistened on the porch. He stepped in front his father and saw the lap of the pink robe was soaking wet. "Dag, Pop. Again?"

The old man scowled at his crotch and both hands clutched the gun. "Shut up. Get out the way. They's something out there."

Wes went inside and got dressed and heard the gun a few more times, each blast making him feel sickly and timid. He shaved and watched a string of blood pulled down from his throat. He was thinking a lot about TJ this morning. TJ in the desert, liberating Kuwait City. TJ back home, tattooed and telling stories about a Mexican girl, some kind of witch who'd married him in some kind of ceremony. TJ flinching a finger and turning his head to red mist in the useless plain of dry grass outside the window. Walking out the yard, Wes mimicked a karate kick and knocked over the sign that read in god we trust. His father called from the porch, "Pussy."

The F-150 had not been new when his father bought it thirteen years before. It bounced and jostled over the deep ruts that ran in front their house. The drive to the nearest grocery store took him about three miles north and at first there had been the urge to just keep driving, but a destination eluded him. A girl named Clara worked the cash register at Cormier's Grocery, and he sensed that she could be a destination, sensed, like a man falling past a line of rope, that she might fill some nagging imperative. The store had one of the short old signs whose letters could be replaced to spell different messages, a light-bulb arrow above the words pointing toward the road. Today it read am i y brothers keeper? yes i m. The oyster-shells of the parking lot crackled like fire under the truck's bald tires.

He'd talked to Clara before. She and the woman who owned the store both believed he'd been in Iraq. He'd told Clara he just got back from the war; a sergeant. Her lips were thin and pink and she had a pointed face covered in blonde freckles, blonde hair like a sunlit lake, and from that sunny field her green eyes seemed to fly outward, or one of them did. Her left eye was lazy or perhaps glass and it wandered discreetly to one corner, as if trying to watch her shoulder.

She was working, but there was a long line, and so he didn't get to talk to her much when he bought ten cans of Vienna sausage, two loaves of Wonder Bread, mayonnaise, milk, toilet paper, and a High Life suitcase of thirty-six cans, and it was okay, because when she smiled at him he lost a significant amount of his speech facility anyway. Absently, he handed her a ten and in a kind of daze hustled out the door.

On the way home he turned onto Big Plain Drive, toward town, and popped a beer. He'd start off thinking about Clara, but then his thoughts would move to memories of the day the refinery exploded. He kept seeing his sister, Anneise, rise up out the field, appearing in the middle of the grass with Barret Wagner, his brother's friend. Loose grass stuck in Anneise's hair and across Lake Quelqueshue a cluster of orange flames bloomed from the metal haze of the petroleum refineries; another boom made the ground quiver, and birds erupted from the trees fencing the shoreline. On the far side of the water, sections of the air had become heaving red blobs, spitting into the lake. The heat was intense, air greasy and particulate, dimpled by gas fumes and heat. His pop and Wagner had run to the stable to secure the horses. One of them had kicked the stall and had broken its leg and its owner would sue for negligence. After that, his father wouldn't board any more horses and the last occasion for work vanished from the farm. Wes and his sister stayed out there watching the eruptions and listening to the wailing sirens. Later on, his father explained to them what had happened, that twelve men had died, but those facts never stole away the beauty of the roiling fire or the sensation, unique and unexpected, that something had happened. Something had busted open the quiet hours of sunlight. He remembered the dry yellow grass that caked his sister's back and the grass stains on her kneecaps.

Back then it had felt like life was not just one thing; it could be other things. Then one day it felt the exact opposite; life was one thing and one thing only, a wait.

Anneise had left home with Barret Wagner when she was seventeen and Wes was thirteen. They hadn't heard from her in a couple years and their father wouldn't speak about her. Wes drank three beers while driving a small circle around the village square and the football field and the old pine mill and the Indian casino just outside the town limits. He imagined that when Clara was his girlfriend, he'd learn the truth about her eye.

When he returned home about an hour later, the green Dodge Shadow parked in the yard cut his reverie with a foreboding, sinking sensation. Clara was inside the house. She was sitting in the living room, talking to his father, and she wore a look of dim horror.

"Ho!" his father coughed. "The war hero returns!" He laughed and brought his oxygen mask up to his face. Clara was standing now.

"I came by cause you didn't give me enough cash. It was nineteen and you gave me a ten. I told Miss Marie I'd just come by and get it. I thought you'd be back."

"No," he said, and set the beer and groceries down.

"I want to hear some war stories!" his father called, then sucked at the mask. He twisted the spigot and the tank hissed.

"Um," said Wes.

Clara started to move past him, shy and hurried, tucking a strand of hair back. She was at the door now and he said, "You want that cash?"

"Oh. Yeah. All right. It was, um, you only gave me ten. So."

"I want to hear some war stories!"

"Shut up!"

"Or, I could just, get it later," she said, opening the door. "Whatever. I mean."

"Okay. Wait." His smile felt so awkward it was excruciating, and he could see his father grinning out the corner of his eye as he pulled two crumpled fives from his pocket. She took them and tried to smile but even her good eye avoided him and she scrambled to her Dodge, started it as if fleeing a crime.

Wes stood in the doorway. A blob of spittle nestled in the corner of his father's crooked smile. He said, "You ought to be ashamed of yourself. To steal your brother's legacy."

"I got a *uniform*. I *was* in Army."

The slit mouth, like a wound in his face, opened and cackled. "You wasn't in no *Iraq*. Less than two months. A washout's what they said. Crazy."

Wes looked out the door to the long fields, the yard signs, the dust cloud disintegrating above the road.

His father counted on one hand. "Mental instability. Panic attacks. Anxiety disorder. Dys-phas-ia." Wes's fists clenched and the dust from Clara's car wafted over the road like a ghostly scarf. His father went on, "You can't fake stuff like that with them. They'd of caught you. That means you're bat-shit crazy."

A hot tide coursed through Wes's face. "I wonder why your whole family ran away," he said. "I wonder why Ma and Anneise left."

His father raised the bottle of Dickel. "The one should of left's still here."

"Everybody's tired of you."

His father lit a cigarette. "You oughta be ashamed. A *sergeant*?"

"Ma hated you. So did Anneise. TJ—"

"Oh, that's *my* fault, I guess. Blame me, you goddamn coward."

Wes marched into the old man's face. "What're you good for except pissing yourself?" Flakes of spit landed on his mottled cheeks and it seemed to please the old man, his eyes flaring with the only vitality they knew.

"What about you? Telling some little girl you're a big war hero. Pretending you your brother."

Wes grabbed the flaps of the robe and jerked his father up. "You didn't have to say nothing!"

"Oh, big man!" His father coughed. "Even as a kid. Sitting out there in the fields. Talking to rocks. You crazy sumbitch."

"Ma didn't think you were much of a man, huh?"

His father swung the nearly empty bottle of Dickel and clipped Wes's cheek, sent him reeling back. "That's it, you pussy. Come back over here and find out what it's about."

Wes snatched the bottle from his father. Emptied it into his mouth while his father groped in the air for it. "Section 8'd! Go talk to your rocks!"

Wes lifted the bottle by the neck as if to bring it down.

"Go ahead, big man!" his father barked, neck outstretched, snarling.

"You let her run off! With Wagner! And you didn't even try to stop it!"

His father lost some of the rigidity in his neck, shook his head. "I hated that boy. Bastard. I hated him."

Wes's arm lowered. "Yeah. Me too."

"Don't talk about your brother, though."

Wes dropped the bottle on the floor and walked to the east window, looked out at the field of high, dead grass. TJ's tattoos were acquired in Mexico, after he was discharged. They were strange, convoluted Indian signs that sleeved both his arms. Black and interlocking, a maze of tribal signature. Wes imagined the markings jerked back, the blast, a red burst in the dawnlight.

"It's not Section 8," Wesley said. "It was called AR 635-200."

"Get me another bottle. It's unlocked."

"You remember TJ talking about that girl that tattooed him in Mexico? A priestess?"

"No."

"No. Cause he never talked to you. 'You're better off talking to those rocks, Wes.' That's what he said."

"Get me another bottle." Finally, his father hoisted himself off the couch with trembling arms. Returned with a new bottle of Dickel.

"You find that bobcat?"

"I didn't say for sure it was a bobcat." The old man settled back on the couch. "They's something out there, though."

Wes turned back to the window, his reflection imposed on the morbid field that was just then rustled by a wind. He heard the sound of his father's gulping, the smacking of his lips. He aims to die, Wes thought, and heard his father chuckle. Then Wes muttered, "It should have been you."

"Say again."

"It should have been you out there. With a gun."

Another chuckle. "It should have been *you*."

"Saved everybody the trouble of having to leave."

"You ever think I wanted her to leave? That ever cross your dumb little mind?"

He still faced the window. Their land was without fences, yet a border seemed definitely construed, limitations drawn of psychic, historical materials. He heard the match strike and smelled the sulfur and then the tobacco of his father's Pall Mall.

"You know, you ain't mine," the old man said.

A pause, and Wesley knew his father was choosing his next words. He'd heard rumors. Anneise had told him something about their mother once, out on the lake. They'd been skinny-dipping when Wes was ten and he'd been afraid to leave the water because of his erection.

"Nope," his father said. "You couldn't of been. You wasn't mine and she didn't even take you with her. What's that say?"

"Who?"

"Who what?"

"Who was it?"

His father shrugged. "Who knows. You mother was a whore."

The news didn't unmoor Wes at all. He'd always felt held outside his own history, his family's, and in the consolations of rock and grass his loneliness had accommodated itself to a secret, imaginary reality. So he'd already inhabited this bastard status beyond any verification.

Burris Prater must have had a shot of guilt, because he spoke in a meager tone toward Wes's back. "It wasn't your fault, though. I told myself. I kept you here cause it wasn't your fault. It was hers. I raised you like my own."

Wes stared into the field. He'd left high school when he was fifteen, after Anneise ran off and after his mother had long ago left to follow a man who traveled with a revival. Three years then where he dug irrigation ditches in the sun. Sat outside with his favorite stones, watching the refineries across the water. Then Army and the hospital. He moved away from the window and looked without expression at the slumped, freckled body under its robe.

"I'm just drunk," the old man muttered. Wes moved past him. "Where you going? They's a Rangers game later on." Wes didn't answer. He closed the front door behind him.

Grazed by sharp, bending blades, Wes cut through the grass and walked to the lake. The refineries resembled a pipe organ, and nothing had lived in the lake for many years except a black and purplish layer of algae. He sat on the moist shore with a beer, crossed his legs.

Time, as in his childhood, could smear here like liquid in sluice, the beat of moments passed by making observations, watching things. Grass, stone, water, cloud. Each observance demarked time and gave him possession of it, became something he inhabited. Sun and sunset, light-dappled water. He could fold time here and have it pass without feelings, turn hours into a moment, feel the stone, and disappear while the daylight crushed down, thick as wax.

Mosquitoes and the overwhelming urge to piss woke him from his trance. A couple hours had passed. He walked inside and found his father sprawled across the floor, the oxygen tank upended and two empty bottles of Dickel beside his body. Wes continued past the body to the bathroom, relieved himself, and sometime during that process he realized the old man was dead.

He walked back in the room and stared at the body. A pool of dark vomit spread under its face, but none of the liquor looked spilled, and so he concluded that his father had emptied both bottles into himself within the space of a few hours. *He meant to die*, Wes thought. *From the moment he woke up this morning.*

It was a little like the day the refineries had exploded.

*

THEY BURIED HIS FATHER IN A CEMETERY OVERLOOK-ing the Gulf of Mexico. Exactly five people gathered under a green tarp that held a sea-colored light beneath it, the way a cloud holds a rain shower. Odor of dead fish. Wesley had the sense they were all standing in an emptied aquarium. The young priest affected an air of liturgical drama, punctuated his phrases with jerky dips and twists of his head. His altar boy kept gazing off at the Gulf, and two cemetery workers looked bored as they watched the simple pine box lower into its hole.

Wesley still thought of him as his father, because he had no one else to picture in the role. Burris Prater had no middle name, and all Wes knew of his paternal grandparents were snippets the old man had always used in an accusatory self-defense. "My daddy made shoes and he left us when I was five. I had two sister and my mother couldn't work because she was sick. When she died I went to work at the plants." He'd married late in life to a younger woman and bought farmland, but the land couldn't produce crops because of pollution that had seeped across the lake and into the groundwater. If he'd had a vision then it had turned on him, twisted itself inside out.

He had his father's truck and what was left of the subsidies, but three weeks later he was still in the house.

The key to the liquor cabinet sat on the mantle and a few empty bottles dotted the shelves. Wes stood at the center of the living room, trying to pitch peanuts into the mouth of one of the bottles and clutching TJ's shotgun in the other hand. On each chair and the sofa sat a large white rock, five of them all together, surrounding him. He'd scrubbed each one clean and selected its placement carefully.

The front door burst open like a starter's pistol, and he whipped around, heard footsteps in the foyer.

The girl at the room's threshold was lean and tan, in short cut-offs and a white tank-top. Her hair was tangled and pulled on top her head. Taut and pleasing, she removed a pair of sunglasses and surveyed the room with a somewhat appalled expression, staring at his rocks.

"Jesus, Wes," said Anneise. "What's going on here?"

"Um."

"Why're you dressed like that?"

He started trying to button the top of his military fatigues, but his fingers fumbled and the gun kept slipping out his grasp. Stunned and exhaustingly drunk, unsure if her appearance was even real, he only said, "I was in the Army."

He realized he'd always felt, if you wait long enough in one spot, everything could come to you.

*

IT WAS ALMOST FALL AND THE WINDOWS WERE OPENED. She came out the shower in a long, faded purple T-shirt that just covered her panties. She curled her legs on the couch and drank coffee he'd made.

"Dead. Jesus. That's so weird it happens now. Right before I come home."

"Yeah," said Wes. He sat on the chair across the room, his fingers gripping his knees.

"Isn't that weird? God. I bet I had a premonition, and that's why I came home."

"Yeah," he nodded and glanced around, as if expecting someone to burst out a closet. A bluish oval of bruise was stamped on her outer thigh. He asked her about where-all she'd been and what-all she'd been doing.

"Oh God, Wes. How could I start to tell you?"

"Well, you were still with Barret?"

"Barret's in trouble. Barret's gone now. But you should tell me about the Army. Tell me about that, Wes. Did you go to Fallujah?"

"No," he said. Her face was strewn with gossamer fractures around her eyes, and the center of her chest looked like it had been sunburned too many times. The skin was finely wrinkled and bunched like crepe paper, reddened, not flushed. "But I was some places. A sergeant. There were, gunfights."

"God. Barret had a gun. Let me tell you how *brave* he was when he had a gun. God. Wes, I been to Georgia, Florida, Alabama, and Texas. I was in Crawford, Wes. I saw the President. He lives there. If I'd known you were in the Army I'd of tried to tell him. I finally made it here on a bus from Corpus Christi. Wes, I was walking and—do you remember Jimmy Dupres? Did you know him? He was at our high school. He's a deputy now. I was walking and he pulled up, and he saw it was me. He recognized me. He's a nice guy. He gave me a ride out here in his cruiser. We were on the Parish Road and he turned the lights on for me. They gave him a siren and he has a gun, too."

"All right."

"What're you so nervous for, Wes? You look like somebody's sneaking up on you."

"No I don't. I don't know. I'm excited to see you."

"You're all grown now. Look at you." She uncoiled her legs and stood, walked to the kitchen to refill her mug. He could see the crescent edges of red panties from behind, and looked away.

He stood and started pacing and was by the window when she came back in and sat down. "Isn't that aces, Wes? That Jimmy Dupres recognized me? He remembered me from high school. He told me he remembered a class I was in."

Out the window the fields undulated, had a character of striving. "I just don't get it now. What're you back for?" She shrugged and looked down into her coffee. He regretted the question, and he suddenly felt he had to be careful with his questions, that this new situation was too fragile and could be broken by their stories. "You want a drink?" That perked her up.

They sat drinking their father's bourbon the rest of the night. He told her about the remaining farm subsidies. She seemed slightly confused about what he'd been doing here, or what he was planning to do, and he was just as confused by her accounts. Anneise told circular storiesthat never closed the loop but spiraled off into different anecdotes, and an incidental description could set off an entirely new narrative, and she would forget the original story she was telling. She put on some music, an old record by the Oak Ridge Boys.

She talked about a group of people who lived in a close grouping of beach shacks owned by an old wealthy guy whose band played every night to the commune; he seemed to have some attachment to the '60s, though he was a little too young to have seen any of it. She talked about Atlanta and Birmingham and the Dinosaur Diamond Prehistoric highway between Colorado and Utah, because she remembered Wes had liked dinosaurs. Wes understood that she remembered things about him that were no longer true. He'd taken all the rocks outside while she was in the shower, and she hadn't brought them up again. He felt she might, though.

She didn't want to talk about TJ at all, and only said, "God it was rough on me when I heard that. I had a wild few months. Rough living." He asked her what had happened to Barret Wagner.

Barret had been with a motorcycle club for the last couple years, and he was attempting forays into stolen cars and drugs. "Long story short, he got in trouble with some people, I think. He had to take off and people were looking for him. I went back to Apollo Village in Corpus, that's what the beach place was called. And after a while I kind of started to realize that I had to forget about Barret and I was like, Anneise, what *are* you doing *girl*? Everybody was naked in the shack and Felan, that was his name, was playing these drums and I said, Okay, maybe four years of this is enough. How many parties do you need to go to? And I don't know, maybe I sensed something, maybe I could feel something. Do you believe in telepathy? Have you heard of that? I met some people in New Orleans that did. They were kind of silly people. But maybe I did know something out in Corpus, like something had happened, and I just felt it was time to come back home for a bit, to see it, and then I get here and he died. Wes. Do you think I could *feel* that he died?"

"Maybe. Sure." He cracked open another bottle of Dickel while a cigarette shook in his lips. A bag of ice sat in a bucket on the coffee table, along with an empty can of Vienna sausage filled with butts that now and then he'd take to the kitchen and empty in the garbage. She smoked more than him.

"I bet that's what it was. I bet I felt him die," she said, and he knew that from now on this would be the mystic heart of a story she would tell people.

"He told me something before he died."

"What?"

"He said I wasn't his."

"Oh." She lifted her glass and her eyes were hooded, lazy. "Course you weren't. I might not be either."

He swallowed and paced along the shelf where his father kept a bent antique bugle from the Civil War. "You ever heard from her?"

"No," Anneise said. "Don't know and don't care. Hey." She held her hand out to him and he took it. She used his grip to raise off the couch and stepped into his arms to dance to the song. "We got the house, at least." She felt heavy in his arms. Close up, he could see more wrinkles and sun-spots along the edges of her face. She brushed his cheek and laughed and they spun once to the music and Wes fell into the couch. She laughed at him and then said she was going to bed.

"All worn out. I'll see you tomorrow. I want to drive into town."

He waved her goodnight and sank into the couch with his drink on his stomach. The room blurred and rocked. The needle hit the end of the record and it kept spinning with a clicking sound like a metronome.

*

A WEEK UNWOUND INTO STRANGE DOMESTICITY. Anneise now believed she was psychic, and had taken to asking Wes questions like "Were you just thinking of a dog? Were you just thinking about Pop?" She said, "Think of a color. Any color. I'll tell you what it is."

She guessed and he shook his head. "Red."

She looked at him with pity, as if he'd forgotten his alphabet. "No, Wes. Green. *Green*."

Wes bought their groceries at a Kroger's in town as he now avoided Cormier's. They ate in front the television, usually around six, when a local station showed reruns of *Cheers*. After they finished their bowls of canned pasta, Anneise took his with hers, as if to clean up, but just left both bowls on a shelf next to the dented bugle, then sat back down with her legs tucked. She leaned on one elbow against the couch's back, her head cocked and held by her hand. There was a browsy, lazy light below her half-dropped eyelids. "Wes?" she said. "Come here, Wes." She patted the cushion.

He stood and sat down beside her, and she turned her head a little, shifted her legs beneath her.

"Whyn't you have a girlfriend?"

He didn't answer.

"It's okay, Wes. Do they make you nervous?"

She bent to lift her beer off the coffee table and her neckline expanded and he could see down to the tips of her breasts beneath the shirt. She sat up and licked foam off her lip. "It's okay," she said. "I just wanted to know."

"No. Not really. They don't."

"So whyn't you have a girlfriend? You're a cute enough guy."

"I don't meet anyone," he shrugged, feeling shrunken, pathetic. "Where do you *meet* them? *How* do you meet them?"

She squinted at him and pondered his words. "I'd think of trying to get into school if I was you. Say McDeere or something. They got some kind of program you could get to, I bet."

He shrugged. "How do I do *that*, though? See, Anneise…" his voice shook and he felt suddenly on the verge of tears. "I can't do *anything*. I don't *know how* to do *anything*."

"Oh. Wes, come here." She leaned forward and hugged him, lifted his face with one hand, stroking the back of his head. "We'll just have to teach you. Okay?"

Her green eyes absorbed his vision, and he had the sense of being tugged gently into them.

A booming from the doorway shook through the walls. His heart skipped a beat, more than one. Someone hammering on the front door with a mallet, maybe. *BoomBoomBoomBoom*.

"Who?" Anneise said. But it didn't matter. There was such urgency in the knocking he knew the only way to get it to stop was to answer the door. He opened it slightly, ready to leap away. The door slammed open and a large, hairy man in a leather vest and filthy blue jeans burst into the foyer. Without turning around he slammed the door behind him, his head whipping from side to side and causing the matted hair at his ears to flap. Wes was sitting on the floor. The man looked down at him and one thick eyebrow raised, the eye red and shaking. It moved to Anneise.

"Baby, by God. Baby baby baby. The whole time, baby, I was only like a couple days behind you. I'd hear 'She just went so-and-so,' or 'She was here last week,' or 'Said she was going home,' and when I heard that one, I thought, well maybe now she'll stay put long enough for me to catch up and baby here you are. Whoo." Barret Wagner again looked down at Wes and lent him a hand in rising.

"God. Damn. Sorry to bust in that way. I don't like being in the open too long. It sure feels vulnerable standing under that porch light. Which one are you again? It's Wesley right? Old Wesley. 'Weird Wes.' Wussley. Wuss. Hey, man. Hey. Goddamn." He shook Wes's hand and with his other stroked the chin of his dark beard. Mud and small debris cluttered its hairs.

The flesh of his arms was tumorous with muscle and bluish tattoos, each a different badly drawn picture, not like TJ's tattoos, which were a system of similar markings rather than individual designs. Wes looked over one of the hairy, spherical shoulders and saw Anneise rushing off the couch, her arms outstretched and her eyes glazed with the look of unquenchable loving fever he'd once seen in people at a revival.

"Oh God, Barret. Did I know you were coming? I think I might of known it. I think I might of *felt* it."

*

WAGNER TOOK A LONG BATH THAT FIRST NIGHT, refilling the tub with hot water each time it turned tepid and having Anneise bring him beers and stay in there, and when she came out, the front of her lavender T-shirt was soaking wet. He'd settled those guys that were after him, he said. That was old news and as it turned out nothing, really. But there was still paper on him, he was a wanted man. It would be good for him to stay there a while before deciding on his next move.

The next day, Wagner had Wes go to the grocery store and buy some provisions, including a number of seeds: tomato and watermelon and cabbage, also rosemary, basil, mint, thyme. He came home to the sounds of hooting from the back bedroom, a thump and squeak keeping erratic time against floor and wall. Wes left the groceries in the foyer and walked back outside to sit at the lake with the rocks.

The day after that, Anneise was up early and tilling rows to plant the seeds. Barret stood at the back door, his shirt off, nappy hair tugged into a ponytail. He was shockingly old, his face brazened and crusty, lumps of scar interrupting his thick black eyebrows. His skin was coarse and unevenly colored, his throat and arms the same fine texture of crepe paper he'd seen on Anneise's chest, but the torso pale and furred with swaths of coarse black hair. He nodded to Anneise in the small field of dirt spreading into the backyard. She was shoving a tiller back and forth like it was a mop.

"Meant to talk you a bit," Wagner said.

"Why do you want to plant that stuff?" Wes asked. He'd just realized that the time it took to grow things from seed seemed to indicate on Wagner's part an intent to remain here, in his house and on his father's land.

"She's the kind needs something to do. That's one thing I always keep in mind about Anneise. She needs something to do.

She's a sweet person, and she's got a lot of love to give, but you got to give her projects, things she can sink her teeth into. Or else she can become confused and do who-knows-what. She just gets bored too easy. That's one of the reasons we always got along: we both have complex minds. But I know how to handle her. She told me y'all just been sitting around everday. Drinking and listening to music and whatnot. So I figured I'd get her to start a garden. I know how to handle her. Give her a project. The girl's mind needs to be occupied, or she's like to get up to anything. There's always going to be a special sort of relationship a girl has to the man who first gutted her fish. You understand what I'm saying? I first shucked your sister's clam, she was fifteen, and that's what she knows. I'm natural to her, like her hair, or like her fingernails." Anneise looked up at them both and waved, wiped her brow, and went back to shoving the tiller to and fro. Her hair was pulled up in a ponytail and she wore a loose, flowered sundress. Wes's jaw was clenching so tightly he heard a molar crack.

Wagner crushed his beer can and let it drop at his feet. "Okay. Why I called you out here. One. I knowed you weren't in no Army. It was TJ. I remember hearing that when I heard about him shooting himself. I seen your papers in the desk in there. Said you couldn't be in the Army. Something wrong with your head. Anyway, just so you know. Anneise don't know right now, but I do, just so you know. Two. We're going to need to be splitting those subsidies from now on. Three ways. Two parts to us and one to you. You know they ain't yours anyway. You didn't do nothing to earn them and if the tax man or whoever finds out your daddy's gone you're going to lose them anyway. Three. You're welcome to stay on here if you want but sometimes a man decides it's time to stop wandering and put down some roots. I think that finding Anneise here and it being where we come from, and with the house empty, your dad dying I mean, it seems pretty right to me that I should marry her and fill her with some babies. You don't like any of that, I understand, but keep it to yourself. I tolerate you, Wes. That's it. And don't think of turning her against me because it can't happen. Like I said, the holes in both your sister's body and heart are molded around my gristle-missile, and she will forever after follow me wherever after that I may lead." He spit on the ground and scratched his stomach, turned his face up to the sun. "Anyways. I wanted to be clear about all that."

*

WESLEY STOOD SLIGHTLY BEHIND DEPUTY JIMMY Dupres, between two of the five police cars whose flashing lights surrounded his house. Dupres talked into a megaphone.

"You need to come on out now, Barret! Keeping the girl a hostage isn't doing anybody no good!" He looked over his shoulder, still holding the megaphone outstretched. "You said they's guns in there, yeah?"

"Yeah. We got shotguns. I'm telling you. He's plain crazy."

From the house, they heard Wagner shout, "She's not a hostage!"

"Well, let her go then Barret! This ain't have nothing to do with her!"

The house was silent and the other deputies, five of them, had their pistols drawn, fingers squirming around the handles. Dupres was tall, broad-shouldered in his crisp tan uniform, but he had an unfortunately recessive chin and rather than a jawline, his face more or less just narrowed into his neck, giving it the appearance of something squeezed out his shoulders. He looked around at his fellow officers, all wearing sunglasses and clearly uncomfortable with just standing there. Three of the cars were stationed in the cordgrass, and two others were in the front. They'd ridden over Anneise's newly planted garden and crushed the three signs his father had kept out front.

"Hey," said Wes, "what's the warrant for, exactly?"

"One in Texas is for narco-trafficking and assault. One in Oklahoma's for indecent exposure and destruction of property. Didn't get the whole story on that one. Something about lawn furniture."

The front door of the house opened and the deputies all raised their guns, hammers clicked, but it was only Anneise, her arms lifted and hands up. She wore high denim shorts and a red halter, and one of the deputies whistled. Her head turned back and forth, taking it all in, and she smiled sheepishly to the officers as she walked with delicate steps toward Dupres, Keeping her arms up the whole time.

"Hey, Jimmy," she said.

He nodded to her and said, "You can put your arms down, hon. He alone in there now?"

"Well, yeah. Hey, Wes. But he's worried. He wanted to know if there's something y'all could work out or something. He sent me to negotiate, like."

"We're not going to be doing any of that, I think," said the deputy, and he touched her elbow and guided her to the rear of the formation.

"Oh," she said. "Well, what's going to happen?"

"Look, Anneise, you got to be honest with yourself about a few things here." Still holding her elbow, he turned her gently toward him and frowned sympathetically. "You got mixed up with a bad man, hon. It ain't your fault, really. I remember him a little. He's always been trouble and your pop prob'ly should of kept him from you but that didn't happen. He's a bad man and a wanted man. As a sworn officer of the law, it is my duty to bring him to justice." As he said the last part, Dupres's face tilted up and off into the distance, and if he'd had a jaw it would have been a noble, soldierly pose.

"Oh," said Anneise. She glanced at Wes. Deputy Dupres had set the megaphone on the car hood, and he grabbed her shoulders and squared her toward him.

He spoke in a halting kind of cadence. "I'm sorry you had to be witness to all this, Anneise. I'd have liked to spare you from it. It's a sour side of justice, when it has to touch the innocent. But I am bound by duty. Can you understand that, Anneise?" He braced her shoulders and drew her closer to him.

"Okay," she said.

"Be glad your brother gave us the tip. This way we're able to come in, get him out your life. You still got time to start over." He touched her face. "Best to think of him as already gone."

"Wait? Wes?" She turned suddenly to her brother, her face crinkled in anger. "Wes gave you a tip? You ratted on Barret, Wes?"

Wes shrugged and took a step back. "Well, look—"

Anneise ran over and started hitting Wes on the shoulders, back and forth, crying, "How could you Wes? He *loved* you. Like a *brother*! Damn you, Wesley!" Dupres pulled her off, and she turned into his chest, burying her face there while he patted her back.

"Mind," the deputy said, "I never have had much respect for the type to sell-out somebody, specially someone's practically family. There's a cowardice there I find hard to abide. A hard-heartedness. But besides what this tells us about your brother's character, I am still duty-bound to the law."

Anneise hugged the deputy and lifted her wet face to gaze up to him. "I *knew* something like this would happen. I *felt* it."

A gunshot crashed and everyone ducked and crouched, Deputy Dupres throwing Anneise to the ground and wrapping around her like a parka. In the echo of the shot, one of the deputies called, "That's me, sir!"

Without rising off Anneise, Dupres called over his shoulder, "What? What was that?"

The deputy called from the side of the house. "Thought I saw something, sir. Out in this field. Looked like a big cat or something."

"Jesus Christ. Holster your weapon. No, wait. Don't. But you're an asshole, Kilpatrick!"

"Yessir," the deputy replied.

"Hey!" They all heard, muffled from the house. "What's going on out there?"

Dupres finally rose off Wes's sister and helped her to her feet. "It'll be all right, Anneise." He stepped back from her and wiped her cheek. "But right now, we've got an armed and dangerous fugitive barricaded in your house, and it's my duty to bring him in."

Anneise sniffled and held on to the deputy's hand, staring up at his mirrored sunglasses and chinless beard stubble. "I could feel that all of this was going to happen, Jimmy. I can sense things."

Wagner called from the house again, "I'm not going to jail!"

"All right, boys," said Dupres. "You heard him." He lifted the megaphone and called, "Have it your way, Barret!" Adjusting his glasses, he held up his hands to shoo Wes and Anneise backward. "Keep back y'all. All right, boys. Swarm."

The deputies rushed the house, five of them scattering around the front and back. One kicked open the front door, ducked aside, and the rest invaded the foyer. They heard someone shout and then an eruption of gunfire filled the white A-frame, the windows blinking with muzzle flashes. At the front and back doors they poured all their bullets into the house. Dupres watched while clutching Anneise to his chest, telling her, "Shh. Don't look, hon."

Wes stood alone, smelling the pungent smoke that wafted outward from the house and spilled over the grass and the cars. When he turned, Anneise was clutching Dupres, and she said, "I always *knew* I'd have a broken heart."

*

THEY'D MADE A TERRIBLE MESS OF BARRET, AS IF HE'D exploded, and Wes was the one who scraped and scrubbed the blood and meat off the walls and ceiling, threw out the rug, and on his hands and knees scoured the living-room floor with steel wool and powdered cleaner that bleached and roughened the floorboards. The cops had dug out the bullets but the holes still riddled the walls. Anneise couldn't stay there, after what happened. One of the deputies had gathered her things and brought them outside to her, and before the ambulance arrived to gather Barret's remains, she had already left for Jimmy Dupres's trailer, which he said she was welcome to use as long as needs be.

Two weeks later the house had been cleaned except for a few tiny dark spots which he'd now and then see that he'd missed, the ragged bullet holes. The Dickel was gone.

He took his pop's old lawn chair out into the cordgrass, dragging it along behind him while holding TJ's old shotgun over one shoulder.

He sat down in the chair, the rough grass taller than his head now. It was midmorning, the sun still low, and a light breeze tickled his skin, the frame creaking at his weight. He stood the shotgun up and held the stock with his feet on the ground. He'd received a letter yesterday. His sister was going to contest ownership of the house. She said that she and Jimmy Dupres would need to move in after their wedding.

The grass rustled like parchment, like seeds in the husks of a kind of marsh plant whose name he couldn't recall. Each stalk of grass had a bright, burning spot at its tip, like comets. Grackles chattered from the trees, unseen, a little hysterical. He thought of TJ in his tattoos. Did he see the sun come up? Had his brother watched for the sunrise, letting it act as a kind of signal?

He leaned forward and pulled the gun toward him till his chin rested on the barrel. Reaching down, his thumb hooked the trigger. The sun's angle changed and suddenly the stalks became like candles holding flames that were each growing more intense and bright, and it seemed he was surrounded by fire. He knew he had to do it, if it was going to get done. Shut his eyes and pressed down on the trigger, flinched and yelped at the same time. The trigger didn't budge, and he had to press the safety off.

Trembling, he moved to deactivate the catch, and when he glanced up, the creature was staring at him through a break in the grass ahead. It was near, maybe eight feet away.

Tawny, the colors of wheat and dust and woodsmoke in evening, its face like an arrowhead, the nose flat and pinkish-gray, the bobcat took a step out, toward him, its feet falling softly as ash, not making a sound. Its eyes were two bronze coins, utterly without pity or regard, only staring coldly, almost without interest, but observing still. Wes's breath caught and his fingers trembled. Smoothly as he could, Wes lifted the gun and leaned the barrel forward until aiming at the creature. The cat began to circle him slowly, each of its movements an implication of coiled power and restrained speed. He let the gun follow, the chair groaning. He turned around in the chair when the cat was behind him, and it continued circling, the eyes flat and nearly daring him, he felt.

His breath stuttered in his ears, and he could taste the sweat now soaking his face.

The cat completed a circle and returned in front of him. The creature studied him, then turned and sauntered slowly back into the brightening grass, crackling the dried stalks, until its colors blended and faded into the color of the field and he could see it no more. A noise thundered from the north field and Wes ran out the grass, looked across the lake as bursts of fire crowned the top of the refineries, and a thick black smoke rose up, wobbling and crooked, with a slanting flow that trailed across the hot blue sky. Thin streamers of fire arced down and sizzled to steam in the water. A searing wind blew across his face and bent the high stalks.

Turning back, he saw to the road, where now a plume of dust rose above it, a rooster tail of dirt kicked up by a car, approaching. A vehicle was coming toward the house. Another explosion and the heat washed over him; he could see the orange and yellow snapping, hear the sirens, and as the dark smoke fled into the sky and the dust advanced on the road, he felt himself there in both streams, both coming and going, staying and leaving all at once.

GRAVES OF LIGHT

NOW MIKE FUSELIER WOULD SOMETIMES WATCH Paul Calder in Moonie's, chasing Wild Turkey with Pabst, and once Mike had seen him snoring out in the sun at Royce-Anne Park, under the WWII memorial. Often he saw Calder simply wandering the streets of West Medora with a confused, absent expression, as if she was something he'd misplaced.

Mike had done some work on their Subaru, a fuel-injection problem, and when he met Paul Calder's wife he'd envied him. Her name was Lara and she was unlike any woman Mike had seen in town. Sleek, dark-hued, lush hair the color of maples in October, she'd worn a short skirt and high leather boots, had said something to Mike in French when she paid for the work, something like "thank you," and his voice got stuck in his throat. He'd never given much thought to older women, but Lara Calder made him suddenly aware of the differences between a girl and a woman. He thought about his own Marie, and she seemed somehow pathetic to him then. He thought of her thick legs and the dopey, bovine look she wore eating malomars and watching TV. All at once Mike understood that nothing you could govern would ever make you truly happy. Lara Calder was a lesson about that, somehow, and while her car pulled away Mike stood behind the counter in a kind of quiet reverence, as when a boy he'd wait to receive the Eucharist.

Now when he saw Paul Calder around town, lost in broad daylight, Mike understood how dangerous it was to covet things, and he believed the truth in what his father had once said, that a man had to be grateful for what he had while he had it, though his father had not been a grateful sort of person.

Felicity Morris saw Paul Calder, too. She couldn't help it because she lived fifty yards down on the other side of County Road 25. The university people usually didn't buy houses out here, and theirs had belonged to a popular veterinarian, a ranch-style built into a hill overlooking the limestone quarry. Now Felicity saw the professor out in his weed-strangled yard with a bottle, sometimes with one of the little birds from the college— his students, she knew. She supposed nobody minded that. She always called him "the professor" in her mind, remembering how puffed-up he'd seemed when he and his wife first arrived. He was much thinner than he used to be, and maybe because of that he seemed less spoiled to her, and he no longer shaved, but to Felicity there was still, even now, a sense of pride to him, an *air*, as if his grief set him above other people. They didn't wave to each other when Felicity would walk into town or back and she'd see him on his porch, lifting his bottle, staring with eyes as cold and remote as the pearling gray light of these fields.

She remembered that his wife had strode around like a pony, like the world was her entitlement. Like she expected you to look.

One morning, shortly after the Calders moved in across the road, Felicity's granddaughter didn't come home until dawn. Janie took the car whenever she wanted and drove it too fast. Felicity knew she had her mother in her. Janie and that Sleaux boy had taken Felicity's Festiva without asking and she now stood screaming at her grandmother in their yard. Screaming about how she had rights, and the whole time the Sleaux boy was in the front seat with his greasy little mustache, laughing, thinking it was some show. Felicity saw past Janie yelling and saw the professor standing on the porch of his ranch house, watching them all. He was still standing there when Janie sped off in the Festiva, the Sleaux boy's hand out the window and slapping the roof, just watching as the dust cloud rolled over Felicity in her nightgown and the car revved down the road.

Felicity had seen the dawn breaking across the fields like gasoline catching fire, the light pooling in the quarry's reservoir, the tattoos on Mitchell Sleaux's arm, and the professor standing there, watching like they were all lab mice. She stayed outside, just so he'd see; she kept her arms folded and stared at him until he turned and went inside his house.

Now Janie and the Festiva were gone, and Felicity walked the mile into the square when she needed something. That's when she was most likely to see Paul Calder on his porch. And she would think, *Go ahead, drink up,* now that he'd learned he was no better than anybody else. Except it seemed to her that he still didn't understand that. The way he carried on. As if he was the only suffering thing in the whole world. The six thousand or so residents of West Medora divide almost evenly into university people and locals who work at the Wal-Mart distribution center or the brick factory or the quarries, and most of those people live on the west side of Jefferson Boulevard, downhill in trailers or small houses with cracked siding and tiny lawns pocked with tires, rusting autos, religious statues. Except for faculty that commute from Bloomington or Indianapolis, most of the college's teachers live near campus in a few subdivisions of restored Victorians that tend to rotate within the university. But Paul and Lara Calder had chosen a semi-remote home in the countryside off CR 25. Paul had told Toby Greer, his colleague in the English Department, that if they were moving out of the city, they'd decided to move *out* of the city. Toby had been a little disappointed when the Calders took the ranch house. He hadn't realized it, but he'd been hoping they'd take the fourbedroom on his street that a doctor from anthropology was trying to sell.

After that year's first departmental dinner, Toby's wife, Vanessa, had accused him of following Lara Calder around all night like a puppy. He didn't think that was fair; he'd only been talking to her about translations of a Chilean poet he liked. Vanessa imitated him when they were back home, wearing one of her sweatsuits, her hair in a knot, and the baby was crying from the sound of their shouting.

Now Toby would see Paul with Amy Churchill, a twenty-year-old drama major. He'd see her petite frame trying to support Calder's weight as she guided him out of Moonie's. She was pretty, but nowhere near Lara's league.

He thought about her. He could admit that.

Toby and the rest of the search committee had voted to give Lara Calder a lectureship when they hired her husband as an Assistant Professor. She spoke four languages and taught a translation workshop. At the party he found himself clinging to certain facts: she'd been with her husband less than two years, they had no children, she liked Nicanor Para.

A few times now Toby had woken up in the middle of the night, and he knew he'd been dreaming about her, but he couldn't remember the dream. He'd look down at Vanessa sleeping, her face swollen, snoring. Then he'd sneak out and walk to David's room and watch him cooing in his crib. He'd pace the hallway between the two bedrooms in silence. Eventually, he'd go to the kitchen and pour a drink and stand there biting his nails, still trying to remember the dream.

*

PAUL CALDER THOUGHT THERE WAS TOO MUCH WIND, for one.

Indiana. The air was never as still as it looked. Another thing was the emptiness, the desolation. It unnerved him. It implied something he couldn't pin down. Maybe it was because he grew up in the South, among congested vegetation, greenery, rivers, marsh. The open plains seemed urgently wrong in a preconscious way. The sun was distant. Too white a light and not enough heat.

On his first drive down, for the interview, he saw out the car window a man in denim overalls, standing in the middle of one of those empty fields. The man watched Calder's car from under a wide, flat hat.

Paul saw a hatchet dangling in one of his hands. In his other he clutched a severed head by its hair.

It was only a stump, the man holding it by its roots. But still, something about the place —Calder felt it *could* have been a head.

Even with those early sensations, he and his wife felt West Medora was fresh air after Chicago. His wife shined here. He took pride in her.

The other women here, even the students, looked bulldoggish to his eyes, thick Midwesterners in frumpy clothes. The women here seemed vaguely embarrassed. Calder saw the looks, and he took some pride in them.

Their nearest neighbor was an old woman who lived with a wild granddaughter, but except for them it was just Paul and his wife and the trees and the view of the reservoir at the quarry, the swirling aquatic colors of the stone. After nine months in West Medora, he and his wife were back in big, intense love. To Paul it was as if they'd arrived together at a place between themselves, a place that had never existed before. Things hadn't always been easy. They'd married quick, after four months, and it was like the old poems say—feverish, the loss of appetite, unquenchable fucking—but within the first year he discovered his wife could bore him. He located a dull resentment in himself. A feeling like he hadn't quite gotten his. Later he'd ascribe that feeling to the fact that once they'd wed, many women seemed drawn to him. Pretty girls approached him. He was poised, funny, sharp. To him it was like he'd finally come into his own, and he felt entitled.

But what he hadn't considered then, what he only admitted later, was that the other women were only drawn to what Lara brought out in him. What having a great woman brings out in a man.

Now he could still get a certain type of young girl, because he was tragic. Because he had the one book and he drank and he was tragic.

Chicago almost killed them, but in West Medora they were true friends, partners in body and spirit. Here, sometimes Calder would see her—spreading butter on toast, say, or shaking her hair out or walking down the hallway, sitting on the couch and scratching Rosco's ear—and he would think, stunned in himself, *Look how beautiful my wife is. Look how cool she is.*

And she had that too, for him, and he could see it in her, and she could see it in him. Sometimes he felt humbled by gratitude. It seemed so funny to him, so chancy. That two people could find each other, that it could be so easy.

Other times, though, not much, but other times he might wonder, *Who is this person*, and, *What have I done*. It wasn't unusual, but he watched her at times with an appraisal, and things like a dimple behind her thigh caused a dim, inarticulate question to circle the perimeter of his thoughts. He wondered if she was good enough for him.

Now he felt bad about that, and he told Amy Churchill that he thought many people simply can't believe anything worthwhile could be theirs. People who want to believe in love, but just can't. They know too much about life. It was like God, like wanting to believe in God, but you know too much. You're riven by doubt.

Now Paul Calder avoided the inside of his house, and he drank too much.

He'd drank too much their last night together, put a dent in the Subaru's bumper when backing out at the bar. They spent their Friday evenings at Moonie's, eating cheese fries and drinking cheap beer, with whiskey for him. She didn't drink like him. It made her sentimental and tired. The more he drank the more confident he felt, the more certain of the future, and he always drank faster and faster until by the time she was tired his vision was blurred and he wanted to stay up all night playing music. He drove them home from the bar in snowfall, with one eye shut, the light snow like scattered dandelions. She was laughing and said, "I used to imagine myself in Paris. All my old boyfriends would commit suicide."

Squinting at the road, Paul said, "They still might." She rubbed his erection beneath his pants, and when they got home she started undoing her skirt on the way to the front door, let it fall to the porch and stepped out of it, looking over her shoulder at him as she vanished into the shadows inside.

The white snow in the moonlight.

*

LATER DON AND PEG RAMSEY, LARA'S PARENTS, hired Duane Consadine out of Indianapolis. The Ramseys were dissatisfied with the West Medora Sheriff's investigation. "It's not exactly CSI down there," Mr. Ramsey had said. "It's not like they have a missing persons bureau."

Consadine naturally began with the husband, but ruled him out quickly. One morning in early April he pulled into the long driveway off CR 25 and found Calder sleeping in the high grass of his front yard with his golden retriever. It was nine o'clock and Calder had a stained and weather-beaten down comforter wrapped around him. He explained to Consadine that he had trouble being alone inside the house. His hands shook and his eyes were so wet that Consadine felt guilty for disturbing the sleep of a man for whom consciousness seemed so intolerable. Inside the detective made a pot of coffee and watched Calder shuffle around, rubbing his arms, until Consadine poured him a cup of coffee and had him sit down.

He explained who he was, and what he'd been hired to do. He asked for her computer, because he wanted to look at her emails and financial records. He'd expected conflict over this, but there was none. Calder told him to take her laptop. Please, he said. Then Consadine watched him rise from the table and grab a bottle of Middleton's off the countertop. Two streams of tears skidded down his cheeks as he upended the bottle. He talked fast and the big blonde dog whined softly under the table.

Calder told him, "I've imagined her face-down in a ditch. I've imagined her with a secret lover in Paris or New York or Mexico. I've imagined her wandering down a country road with amnesia. And these people—" He wiped his mouth and gestured at the world outside the house. "—these people to me. They've become like part of some conspiracy. The sheriff. He thinks she just left me. But if that was true, she'd have taken the dog, right? He's her dog. She'd have called her parents. And why make a grocery list?"

Consadine listened to him for almost two hours, until Calder had drank enough to put himself back to sleep, and he left him on the couch with the dog curled at his feet. It was terrible to witness, like a form of real damnation. As he shut the front door the laptop computer under his arm felt dense, a weight more like stone.

As Consadine studied photographs of Lara Calder, read her correspondence and writing, he began to sense the profundity of her husband's shock and grief. Obviously she was a beautiful woman, but there was a quirk to her expression, a keen edge, and he guessed that she hadn't been good-looking growing up, didn't come into that until later. In his experience, people born beautiful tended to lack character, and she did not. He could see it in her various tones—playful, funny, aggressive—the rigor of her intelligence, the way it was informed by a basic kindness, a real curiosity about things. She'd be the type to haunt exes, and he imagined them trying to stay in touch, holding out hope for reconciliation. All of a sudden he could smell his ex-wife, the one in Florida; the scent of her breath in the morning was on the air. He learned about Lara's high school in Hillsboro, a green and lonely town only slightly larger than the one where she'd vanished. Old photos confirmed—she was gawky, bookish, plain as a teenager. Traced her back through graduate school at UNC—her twentieth birthday and suddenly she was a knockout—to a year she spent in Paris for Stanford and then her time in Chicago as a lecturer at Northwestern, where she'd met Paul Calder.

Consadine thought to track down Lara's exes, what ones he knew of. His definite instinct was that her disappearance somehow involved a man. She'd be the sort of woman men assaulted with yearning: alluring, and smart enough to baffle and frustrate them.

But three months of investigating and Consadine had gotten nowhere, and when her parents could no longer afford him he kept her pictures and documents near at hand. Even later when he'd packed those things up and met his next wife, Duane Consadine would occasionally check the website her parents maintained, and he'd understand that Lara Calder had stuck herself in his mind, the idea of her. She'd become a shard of unknowing. One of those things you just have to live with.

*

THE MORNING AFTER THEY GOT DRUNK AT MOONIE'S, after he'd dented the bumper on the Subaru, Paul Calder woke up alone. Horror shot through him. He was overwhelmed with a crushing fear that Lara was gone, that this separation from her was permanent. He jumped out of bed and ran across the hall, shouting her name.

She was in the kitchen, drinking juice and making a grocery list. She was dressed to work out, in spandex pants and a tank-top that bared her midriff. Rosco was staring up at her, bug-eyed and tongue flopping because he knew they were going for a run. When Paul found her he was free to notice his priapic hangover. She looked over her shoulder and chuckled at her husband, asked how he felt.

He moved behind her, reeking of booze.

She was on the table with her legs thrown around him, the spandex coiled on her ankle. The table banged across the floor and scratched the linoleum and she laughed like mad, hollering at him.

He'd remember the table hitting the sink, then slamming the counter. Rosco barking, hopping around, his nails clicking on the floor. He'd remember her tugging at his hair.

He collapsed when they were done and she just laid there, and he looked up and watched himself dripping out of her, onto the table. He'd remember her hair splayed in all directions, the tank top rolled above her breasts. She'd blushed like a map of blood— she had sensitive skin and he could watch her moods play out on her flesh. She laughed. She looked so pleased. He lurched up and started licking her. He felt penitent.

About an hour later she finally went for her jog, skipping out the door with the dog. Paul was excited because now he could have a drink, which would help his hangover.

He'd always be grateful they'd made love that morning, grateful they'd had that.

At some point he fell asleep on the couch, and it was after three when he woke up. Afternoon, bright. He stepped outside. The car was in the driveway. He called for Rosco. The fear he'd felt earlier returned, but stronger, fuller. He was scared the way children get, like there was a siren in his head.

He grabbed the phone and tried her cell, but it rang from her purse in the bedroom. She hadn't taken them with her. Either she'd come back while he was asleep and went out again, went out with the dog again, to do something that didn't require a purse, or she'd never come back at all. He told himself to settle down.

He took a shower, portioned out the next two hours with little nips of Jameson, made notes for his next book, a big novel that he would never write.

After five o'clock, Lara still hadn't returned.

He noticed the dent in the Subaru where he'd hit the pole the night before. He drove down the road and saw the old woman across the street, watching him. It seemed like that was all she did when her granddaughter was gone, when the car in their yard was gone. She'd stand outside and wait for it to come back, and he had sympathy for her now, her stasis.

He drove down by the park, the trails Lara used. A gray, bronzed evening with brown clouds. He drove around the campus and back up along the limestone quarries and out past the Wal-Mart and past the tennis courts and almost to Crawfordsville.

He told himself, it's been another hour. She'll be home when I get there.

He needed her to be there so badly, he'd never noticed before. There was nothing he could compare this fear to, not even as a child, when he was often scared. But she wasn't home. There was a message on the answering machine and his stomach knotted as he played it.

It was a Medievalist in his department. She said, "Paul? It's Louise Formicella. I've found your dog."

She said she found Rosco wandering around near the courthouse, with his collar on and leash dragging. He was alone. She said she recognized him and brought him to her house.

His heart seized. It was like he'd known already what was going to happen. Like he knew it the moment he woke that morning—that all day, he realized, this thing he knew had skirted the periphery of his awareness. Like all day he'd been trying to deny what he woke up knowing.

Which is that his wife had vanished off the face of the earth.

*

THE OTHER MAN DIDN'T NOTICE WHEN PAUL CALDER came into Moonie's, but Mike Fuselier did. He'd been thinking about Calder ever since he saw the picture of his wife on the news last March, since he'd started seeing him stumbling around town. Mike was drinking at the end of the bar with his Uncle Ray, who owned the garage, and he watched Calder order a whiskey with both hands on the railing as if he had to hold himself up. Mike thought about Marie, about what he'd do if she vanished. He couldn't deny a submerged wave of relief at the thought.

He saw Paul Calder spot the other man and take his drink to the back booth where this guy had been nursing a beer by himself. The man looked up when Calder's shadow fell over his ashtray. Uncle Ray was talking but Mike had his ears cocked to that booth. Calder was rail-thin, his sharp cheeks jutting above a ragged beard. He heard the other man say, "Paul. God, man. What can be said?"

Calder didn't answer him. He rubbed the rim of his glass and looked around. "How to make rooms not feel like boxes," he said.

"What?" said the other man. "You want a drink?"

"How to make days not feel like boxes," said Calder. And when he said that, it touched off something in Mike Fuselier, some way he'd been feeling—like it had described something he understood. And he didn't know why, but he started thinking about Marie, and about the ways he thought about her.

Paul Calder massaged his chin and stared at the other man. Then he pushed his glass away and said, "I'm wondering, Toby. Why is it my wife goes missing, but I hear *you* leave a committee meeting in tears, that your wife's kicked you out of the house. Why is *that* happening, Toby?"

Toby drank from his beer and set it down. "I think that's my business, Paul."

"You should come to my place, Toby, you need somewhere to stay. I got lots and lots of room."

Toby's fingers curled around the edges of the table, and he took a deep breath. "I've been seeing you around with Amy Churchill, right? What is she, twenty?"

"Hey, Toby." Calder leaned over the table. "Is there something you want to tell me?"

"What the hell is that supposed to mean?"

"Go ahead. Just tell me. I remember you mooning over her."

"I'm trying to be civil, Paul. Out of sympathy." Now you could see the other man getting nervous, squirming in his seat.

"We laughed about that. Me and her. Lara and I. Did you think you had a chance?"

Toby squeaked out an almost-stuttered 'fuck off' that made Mike embarrassed for him.

Paul Calder launched himself over the table. The ashtray flew, tossing grit everywhere, the bottle spun to the floor and bounced, and before the other man had a sense he was in a fight, Calder's hands were wrapped around his throat, and he growled, "*Tell me. Tell me what happened.*"

The bartender yelled at them, and Mike and his uncle jumped off their stools, because the other man's face was turning purple and his eyes were bugging, and it was obvious Paul Calder meant to murder him. Mike heard him say, "*Tell. Me.*"

They lifted him off and Mike said, "Mr. Calder! Come on, Mr. Calder!" When he stopped struggling they all saw the tears streaking his face, his trembling lips, and when Ray let him go Calder dropped to his knees.

The people in the bar just looked at the other man, Toby Greer. He dusted himself off, rubbed his throat, and he seemed ashamed to meet their eyes. He rose and lurched out the back door. Then Mike and his uncle propped Calder at the bar. Everybody knew who he was, and the bartender served him a coffee.

He said thanks and sat with his head bent, staring at the rail. Mike's uncle had turned to talk to Jim Prentis, and Mike realized they were doing Mr. Calder the courtesy of ignoring him. But Mike wanted to talk to him. He thought it might be possible to tell Paul Calder about that day his wife picked up their car, that there could be a way to tell her husband that he had admired her, and not in a disrespectful way, and so he'd admired him, too. But he felt ridiculous to even think it. Then he was going to say something friendly, something harmless, but that seemed stupid too, and yet he felt he *needed* to say something, so he described this place he knew in a field near the southeast corner of Raccoon Lake. A square plot of dirt hidden in the high scrubgrass.

Mike told Paul Calder that he came upon places like that now and then, places where grass doesn't grow, rectangles of dirt. Calder watched him with spent but intense eyes, paying attention, and so Mike continued and told him how his father had first showed him such a spot, a barren mound, and explained that it was a grave. "A secret grave." And while he was telling Paul Calder about that, he was also thinking about Marie, about how sad she'd looked that morning when he left for work. He'd been short with her, but she had just kept her head down at the breakfast table, eating a donut, and now, thinking about it, she looked so sad that his heart broke. He saw her as he told Paul Calder about those odd plots of land you could find hidden in the forests and fields, the secret graves.

His uncle and Jim Prentis heard him talking, though, and they'd stopped to listen, and Uncle Ray said, "Mike, what the hell are you talking about? Leave that man alone."

Mike lost the thought, or his reason for telling it. He asked Calder if there was somebody he could call for him, and he gave Mike a girl's number. Mike called her and she came to the bar. Her name was Amy and she looked younger than Mike, younger than Marie, a blonde, pretty. She walked Calder out the door.

Mike stayed at the bar for a couple more beers. He kept picturing Lara Calder and thinking about those small rectangles of bare dirt where grass wouldn't grow. He finished his third beer and went to the pay-phones by the restroom. He called Marie.

"I was just checking in," he said.

"Surprise, surprise," she said.

Meanwhile Amy Churchill drove Paul Calder home in the Honda Accord her parents bought her when she graduated from Washington High School. She'd liked Paul's class best when he discussed not his own writing but the work of someone else he admired. The passion and excitement in his voice, the complex unfolding of his mind. Through him she'd discovered Wharton and Porter and Munro. He could still talk about books. It was a good way to draw him out.

She felt sorry for him and sorry for his wife. When she'd first seen Lara Calder, the way she dressed and held herself, Amy couldn't even be jealous. She thought that Lara Calder was the sort of woman she wouldn't mind growing up to be, and hoped that one day she possessed that kind of confidence and poise, and she knew enough to know the doorway to those things was experience. She felt that Paul could help her in that becoming, like he could be a kind of education. He was lost and exhausted but still a type of man, a talented man with a deep, receptive soul, one that needed to be nurtured back to life. Wouldn't that be something, that kind of experience? Wouldn't that be a privileged sort of material, to save a man like that?

As they turned on his street they passed an old woman walking the dusty road. Paul noticed, sat up straight and looked back at the woman.

"What?" Amy asked. He didn't answer.

He took a hot bath while she heated a frozen pizza and fed the dog. When he finally got out of the bath the pizza was cool, and he said he wasn't hungry. He had a towel on and stared down at the floor. He said, "That woman. Down the street. She used to have a car. And a granddaughter. But I haven't seen her or the car since Lara disappeared."

Amy didn't understand what he meant. Sometimes he said things, gave theories about his wife, and they didn't always make sense. It was more than a little paranoid.

He poured himself a drink and told Amy that he'd fallen asleep in the bathtub. He said he'd had a dream. His voice became flat and very distant, as if he were receding, and its dead, stilted tone unnerved and injured her in a way she didn't understand. He told her that in his dream he saw a fresh plot of bare dirt in a field of high grass. He said there was a single dead dandelion on the plot, and he said that he knew how the weed had died.

"It died," he said, "when its roots groped down into the soft, new earth, searching for purchase. Like a thief's fingers. Winding past soil and rock and bone until its roots struck the jade engagement ring worn on the finger of a corpse. My wife." He opened his hand in the air, like a magician. "And the roots just stopped. And died."

He didn't say anything else about it, but for Amy a darkening had occurred. And later she became upset, and didn't know why, but she went back to spend the night in her dorm.

In the moment after that dream the shift first began to take hold in Paul Calder. He had a sense. There'd been an accident. Before that, he'd somehow thought he still might see her again.

He didn't know when, what the precise dimensions were of his adjustment, but one day he was able to accomplish small tasks, to think beyond the present moment. Amy helped him box up Lara's things and put them in the spare bedroom, and seemed grateful they were doing it. And later, he was even able to keep the door to that room closed.

Moving away from his wife, he began to resent her, and he understood then that he'd never loved her correctly. He didn't have time to learn to love her correctly. He felt bad about that, because she had loved him.

She became an alternative for his life, a branch of time that continued somewhere else, outside this existence. This branch, the one he was on, had been pruned.

And in her abiding generosity, she'd left him with a final gift. Lara had marked him, given him a definition, one that winnowed his life to very specific dimensions. Lara had made him tragic.

Now there was no need to strive or write or add to his meager professional achievements. In the eyes of everyone he had lost a great, great deal, and if he wished, he never had to recover.

People understood. They gave him two years sabbatical.

It occurred to him that he'd waited his whole life to be this sort of fuck-up.

He'd always feel that he could have gotten better, he just chose not to.

He really couldn't see the point.

*

FELICITY MORRIS SUPPOSED HE'D STARTED LIVING indoors again, with the cold weather coming, but she saw him once more in the fall. He was with a young girl at the football game. It was a big year for West Medora High's program. They were picked in newspaper polls to win the state AA title. Most everybody was turning out for those games.

She went because it was something to do on Fridays, and Bruce Chenault would take her. Since Janie had left, he'd give Felicity rides in his Toyota truck when she needed. He was a widower, and Felicity had known his wife. They'd all attended First Pentecostal. He was older than her, almost eighty, but spry and sharp and good company when she cooked too much food or wanted to see a movie in Plainfield. His face was flat and wizened, with a burnished, tempered quality to his complexion. If he wasn't in church or a restaurant he always wore a net trucker's cap, but still had a shock of white hair crowning his scalp. He kept his eyes on his shoes a lot. He listened to her.

Their seats were about five rows up, near the aisle, and they watched the teams warm-up below. It was late October and Bruce had brought them a thermos of coffee. He poured her the first cup and she blew steam from it while watching the cheerleaders near the fence kicking. Some men whistled.

The team was now 5–0 and she felt good for those boys, the way their accomplishment leant everybody in the stands a pride, and it meant they'd done something right, because they were their boys, from their town, and Felicity smiled to think that. Bruce caught her smiling and as if he needed something to do he looked away and sipped his coffee, wincing from its heat. He managed his land by himself still, and in autumn he smelled pleasantly of bonfires.

Early in the second quarter the visitors scored for the first time when the home team let a receiver pull down a long pass with no one behind him. The stands took flight with disappointed sounds, boos, laments, even though they were ahead by fourteen. Then Felicity heard, everyone heard, one man's voice shouting. He was screaming, cursing, howling. Saying horrible things.

Mike Fuselier was there, and he heard too. He was sitting next to Marie, her belly just starting to show, and she shrank into herself as the voice behind them continued. Like most of the people, Mike turned around to find the source of the shouting.

Toby Greer turned too. He was there with his young son, David, and his wife Vanessa. She'd taken him back a few weeks earlier. He saw Paul Calder standing near the top row, waving a big cup of something, shrieking his head off. He cursed at the referees, the other team, WMH's own coaching staff.

He said things Felicity had honestly never heard before, and he seemed to be not just screaming to the people on the field, but to the people in the stands, all of them. You bunch of this-and-thats. You can eat this-and-that. The sky behind him was black and filled with stars.

In the past Felicity had felt herself wanting to talk to him, but there was no way she could. She saw the two sheriff's deputies working their way up the stands toward him, saw the young girl beside him cringing, tugging his waistband, trying to get him to sit.

He certainly knew how to milk it, Felicity thought. Still, in the past she'd wanted to talk to him.

His wife was gone, and her granddaughter gone, run off with Mitchell Sleaux and her Festiva. So who was this man to expect justice, to drink and rail like a maniac when he didn't get it? Justice, when there were women like his missing wife, women who, by right of birth, had already swept the field clear of things worth having. Felicity felt that things which had been denied her granddaughter had been given to this other woman in abundance. So the idea of justice was already something of a crock, deprived of power by the basic facts of life.

Even so, at times she had wanted to speak to Paul Calder, because they were both alone. And whatever had happened, they'd become alone on the same day.

Felicity kept facing behind and watched as the deputies approached Calder. The girl with him tried to talk to them, and when one of them reached for the professor he dropped his drink, and Felicity saw it spill in the night air, sparkling against the lights and frozen for a moment like a floating scarf.

He saw her. Their eyes met.

Then he stopped struggling with the deputies. He lowered his hands and while they took him by the wrists he didn't look at them, only at Felicity, staring past all the other faces and still staring as the deputies led him toward the aisle.

She must have had her hand to her mouth, because Bruce touched it gently, and his dry fingers grazed her lips. He said, "I'm sorry you had to hear that kind of language, Lissey." She was shaking and he gave her his jacket.

She waved the matter off, but felt ashamed as she watched Paul Calder led out the exit. Mike Fuselier watched, and Toby and Vanessa Greer watched too, as Paul was taken outside the fences and Amy Churchill followed.

When Bruce brought her home that night, he took her hand and asked Felicity if he might come inside.

She wanted so badly for him to, but she was thinking about the professor, and about his wife and her granddaughter, and some apocalyptic notion seemed to pass over her, a shadow or darkness, something she saw reflected back in the folds of Bruce's face, the depth of his wrinkles, the shattered blood vessels in his skin. This idea—that everything we do, no matter what, is in vain.

He must have seen it in her eyes.

She said she was tired, and she walked herself to the door. She still had his jacket. It was an olive-green windbreaker and now, weeks later, it hung in her foyer, waiting for him to return. She could see the jacket hanging there from her rocking chair in the living room, and seeing its hollow, limp shape, the shadow it cast on the wall, she would feel angry at Paul Calder.

It seemed like pride to her, his behavior. It seemed like pride and entitlement. The way he carried on.

As if he owned abandonment.

As if he was the only person in the world who'd ever lost something.

ACKNOWLEDGMENTS

Among various kindnesses from both friends and strangers, this book would not exist without at least the following people. They have my deepest gratitude and appreciation:

Matt Clark, 1966-1998

C. Michael Curtis, for his faith and generosity

Skip Hays, for patient instruction in reading, writing, and more practical matters

Thanks to Kate Nitze for all her enthusiasm and efforts on my behalf.

I owe an additional debt to the great Yasunari Kawabata, whose "Palm-of-the-Hand" stories suggested an anecdote recounted in the first part of "Two Shores."

www.ingramcontent.com/pod-product-compliance
Lightning Source LLC
Jackson TN
JSHW081328130125
77033JS00014B/457